To Me
I Wed

ALSO BY K.M. JACKSON

Holiday Temptation
(with Donna Hill and Farrah Rochon)

The Unconventional Brides Series

Insert Groom Here

To Me I Wed

An Unconventional Brides Romance

K.M. JACKSON

Kensington Publishing Corp.
http://www.kensingtonbooks.com

DAFINA BOOKS are published by

Kensington Publishing Corp.
119 West 40th Street
New York, NY 10018

All Kensington Titles, Imprints, and Distributed Lines are available at special quantity discounts for bulk purchases for sales promotions, premiums, fund-raising, and educational or institutional use. Special book excerpts or customized printings can also be created to fit specific needs. For details, write or phone the office of the Kensington special sales manager: Kensington Publishing Corp., 119 West 40th Street, New York, NY 10018, attn: Special Sales Department, Phone: 1-800-221-2647.

Dafina and the Dafina logo Reg. U.S. Pat. & TM Off.

ISBN-13: 978-1-4967-0570-9
ISBN-10: 1-4967-0570-X
First Kensington Mass Market Edition: May 2017

eISBN-13: 978-1-4967-0571-6
eISBN-10: 1-4967-0571-8
Kensington Electronic Edition: May 2017

10 9 8 7 6 5 4 3 2 1

Printed in the United States of America

To Will
Your love takes me from enough to more than.

Acknowledgments

Though writing is a solitary endeavor, no book is truly written alone. Because of that, there are quite a few people I'd like to thank for helping me through this process and for mainly keeping me sane and pulling me out of my own head when I most needed it. Because, though it's fine for a while, woman cannot live by social media alone.

As always first and foremost thank you to God for being my rock and by my side when there is only my voice and no one else's.

Thank you to my Dear, DH, Will, for always being an inspiration. You remind me that love is in the small moments.

To my children, Kayla and William, for always being a driving force. And to the rest of my family for being the grounding that keeps me laughing at what most would cry over.

All the gratitude in my heart goes out to the phenomenal team at Kensington Publishing. To my editor, Selena James, I never imagined it could be this good. All of you at Kensington are jewels to work with.

Thank you to Team KMJ, who never fail to remind me of what a privilege this writing gig is. And to Amy and to Dana, you both are treasures.

Karli, Wendy, Kiya, Patrice, Patricia, Eileen, Jackie & Marva. I'm throwing kisses and confetti to my amazing friends who truly lift me up with joy each and every day just by being who they are.

To: Farrah, Adrianne, Shelly, Lauren, Deborah, Sofia, Katana, Cheris, Falguni, Megan, Sonali, Kaia, Synithia, Stacey and all my supercool Destin Divas. If we're doing like the young chippies do and calling out squads, then mine is LIT!

Yes, I'm a lucky woman indeed. But please don't pinch me, because I don't want to wake up anytime soon.

And lastly, Nana, your heart beats on.

All the best,
KMJ

Chapter 1

"You're not just gaining a wife, you're getting my best friend." Lily Perry took one look at her sister, Sophie, and realized her mistake. *Shit. Now I've done it.* Did she really just use the same best friend line on Sophie that she had with Sophie's twin, Audrey, at her wedding? Or was it Peggy who she used that line on when she married Marcus? Her sisters had been getting married left and right, and all the weddings and toasts were starting to blur together. You'd think they were in some sort of great marriage race.

Lily looked around the banquet room of the VFW hall and caught her mother's sister, Aunt Ruby pulling a face and whispering something to her newly engaged daughter, Nikki. Lily swallowed back a grimace. Jeeze, even Nikki was jumping the broom. At the rate her family was going, there would not be a broom or a groom to be snagged in all of the Rockaways. Not that Lily was actively looking for either. She had a vacuum in her apartment for sweeping, and, well, for other tasks, if her dating life hit a lull she had an electronic device to take care of that too. It was way more reliable than men anyway. Still, Lily glanced left and caught her mother, Renée Henton-Perry, staring too. The hyphenation in her name was still new to her and intentionally left off the wedding invitations. She preferring to keep things simple she said and going the traditional route of Mr. and Mrs. Perry request the honor blah, blah, blah and so forth. Her hair and makeup were flawless, as usual, and her skin was smooth and unlined. The untrained eye would never determine that she was the mother of six grown daughters—four married—with a grandchild on the way. One would also not know that right then she was highly pissed. But Lily knew. She caught the glint of disapproval in her mother's eye and the ever-so-slight pull of tension around her perfectly lined mouth. Lily wondered if it was due to her speech faux pas or the fact that, one table over, Lily's father, Philip Perry, was sitting with his arm draped casually around his current girlfriend, who was happily sipping on her pink cocktail and batting her long, glued-on lashes.

Lily cleared her throat as her cousin Nikki smirked and rolled her eyes in her direction. Unperturbed by her cousin's cutting glance, Lily raised her glass higher, giving her sister what she hoped passed for a glowing smile before turning to the crowd. "I'm the luckiest woman in the world to have been blessed with the world's best sisters. And to all my brothers-in-law, you'd better treat them right, or there will be hell to pay." She then directed her final words to her newest brother-in-law, Simon, who looked ecstatic to be marrying Sophie. His big blue eyes shined brightly for her as they had every day since they'd met in Sophie's improv class.

Both budding actors, they made a slightly sickeningly perfect couple. Sophie with her cocoa-brown skin and finely chiseled model features, and Simon with his wavy dark hair and captivating eyes. They looked like a couple in an aspirational car ad or in the picture that comes in the picture frame that you replace with your mediocre second best. Plus, they were always smiling and complimenting each other. If Lily didn't know them in person and up close, she'd swear their love was faked for some reality TV show. Lily smiled at her new brother-in-law and continued from her heart. "Simon, I'm not worried about you. Your love for Sophie has been shining bright since day one. May it shine on forever." Lily turned back to the now-beaming crowd. She had them. Hell, even Aunt Ruby was blinking back a tear.

But just as Lily took a sip of her champagne, she caught sight of a sneer from freaking Lacy Colten. Ugh, why had Sophie invited that man stealer? A nemesis since high school, Lacy was well known for frequenting weddings to get free booze and easy prey. Lily watched as Lacy stopped sneering, quickly sat up straighter, and stuck her already-on-display double Ds out even farther as she looked across the room, no doubt at her next victim. Lily's eyes shifted.

It was him, and surprisingly, he was staring at her, not Lacy. Oh crap. His eyes so dark and intense they reminded her of hushed quiet in the dead of night. Midnight. Lily frowned as the heat of his stare penetrated her being. Working her over from the inside out. Stirring up feelings that she'd long told herself she was well and good over. What the hell, dude?

Mind your own business. Lily pointedly tried to look in any direction but his as she wondered what he was doing there and mentally cursed Thomas for backing out at the last minute and leaving her to attend this wedding on her own. She'd fix him the next time he needed someone to attend one of his boring corporate functions and one of his usual cookie-cutter airheads just wouldn't cut the mustard.

"Your toast was great," Scott, Simon's brother, said as he took his spot to make the best man's toast and thankfully pulled Lily's attention away from Midnight and back to the task at hand.

"Thanks," Lily said, her voice slightly shaky.

Why was he staring so dang hard? As a matter of fact, why was he there at all? Lily knew he was a friend of Simon's, but were they really close enough to warrant an invite to an intimate family affair? She snorted to herself. Hell, Lacy was there. Seems anyone could get into this party. But still, she couldn't believe she missed his name on the guest list. Wait, she couldn't believe she missed his name all together, as in the fact that she couldn't remember it. How could a person not remember the name of another person she made out with pretty hot and heavy one night? Lily inwardly shifted as she wondered what her mother would say to that. She'd probably purse her lips so hard she'd pull a muscle. But still, there it was. For the life of her she couldn't remember his name. Not that it was all that much of a bad thing. The not-remembering-his-name deal Lily considered it a bit of a triumph, as after their hot-and-heavy make out session on the beach those months ago he went radio silent with zero communication sent in her direction. So Lily made it a point to not dwell on him for longer than the week she'd given him to call and then mentally erased his name from her "give a crap" database.

Still Lily worried at her bottom lip. It was a short name, that she knew, and her face heated up when she recalled that his name was the only thing that was short about him. Lily felt the heat rise in her cheeks to a near boiling level as she looked back at midnight eyes and caught a distinct raise of his brow just as she was turning to take her seat once more. It was as if he knew what she was thinking. And it was then that she almost tripped on the hem of her dress, getting it caught in the toe of the stupid dyed-to-match satin-and-sparkle shoes that Sophie insisted they all wear. If it were her day, there would be no matching dresses. Come on, no one dress flattered everyone and dyed-to-match. Please. The horror. This was not nineteen ninety-eight. Had she not taught Sophie anything?

Lily righted herself with the back of the spindles of the rented gold chairs, and once again her eyes connected with Midnight's. He smirked and raised his beer in mock salute. The freaking nerve.

Lily squelched her blush as she turned away and tried to focus on Scott's speech. He was going on about something to do with a keg and a goat, and she told herself she really should have vetted what he'd planned to say. It was a rookie move leaving the best man's speech up to chance. More than one fight has broken out due to mention of a boys-gone-wild bachelor party.

Lily shook her head as the crowd laughed and her thoughts went back to Mr. Eyes. Maybe he was the plus-one of another guest. At that thought Lily got a surprising and completely unwelcome knot in her stomach. What should she care if an old hookup was a plus-one at a wedding she was attending? That wasn't awkward at all. Well, not all that much. And what was he doing looking at her like that if he was someone else's plus-one? She let out a deep breath and did a quick flip in her mind, his overly dark, midnight eyes taking Lily back to their first and only meeting the summer before, on the beach where Sophie and Simon were on a not-quite-date with a group of friends and she tagged along, still feeling slightly salty after Thomas giving her his little speech about their not being mutually exclusive. Well, hell, she'd wished she'd had known that bit of bullshit before she'd gone and turned down her fair share of good-looking man candy while he was tipping around the city spreading all his joy. For the life of her she didn't know why she still gave Thomas the time of day. And now here she was, obviously dateless, when he was supposed to at least be available as her plus-one, mutually exclusive or not. They had an understanding.

No matter though. Right now Lily was focused on Midnight, and she couldn't help but note that he looked just as good now as he had then. Though now he wore his hair shaved close to his scalp, and he had this scruff that looked quite, well, touchable in a rough but irresistible way on his chin. And his shoulders, which were wide then, seemed even wider now. As a matter of fact they were practically straining the hell out of his black suit jacket. And just as he'd done on the beach that afternoon, where they'd shared beers and tacos then later quite a bit more, making out under the dock, he was looking at her as if he could see right through her dress, past her mask of calm reserve and down to the fact that just his stare was making her hot as hell. Forget the champagne, maybe she needed a cold shower.

Sophie leaned over to Lily and patted her hand. "Nice toast, sis," she whispered between smiling clenched teeth. "I liked it the first time I heard it too."

Lily shook her head and turned her younger sister's way. "Can you cut me just a little slack? You gave me only three months to put this shindig together, and I pulled out all the stops for you, calling in many markers with my vendors, mind you—even passing on a job in order to slip you in. So sorry if I bungled the toast, but you have to admit the rest of your day has been perfect."

Duly chastised, Sophie shook her pretty head in agreement. Yes, it had been perfect, Lily knew that. As a high-end social event planner, Lily was just getting to the top of her game, or at least she could envision the top from where she was standing in the valley. And she had been working overtime for her sisters as of late. "Thank you, this day has been wonderful," Sophie finally said. "I just wish you would be in the moment with me and stop to enjoy what's going on. You're not a robot, you know. And we're family, I'm not just any of your other clients."

"Of course you're not just any other client," Lily started just when the DJ decided to strike up a particularly annoying nineties dance track that had the crowd quickly exiting the dance floor and heading back to their seats. Lily frowned and looked at her sister. "If you were any other client, I wouldn't have let you hire Awful Roy from high school to DJ this gig." She let out a sigh. "But thanks to me and my

extraspecial way of treating all my clients like family,
I'm going to handle this for you and go kick some
sorry DJ ass right now to get this party on track."

As Sophie let out a breath and shook her head,
Lily headed in Roy's direction, a new and improved
set list the only thing on her mind.

"So when is it going to finally be your turn to walk
down the aisle? You can't let your sisters have all the
fun."

Really? The slightly slurred voice came at her
from behind and instantly ruined Lily's semi-good
mood after the Roy smackdown. Just when things
were starting to get back on track. People were dancing once again; DJ R-Town, aka Roy Husker, had
promised no more songs with the words *groove* or
celebration in them; and Sophie was currently booty
shaking in a semi-disrespectful way around her long-
time love, newly minted husband, Simon.

All was in place and running beautifully. Not to
mention the normally slightly drab VFW hall on the
North Shore of the Island had been transformed to a
bridal oasis. All done up in Sophie's colors of laven-
der and rose. It took Lily pulling quite a few strings
with some of her vendors to get everything in place,
but when they heard the wedding was for her sister,
none of them would turn down the opportunity to do
Lily a favor with hopes of being called upon for some
of her more high-profile clients.

Yes, the day was going well, or at least better than
expected given the fact that she was once again being
showcased as a bridesmaid. It wasn't all that much of
a problem, despite the shoes, but she was a surprisingly dateless one, thanks to Thomas and his unreliable ass. Well, that just made things unnecessarily

inconvenient. He was supposed to be there for her as a buffer against stupid-ass questions like this one.

Lily gave herself a mental kick. She should have known the question was coming. Even with Thomas by her side at Audrey's wedding, she hadn't made it out without the big M question coming her way. She didn't know why she'd thought she'd make it through this one. Maybe it was the long lull that gave her a false sense of hope that just once she'd get through one blasted family wedding without the focus turning to her lack of a significant other. Today it was Uncle Gene holding up the singleton mirror as he jabbed at her with his not-so-innocent questions. Lily turned away from her inspection of the ice-cream martini bar to face a bleary-eyed Uncle Gene. She tried her best to reach the back corner of her heart to come up with a retort that was, if not kind, at least not the "step off and mind your own damn business and while you're at it maybe lighten up on the whiskeys. Oh, and by the way, my eyes are up here, Uncle Gene" retort that she really wanted to blurt out.

Nope. Lily knew that comeback wouldn't do, so she sucked in a breath and forced a smile for her half-drunk, but mostly harmless, uncle. She was just about to say something when out of the corner of her eye she caught him staring at her . . . again.

Okay, this was getting highly uncomfortable if not wholly unwelcome. It wasn't like he was an unattractive man, he was quite the opposite; she just wasn't in the mood for flirty games. Well, not much. She looked past Uncle Gene to sweep him with a brief glance. Hell, it wasn't like Thomas showed, or like they were exclusive, Lily thought as she twisted at her lip. And if he were a plus-one, well, where the hell was his date?

Lily glanced again. Broad shouldered and tall, even by her standards, which meant exceptionally tall since she was five foot ten, Midnight was handsome in that slightly rough way that went against her norm but was just her thing back when they hooked up. With his smooth, tanned skin; full lips; and now that close-cropped hair, he had her instantly thinking of how luxuriously bristly he'd feel beneath her palms. But it was his eyes that really pulled her in. Framed by full brows, they were deep set, dark as pitch, and after all these months still made her feel as if he was seeing way too much. As if he knew what she looked like under her clothes, past her Grecian-styled one-shoulder dress that matched her sisters' but was a darker shade of rose, highlighting her status or, as some would think, shame, as maid of honor. The dress skimmed her generous curves in a flattering way but was still modest enough to not cause a stir. But with the way Midnight was eyeing her, she may as well have been naked in the middle of the VFW. It was as if his eyes caught it all.

It was then that Uncle Gene snapped his fingers in front of her face. "Earth to Lily. Girl, are you listening to me? That last boyfriend run out on you due to your lack of hearing?"

Lily felt the rage start at her toes and work its way up. Screw niceties. Uncle Gene had gone too far that time. She opened her mouth to let him have it when another voice entered the fray.

"Shut your drunk behind up, Gene, and leave the child alone!"

Lily couldn't help the smile that quirked at the

corner of her lips as Uncle Gene's face fell with the verbal smackdown from her grandmother, Delilah. Immediately, he flipped from being annoying Uncle Gene to being Gene, set upon son-in-law. "Aww, come on, Mama Dee. I'm just teasing her. I don't mean any harm."

Mama Dee leveled him with a hard stare and a wave of her regal hand. "What you need to be doing is stop worrying about everyone else and go get your wife so she stops harassing all the eligible groomsmen on the dance floor." Mama Dee shook her head as, in unison, the trio turned and looked toward the dance floor to get a glimpse of Aunt Ruby as she turned a two-step into three, confusing her young dance partner as she swiveled around him in her glittery ensemble, each time she passed his backside giving it a swift and hard bump with her hip. Mama Dee shook her head. "When will that child learn? Now, I'm all for a bit of fun, but at least do it on beat and with the proper undergarments. Her hips about straining the life out of that skirt. I thought I taught her better."

Lily couldn't hold back and snorted as Uncle Gene shook his head and put his drink down on a passing waiter's tray as he ran off to rescue the groomsmen from Aunt Ruby. "There," Mama Dee said, "that takes care of him." She leaned back a bit and gave Ruby a long stare. "Now, what are we going to do about you?"

Lily frowned, then let out a breath. "I didn't think I needed doing, Mama Dee."

Mama Dee released a small huff and shook her head, sending her gray curls bouncing. "Well, you need something. Running from one corner of this hall to the other, doing nothing but giving orders, and if not that then holding up the wall or warming the chairs."

"But I'm the wedding coordinator," Lily argued. "It's my job to do all these things. To make sure everything runs smoothly. If I don't, who will?"

Mama Dee just shook her head harder. "You can't run forever, girl. It's not your job to take care of everyone in this family. I don't know when you're going to learn that. It's your biggest fault."

Lily pulled back. "My biggest? You mean I have more?"

Mama Dee laughed and rolled her eyes. "Besides being conceited to a fault? No, honey. That will just about do it."

Lily laughed and gave her grandmother a hug. When she pulled back, Mama Dee was eyeing her once again. "What now, Mama Dee?"

"Nothing dear, it's just that I thought Thomas would be here with you and I'd at least get to see you have a dance today. You two have been going out how long now, nine months? Or is it a year? Isn't there a pot he should be getting off right about now?"

Lily once again let out a huff as she looked into her grandmother's eyes, the ones so very like her own. "Oh, Mama Dee, not you too," she croaked. "I can take it from anyone else, but I thought for sure you would be on my side. You know I'm not worried about getting married or even settling down. All my sisters may be eagerly tying themselves to a man, but I'm perfectly happy with my life as it is. Can't a woman be fulfilled just being on her own? Why must marriage always come up at these things? I mean, come on, there has to be a reason they call it settling down and not something like trading up."

When Mama Dee scrunched up her face and gave Lily a dark look, Lily realized that they were at a wedding and she really didn't want to get one of Mama Dee's famous tell offs in front of these people. "Okay, I get it. We're at a wedding and I'm sorry. I didn't mean to get mouthy. But just because we're here and I'm the planner and once again maid of honor, emphasis on *maid*, doesn't mean I'm fair game in the get-Lily-married contest. I have my own apartment that is close enough to Manhattan to be considered the city, good friends, and a career that is just now really taking off. I'm making quite the name for myself. Isn't that enough?"

Mama Dee rolled her eyes again as she sighed. "Calm it down, child. I swear, your blood pressure must be higher than half the seniors here. You need me to walk around to see if I can score you a nerve pill?"

It was now Lily's turn to roll her eyes. A person could never outtalk Mama Dee, and she didn't know why she tried.

"I'm not talking about marriage," her grandmother continued. "I was just getting on you to have a little fun. You organized this whole thing for your sister and the sister before her and the one before that one. Your life is all about taking care of others, and I don't see anyone taking care of you. Hell, I did not see you dance more than once at either of those weddings, and that was for the mandatory bridal party dance, and you practically frowned your way through those. You know, that's not the way I taught you girls. You're supposed to live. Live and fully breathe in every moment. " Mama Dee put her hand on top of Lily's, the cool, powdery feel giving Lily the comfort that it always had since she was a little girl. She looked Lily straight in the eyes before saying, "Now, I'm not going to lie, Nothing would make me happier than seeing you walk down the aisle one day to join up with a man who deserves someone as amazing as you are. But until that day, and even if it don't come, I'd just be content to see you kick up your heels a bit and sew a few oats." At that Lily grew slightly warm and her eyes shifted. There he was again. Standing slightly off to the side, over by the door to the kitchen with his dark eyes trained her way. Lily swallowed and forced her gaze back to Mama Dee quick enough, she hoped, for the sharp-eyed women not to have caught her staring.

Mama Dee raised her brow. "Like I said, sow some oats have a little fun, girl. Hell, just because your daddy was a shit, that shouldn't turn you off the institution. You know your grandfather was the love of my life."

Lily couldn't help sighing. "Mama Dee, you were Granddaddy's second wife and he was your third husband."

Mama Dee looked at her like she was speaking gibberish. "And so what? That just proves my point. We both didn't give up and kept at it till we got it right. You take your lessons from your elders, child. I know what's right. Live it up while you can. Life is always way shorter than we expect. Shoot, your sisters all have one marriage up on you already."

At that ridiculous declaration Lily couldn't help but laugh. "You're incorrigible, Mama Dee. Hush, or some may think you're already on to the next marriage for these newlyweds." She knew her nutty grandmother thought it was awful the way her mother had not remarried after her father left. She was always urging her to sign up with an online dating service and get back out there.

"I'm wishing no such thing. I just love love, and I want it for all my girls. If they can have a fraction of the joy Deacon and I had, that would be enough. I don't want them settling for anything less." Mama Dee's eyes went slightly glassy as they always did when she talked about Lily's late grandfather, the love of her life. Lily didn't understand that type of glassy-eyed love. She'd seen it but didn't get the feeling, and part of her hoped she never did. She had a sense that the loss of a love like that was something she could never recover from. She knew deep down that her mother hadn't.

Mama Dee reached over and ran a hand over Lily's cheek affectionately. She smiled, and then looked back at the dance floor, jutted out her chin, and pulled a face. Lily turned to see her Aunt Ruby now shimmying her sequined booty around the confused groomsmen and a finger-popping Uncle Gene had joined in. "Now you need to find you someone and get on out there. You can't let your old aunt have all the fun. Go on and show her how the young girls do it."

Lily started to shake her head no when a low voice rolled in from over her shoulder. "That was just what I was about to say."

Startled by the unexpected sexy, gravelly voice, Lily jumped back, but the sparkle of approval in her grandmother's sharp eyes let her know there was nothing to fear. Quite the opposite. Lily turned and looked deep into Midnight's eyes that saw too much and that she knew a little too well.

Despite his slightly intimidating look, he was smiling down at her. Damn, he was tall. Taller than she'd remembered or even guessed while spying him from across the room. So tall she had to crane her neck to get a good look at him, which was annoying and not something she was used to, so Lily took a quick step back, causing her heel to get caught in the chiffon hem of her dress. Oh hell. But he was quicker than her klutzy feet. His arm jutted out swiftly, his large warm hand going for her bare elbow and pulling her against his rock-hard side with a rather indelicate "Oomph!" Lily quickly pushed back against his chest and straightened herself, this time more careful as she stepped back and found a way to look down her nose at him while still looking up. "Excuse you."

He smiled wider, and it was completely unnerving while being totally disarming. "Excuse me, or is it you? I guess both of us are at fault with that one," he said. His voice as rough as the look of the hair on his strong chin.

Lily felt her brows draw together. "Do you, now?"

He chuckled, then put out a hand, which she looked at as if he was sticking out his foot for her to shake. Midnight shook his head slightly and then directed his attention to Mama Dee, whom Lily had forgotten was standing there. But one look at Mama Dee let Lily know she was having the time of her life taking in this exchange. "Hello, I'm Vincent—"

"Vin," Lily interrupted on a surprised breath as he turned to her with a smile that was altogether devastating before turning back to Mama Dee.

"Yes, Vincent Caro," he said. "But my friends and old acquaintances all me Vin. Just bumping in to ask Lily here for a dance. That is, if you don't mind my interrupting, ma'am."

Mama Dee grinned wide and took Vin's hand when Lily wouldn't. But then her eyes narrowed. "Have we met? I feel like we have."

Lily gave Vin an intense up-and-down inspection. He shook his head. "I don't believe so, ma'am."

Mama Dee let go of his hand and shrugged. "Well, it's something about your face."

His eyes widened. "I don't know if that's good or bad."

Mama Dee winked. "Trust me, baby. In your case, it's good. If it was bad you'd have already been sent on your way."

Vin pulled back with a laugh. "I don't doubt it, ma'am."

As Lily took in the scene, she was digesting his name, once again letting it fill her memory banks. Vincent Caro. Vin, yeah, that was it. No callback Vin. She should have remembered. She'd thought for sure when they'd exchanged numbers he'd call her. He was Simon's friend after all, and Simon didn't seem a no callback kind of guy. And silly as it was, she wasn't a first callback kind of women. Nor was she a texter. She wasn't into guys that had her chasing them down for a response. He'd asked for her number first, he'd should have been the one to initiate the call. That was that. Rule number 23 in the Laws of Lily. No amendments necessary. Not that his not calling back was the biggest deal. During that time she'd really thrown herself into her work, and it paid off. She'd gotten her business well established, and though she wasn't in any sort of committed relationship, much to the chagrin of her family, she was happy. Back then she may have considered herself hurt over him not calling. Not now. And though Lily knew those types of things were not something she could truly avoid, she didn't see herself encountering that type of hurt in the immediate future.

And truly it wasn't as if she was surprised by Vin's brush-off. Sadly, hurt a bit, but not all that surprised. After seeing how her father had moved on from her mother, from all of them, despite all his so-called love of family, Lily wasn't easily surprised when it came to affairs of the heart and unreliable men. She had been there before, seen the hurt and the pain up close and vowed never to get bent out of shape over a noncommittal, noncommunicative man ever again. Lily finally spoke up. "I'm sure she does mind your interrupting."

Her emotions were her power, and it was something she'd never give up. Vin. She mentally snorted his name. She should give him a thank-you. In a way he'd freed her by not ever calling her. It was with that thought that her grandmother's voice brought her back to the scene at hand. "Lily, stop acting like you were raised in a barn and shake the man's hand."

Lily let out a low breath and looked at her grandmother. But Mama Dee's raised brow let Lily know she was out of hand. Completely. She looked back over to Vin. What was she doing? Here was a perfectly handsome—handsome and tall, mind you— man showing interest, again, where Thomas was perfectly MIA and she was acting like she was all of thirteen instead of pushing thirty. So what if they had a sketchy past? The past was called the past for a reason, and he was in front of her looking hot right now. So what, he'd snubbed her after their first encounter. That was then. She was a grown woman and in the driver's seat of her life. She could see him clearly for what he was, and right now it was time for her to start having a good time. That sealed it. Mama Dee was right. The moment had come for her to have a little fun, and Vin may be just the answer.

Lily uncrossed her arms and smiled as she stretched out her hand. "Nice to see you again, Vincent."

He raised a brow at the use of his full name, then took her hand in his. Lily couldn't help but wonder if the immediate sensual pull was something that only she felt as he gave her hand a shake. Probably so. A man like him more than likely weakened knees everywhere he went without a care for the women he left crumbling in his wake.

"So, would you like to dance?"

Lily's hand went still and she blinked. She blinked again before pulling her hand from his and, as casually as she could, crossing her arms once more. She glanced over at her aunt and uncle getting busy to a nineties dance track. Yeah, dancing didn't look so fun right now. "No, um, I wouldn't say that I would. But maybe the next song?"

Suddenly the music changed and a slow ballad came on. "And this song is perfect," Mama Dee spoke up without missing a beat. "Why, I was just saying the dance floor needs more young blood. You two get on out there and do my old heart some good."

Lily shot her grandmother a semi-sharp look but knew it would go no further than that. She could never deny Mama Dee anything, just as her grandmother could never deny her. They were like that.

Though Lily had four sisters, she and Mama Dee always had a special bond. Her recent health troubles only served to remind Lily just how precious that bond was. She let out a sigh as she looked her grandmother's way. "You don't play fair, lady."

Mama Dee chuckled, the sound of her laugh light and musical, letting Lily know it amused Mama Dee to no end that she'd won the latest round with Lily and her man situation. "Now, when have I ever? Go on out there and have fun. Put on a show they won't soon forget."

Chapter 2

Vin took Lily's hand and led her onto the dance floor. As he did, he tried his best to ignore the immediate and almost visceral pull in his groin. He told himself he could handle this. That it was good to get excited. Lately he'd become bored with seeing women as all the same, just cookie cutter versions of one another, so this unexpected thrill was a welcome sensation. But he was having trouble dealing with the highly annoying twinge that was dangerously much higher up. The one hovering close to the left side of his chest. That feeling, while not new, was one he'd told himself was long buried and better left forgotten. Something he hadn't expected to feel again and frankly, didn't know if he wanted to feel. Especially since it was safer not to.

Seeing her again just about knocked the breath out him, but to Vin's credit, he had to admit he'd played it off pretty well. Why shouldn't he? He was the king of cool. At least he played the part well enough. He'd half expected to see her at the wedding. Okay, fine, he knew he'd see her at the wedding; she was Sophie's sister, after all. Honestly, he was surprised he'd never run into her these past few months in and around town. Part of him fully expected to. Maybe even wanted to, though he knew it was way too late for any sort of rekindling. Besides, that's just the way things went out on the Island. When the season ended, only the locals remained and everyone else went back to their lives commuting to and from the city, where the real money was to be made. He knew that. He also knew that though she was a local girl, she spent most of her time in the city, venturing back home only for family functions, as it were.

Still, the way he'd handled things with her before pretty much sealed the deal on any replay of what they had that day on the beach. Not that he blamed her. He'd never called. Time had just slipped away as he'd buried himself in the launch of his restaurant. He'd had to give that his all. Putting everything he had, time, energy, the possibility of relationships, into the dream his mother instilled in him before she'd passed—died. And Vin knew then that he didn't need the distraction a woman like Lily Perry could bring. Besides, it wasn't as if she called him either, and though that thought was sobering, Vin had to infer from that that his not calling was no big loss to her. The way she'd come on to him that day and night under the docks, well, she just didn't seem the type to wait for a formal invitation when it came to going after something or someone she wanted.

Even with that fact, here he was. When Simon invited him to the wedding and requested his empanadas, Vin—like a silly schoolboy instead of a full-grown man—thought . . . maybe. His mind went to the docks, and her eyes and those luscious lips that he'd never quite forgotten, and for a moment he thought there could be a chance for, he didn't know what . . . just, something.

Vin forcibly pushed the ridiculous feeling of *maybe* aside as he took Lily in his arms and tried to look at the situation objectively. This was no big deal, he told himself. She was just a pretty woman he was dancing with at a friend's wedding. Hell, that in itself made the situation pretty extraordinary. Vin didn't dance. Just like he didn't waste time on silly thoughts of *maybe*. That was something he hadn't done in longer than he could remember. *Maybe* was for dreamers, and he liked to spend his time now firmly planted in reality and absolutes. The only dream he dared believe in, thanks to his mother, was his restaurant, Canéla and at least with that he had some bit of control over it.

But as the music took on a sexy strain, and Vin got his first real feel of Lily Perry in longer than he'd care to remember, his arms and his betraying heart couldn't deny the perfection of the moment. The woman was lush. No petite flower, despite her pretty name, Lily was tall and, for lack of a better word, sturdy. Vin almost pulled a face as the odd word entered his thoughts and he tripped over her feet.

"Ouch!"

"I'm sorry," he stammered out. *Shit*. So much for his cool factor. He needed to focus. But looking into her big brown eyes, eyes that were at the same time cunning and still innocent, and getting a glimpse of the direct challenge in them made him want to kiss her until her sooty lashes fluttered and those eyes rolled back in her head.

Why was she so perfect? So put together and so

damned cultured? She was from here. And not the fancy part of here either. She was a town girl, but the way she carried herself you would think she lived in one of the high-priced estates a few exits down the highway. The ones where the residents didn't fight bumper-to-bumper traffic on the weekends but had helicopters fly them in from the city. Vin remembered she was that way at their first meeting too, out on the beach. Not as loose and carefree as her sisters but so carefully buttoned up and tamed that it was as if she was looking down on everyone even when she was supposedly just relaxing. She gave him the shock of his life when she followed him under the dock and gave him a memory that to this day still made his most erotic dreams pale in comparison, and all they did was make out. Make out! What grown-ass man ever said those words?

"Are we going to just stand here, or should I take the lead?"

Vin blinked and mentally kicked himself. *What the hell, man? Get it together.* There'd be no fluttering or anything close to it if he stood there like an idiot all night. Vin attempted a shuffle and sway, then proceeded to step on Lily's crystal-clad foot again.

"Do you mind? I kind of need these feet for walking tomorrow." Her tone was cool and detached and let him know he was failing monumentally with his attempt at impressing her.

"Shit! I'm sorry. I'm better in the kitchen than I am on the dance floor. Hell, I'm better at so many other things than dancing."

She looked up at him with a definite spark in her eyes. "Other things?" she drawled out. "I remember."

Vin chuckled. Her flirtation caught him off guard.

He'd almost forgotten how quick she could be, but that's what he'd liked about her.

"Maybe I'm talking about your cooking. Not that I've ever tasted it." Her gaze narrowed. "I remember Simon saying something about your having a stand on the beach. You still working there?"

Vin nodded. "I own it, actually. Along with my mother." He frowned. He wasn't sure why he felt the need to be sure she knew that. What did it matter him owning what? And why add in his mother? She was gone. The thought never failing to bring a dull pain to his chest. "I'm sorry. What does it matter my owning the stand or not?" He forced a smile then. "Yes, I still have the stand and I open it seasonally, though I have another venture in the works now."

Lily nodded. "That's okay. You should be proud of your accomplishments."

With her calm reassurance Vin felt his heart rate slowing to normal and felt literally and figuratively on better footing. For a few moments they were quiet and swaying as one on the dance floor. Vin fought not to get swept up and let his mind wander to anyplace further than the moment they were in. He knew it was safer that way. It was the way he'd been living. The way he'd survived the past year after losing his mother. He'd learned to live in the moment, focus on work, and enjoy the little pleasures of life as they came. To expect any more than that was naïve. Expecting or anticipating was a fool's game. Tomorrow wasn't promised, so he let that be, just as now with Lily in his arms he swayed and went the way the wind took him. Although strangely, it seemed to never take him that far from home.

The breeze picked up and sailed through the open

doors of the balcony, where there were more guests mingling, filing into the hall of the VFW.

Vin watched as the few free tendrils of Lily's up-swept hair breezed across her face and against the length of her regal neck. She was lovely. Probably too lovely for him. Not to mention too much of a nice girl in that way that he knew deep down she'd be, despite all that talk he'd overheard between her and her grandmother about not wanting the whole settle-down, white-picket-fence life and the whole "come on let's get hot and heavy under the docks" femme fatal character she played at with him. He knew the look, and she had it written all over her face. Well put together, accomplished, yes, she was all of that, but she was also Sophie's older sister. And the fact was that the Perry women seemed to have been bitten by the marriage bug big-time. Despite his surprisingly putting down even deeper roots in town with his restaurant, that didn't mean he wanted to settle down. Family life was not for him. Although he knew his stance was not the dream his late mother had for him, he also knew it was part of his survival right now.

Even so, the way her curves were fitting so nicely in his hands and lining up with his body in just the perfect way took him back to that amazing evening under the dock and had him wanting to line her up but good in the horizontal way. Made him for just a moment want to change his stance on all he thought he knew about himself and go back to that night and call her back even before she'd gotten home. It made him curse every wasted moment between now and then when he should have had her in his arms. They'd only gotten so far that night under the dock. Under the dock. How very high school of them both.

Two grown adults. Not to mention the fact that they didn't go all the way with having full on sex but both working each other to a state of complete satisfaction, so much so that he had a terrible habit of comparing many women since . . . to her. Vin supposed, though it was contrary to anything that made good sense, that was one of the reasons he'd never pursued her. She had the dangerous ability of instantly pulling him in. Making him want to be with her, be near her so much so that it was practically a need. And shit if that didn't scare him. He told himself he never wanted to feel a need for someone, anyone. Not ever again.

Lily gave a short cough, and when he brought his gaze up from her hips and back to those pretty eyes, they had lost any hint of playfulness. "Honestly, if you pulled me out here to just step on my feet and gawk at me without offering up any conversation, I can move on. It's my sister's wedding and I'm plenty busy. I have much better things to do than waste my time on the dance floor with you."

The biting tone of her honey-dipped voice pulled Vin up short, and he frowned. Quickly snatched out of his momentary fantasy he was grateful for her sharpness; it bolstered his courage and told him he could handle her, that the distance she inserted made him stronger and let him know he could pursue her and come out just fine. "You call a dance at a wedding a waste of time?" he countered.

Lily cocked her head as she easily glided left and then right, dipping a little, leading him around the dance floor. Wait. *When did that happen?* Damn, the woman was bossy. "I call this dance a waste of time. I don't engage in pursuits that don't lead to anything. Time is too precious."

Vin took that as a cue and ever so slightly tightened his hold on the small of her back. His fingertips inched along her spine as he attempted to shift their direction and take the lead. But the quick shift and stiffening of her spine let him know she wouldn't be giving in so easily. "That's funny, I consider this a perfect way to spend what could be an otherwise dull afternoon," he said.

The wind blew again, and she moved her hand from his shoulder, leaving him cold as she tucked her wayward hair behind the pretty shell of her ear. "If it's so dull, then what are you doing here?" she countered, not letting his remark pass. He should have known she probably wouldn't take too kindly to having her sister's wedding described as dull.

Vin cleared his throat, silently cursing the nerves suddenly lodged there and hoping to cover them up. "Simon is a friend, and I promised him I'd come and bring some of my empanadas that he likes."

She pulled up short then and stopped swaying, looking at him hard. "So you're that friend. I should have connected the two."

Vin felt his brows draw together. "I don't know how I should take that. What does 'that friend' mean?"

Lily shrugged, her beautifully sloped shoulders rising and falling in dismissal as she picked up the dance again. She really was a natural leader. The way she had no problem taking control made Vin wonder what she'd be like in bed. Could she ever give up control, and would it even really matter? Somehow he doubted it. "It's nothing. I helped my sister out with the menu and, for the life of me, couldn't figure how your empanadas would fit in with our southern

soul food theme, but for some reason Simon dug his
heels in and insisted on them."

Vin had no comment but instead shrugged himself. Simon wasn't the first to dig his heels in when it
came to his food, and he probably wouldn't be the
last. What could he say? His food was good and he'd
make no apologies for that.

"What?" Lily asked, her eyes widening. "You don't
care to elaborate, just a shrug?"

"There's nothing to elaborate. I'm flattered Simon
enjoys them so much that he was willing to go to bat
for me, but I didn't mean to cause marital discourse,
especially not before the happy couple tied the knot.
I'll have to find a way to make it up to Sophie."

"Hmm."

Vin paused in the dance, causing her to momentarily stop and hit his chest, the feeling stirring him
to no end. He looked down at her while telling himself to check his schoolboy, hormone-ish feelings.
"That's not too ominous a sound."

She shook her head. "It's nothing."

"Well, it was a whole lot of nothing."

"It's just that I'd not heard Simon or Sophie talk
about you all that much. I assumed you weren't that
close."

Vin paused. The music continued while he held
her in his grasp and looked her in the eyes. "So are
you saying you wondered about me?"

Lily frowned, her full top lip curling just a bit as
she cast her gaze somewhere past his shoulder. "I'm
not saying anything of the sort. Just making conversation and letting you know that neither your name
nor your empanadas ever came up." She shrugged.
"That's all."

Now it was his turn to say, "Hmm."

Lily looked up at him, her expression a definite twinge of annoyance with an edge of exasperation. Vin grinned when she frowned harder.

"I'm just surprised," he said.

She looked him in the eye again. "What in the world for? Is your ego so big that you feel you'd be the cause for conversation over the course of this past year?"

Vin thought long and hard. He could feel the tension in her back as her spine went impossibly more rigid, but she looked so pretty as the anger bloomed in her mahogany cheeks; all he wanted to do was kiss her. "Of course not, it's just that my empanadas are that good."

She shook her head slightly and rolled her eyes, though at the same time there was the slightest hint of a quirk to the corner of her mouth. For the life of him, he wanted to bend down and kiss her just then. Whoever the fool was he'd overheard her talking to her grandmother about who didn't show today was losing out . . . big-time.

Just then a waiter dropped a tray, the clang turning everyone's head. Lily winced, then looked up at him. She gave him a half smile as she started to pull out of his grasp, but her eyes held what he thought was a twinge of regret. "Sorry, but I've got to go and put this fire out."

"Do you? But we haven't finished our dance. Can't someone else do it? Don't you get to take a break sometimes? Let loose and enjoy yourself a little bit?" Taking a chance, Vin pulled her in closer, bringing her body flush against his so they were chest to chest and thigh to thigh. Though she gave him a little resistance, she leaned in, and the chance he'd taken was worth it, because she felt like perfection and smelled equally as delicious. Like spring rain and honey. The urge to lean down and taste her on that spot between her neck and shoulder, where that tendril of hair curled so prettily, was almost overwhelming. But her mind was already elsewhere, and her body was soon to follow as responsibilities won out and she pulled away, looking up at him. "You're a bit of a pain in the ass, Vincent Caro."

"And you should take a little time and taste what I have to offer, Lily Perry."

The beauty of her smile brightening her face, bringing a light shimmer to her pretty eyes as she eased out of his embrace was worth his quip. "I already did, remember?"

The words brought him both regret and longing. "How could I ever forget?"

Lily walked away from Vincent Caro slightly unsteady on her feet. She was hot and shaky but trying her best not to let it show. Thank goodness for the dropped tray, because if the tray hadn't hit the floor she was sure she would have. That or be swept up in the arms of all that man like some sort of romance heroine. It was so unlike her, but damn it, being in such close proximity to him it was hard to keep her knees from weakening. Vincent Caro was a lot to take in all at once, and she had never considered herself shy when it came to men, despite Uncle Gene and what he thought he knew about her status.

She let out a long breath as she scanned the mini-desserts before they were due to go out. In addition to the traditional wedding cake Sophie wanted an assortment of mini-dessert bites, since she'd never been one for cake. Lily had tried her best to keep her usual thread of control as she did in every tense situation, but still she picked up an individual peach pie and brought it to her lips. She'd found it incredibly hard to hold on to her sense of control when it came to him, not to mention everything on him was hard and, well, solid. From his chest to his arms to his thighs. When he pulled her against him out on the dance floor, her mind raced back to their time on the beach. Wandering to that unforgettable moment, the one that kept her up more nights than she'd care to admit after their encounter was over, making her feel both mentally and physically weak. She finished the mini-pie and looked at the now clearly evident space it left on the platter. *Shit*, she thought as she wiped her fingers on a napkin and then quickly rearranged the rest of the desserts to fill in the spot. She thought she was over Vin. Over searching for that swept-away feeling, but encountering him, being so close to him, had done nothing but stoke a merely dormant fire that was smoldering but nowhere near dead. She was afraid that if they'd gotten any closer on the dance floor she'd have scandalized the place and figured out just how hard he could be. How reckless she could be. A smile pulled at the corner of Lily's mouth. Not that that would be a bad thing at all. Just it would be a little too much for her family to handle. Sexpot Lily was way off the idea of the image they had of her, so no use for her to go bursting bubbles now.

So what that Thomas had bailed on her and not come through with escorting her to this wedding. It

was his loss. They weren't mutually exclusive, and as
it turns out had never been. Lily let out a slow breath.
To think she had actually considered hooking up with
Thomas this weekend. For old time's sake and well,
it had been a while since she'd considered being with
anyone. A long while. No matter though. Even the
thought of him now paled in comparison to the man
Vin was. Besides, the real annoyance was over the
time wasted with him and the fact that she had to
endure the wedding and the constant scrutiny of her
family alone. But she couldn't come down on
Thomas too hard. It wasn't like there was any real attachment or commitment made between the two of
them beyond being available for business deals and
family functions. Sure, for a while she thought they
were a thing. He hers and her his, but now there was
clarity and she wasn't tied to him. She wasn't tied to
anyone. He was a convenience for her just as she
was for him. Hell, a suitable escort was not easy to
find in her hometown. It was almost as hard as it
was to find a safe, passible and most of all satisfac-
tory screw.

Lily left the kitchen and went out to check on the
guests. From across the deck where she was now
standing, her eyes shifted once again to Vincent Caro.
He was talking with another of the groomsmen, and
they were laughing it up in that way that guys do
when his slightly hooded eyes slid to hers for a
moment, the heat of his look practically gluing her
DTM sandals to the wood of the deck. Lily uncon-
sciously licked her lips, letting out a necessary sigh
right as her little cousin, Chantal, pulled at her skirt.
She looked down. "Cousin Lily, is it time for cake?"

Lily blinked, bringing her wide-eyed cousin into

focus. Chantal's words came out on a lisp, forcing
Lily to focus on the job at hand. What was she doing?
Whew. Maybe it had been too long a dry spell. She
had a wedding to run and, family or not, she had a
reputation to uphold when it came to her work. Lily
frowned. She would have been so much safer if
Thomas hadn't bailed and had given her a much
needed buffer for her ridiculous hormones. She
didn't have these types of distracted brain freezes
with him around. *Focus, Lil, focus.* She mentally said
the words with determination and then smiled down
at Chantal. "You're right, honey, it is almost cake
time. Let me quickly get things in place."

She ran off toward the kitchen again, throwing up
a mental block against the broad-shouldered Vin Caro.
Along the way, she gave directions to the staff and told
the DJ to announce the cutting of the cake, which
blessedly gave her something else to think about. Passing a nearly empty tray, her eyes glanced to the few
golden brown meat pies left. She was tempted to try
one of Vin's empanadas but resisted. But Lily knew it
was a moment on the lips that she just couldn't afford.

Successfully having dodged the bouquet during
the toss—after catching two she didn't need to add
another to her collection—Lily was moving bits of
cake around on her plate when an empanada slid into
her field of vision. "Can I tempt you with something
hotter?"

She looked up into Vin's nearly black eyes with a
cautious side-eyed glare. "Come on, you can't be
serious with that line."

He shrugged and eased down into the empty seat

next to her, recently vacated by Simon's brother Stan, whom she hoped was resting off his liberal use of the open bar and not going in for another round. "That depends on if you think it's funny, corny, cute, or desperate."

Lily chose to keep her opinion to herself. It wouldn't do to tell him that she found his tactics cute and sexy, not to mention that the food in front of her looked like it tasted better than the cake she'd ordered, which, to her horror, was dry and crumbly. The baker was new to her and had come highly recommended by Sophie. Although the baker's skill with decorating was almost unmatched, he seemed to be a disaster when it came to the actual cake under the frosting. Lily was mentally kicking him off her prospective vendor list. But pushing thoughts of the cake aside, Lily gave Vin a slow up and down as she let out a long sigh and picked up the warm empanada he was offering. She brought it to her lips.

Lord, why did you do it?! The dang empanada was delicious! The outer crust was light and flakey, not at all crumbly but melt-in-your-mouth delicious, while the meat-filled center was both savory and sweet with just enough spice to give you a bite back that was a perfect shock to your senses. "No wonder Simon insisted on having these at his wedding." She opened her eyes wide and looked at Vin, catching the smug half smile on his lips.

"I told you my talents were not on the dance floor," Vin said from by her side.

Lily nodded as she chewed and swallowed. She wanted to argue with him—no man should be that cocky about his abilities—but she couldn't. He was right. "You made this?" she asked, almost shocked that he could look that good and still have that type of skill. Lily shook her head.

One brow went up. "Why would I lie?"

He had a point there. Lily gave him a smile. "Well you, sir, are dead wrong for doing it." She finished the small pie in two bites and would have been satisfied with maybe two more. As if reading her mind, he grinned again and the small action was like a stinger right to her chest. He really should carry a warning with that smile.

"You're quite sure of yourself, aren't you?" Lily asked. She then looked around the room. The reception, like all of her family's functions, was just getting into full swing. Normally after cake, folks would be making their exit, but now was the time for her people to really let loose. She saw a couple of cousins making requests from the DJ and knew that yet another popular line dance was soon to come. Lily glanced from Vin to her sister, who was shimmying with Simon and laughing happily up into his face. She looked so carefree and wide open, as if her heart couldn't hold all her joy. As Lily watched her sister, she got a brief lump in her throat wondering what that must feel like, must be like, to laugh with such abandon looking at the man you loved and having him look back at you the same way.

But in that moment the music changed and, just as she feared, hands started to clap, feet stomped, and the slide was queued up. Multiple cousins pointed at her, and in a quick panic to avoid cha-cha-ing for the next twenty-five minutes, Lily grabbed Vin's hand and tugged him up. "Save me. Please."

He looked at her, wide eyed for a moment.

"I'll do anything to not slide left then hop right for

three songs straight," she said by way of explanation, tipping her head toward the dance floor. They both turned to look, and there was Aunt Ruby leading the charge. Her ample hips swayed left, then right, to the heavy beat of the song's bass while the singer rapped the steps and DJ R-Town mimicked his words, his mouth too close to the mic so his voice came out deep and statically.

Vin squeezed Lily's hand and let her lead him. "Consider me your knight," he said as he followed her out to the deck and onto the stairs that led to the parking area below the VFW. Once there they encountered a couple of the busboys on a break having a smoke. Lily's instinct was to speak up and get on them about finding other things to do when they were on her—well, her sister's—clock, but she was currently on her own escape grind so thought the better of it. Besides, she had just taken off to do who knew what with a guy she knew she had no business being with, so who was she to lecture anyone at the moment? She pulled up short then, as better judgment threatened to seep in, causing Vin to stop between cars and stare at her. "You all right? Where are we going?"

Lily let the question weigh on her for a moment while she thought it over. Where was she going? She hadn't thought things through. In the moment all she wanted to do was get out from under her family, away from the suddenly oppressive feeling of overwhelming revelry and joy and get away with the dangerous and delicious-looking and, now she knew, extremely talented in the kitchen Vincent Caro. He looked her up and down, his eyes raking over her body in that way of his that had her feeling exposed in the best and most heated of ways, when she suddenly knew the answer to her question. She made a mental note to send Thomas a thank-you for his no-show once she got home. Giving Vin's hand a squeeze, she pulled him behind her once again. "Just follow me."

They rounded the building and followed a small path on the back side of the hall to an old utility hut. It was locked, as Lily knew it would be. But she stepped carefully to the back of the hut, where there was an old wooden bench that she remembered from her childhood days of playing hide-and-go-seek with the cousins. This spot was wooded and hidden, but the view from this point was almost as good as from the VFW balcony high above them. You could see past the woods, down to the beach and the magnificent ocean beyond.

"How did you know about this?" Vin asked, his voice low and closer to the back of her neck than she had anticipated. Lily turned to him and smiled, trying to keep it casual while feeling anything but.

"I used to play here as a kid. When my dad would come to the VFW. We didn't care much for hanging out inside."

He nodded. "That's funny. I thought I knew just about every hidden spot on the island."

It was her turn to nod. "And that's funny; I thought I knew just about every hidden chef, but here you are."

Lily took a step forward and came chest to chest with Vin, looking up into his onyx eyes. "So, are you going to tell me your recipe for those empanadas? I have quite the influence, you know. I could steer some business your way."

He grinned at her, only slightly but enough to make her want to ease forward and lick at the upturned corners of his mouth.

"Your influence is quite welcome, Miss Perry, but I'm not one to cook and tell." His tone was dark and teasing and set all her nerves to tingling.

Feeling slightly heady on her wedding toast wine and pulled into the haze of his deep eyes, Lily eased forward to finally get a taste of his full lips. They were soft. Softer than she remembered, and it surprised her from a man who was as hard and angular as he was. She tipped out her tongue and let it gently lick at his fullness. When he let out a low growl and snaked his arm around her waist, pulling her in close, he let her know he wasn't nearly as soft or tame as his lips let on.

His hardness and heat turned Lily on immediately and sent her head spinning. She could hear the light strains of the music from overhead along with thump, thump, thumping of the sounds of the guests moving in unison on the old wooden deck, or maybe that was the thumping of her heart, Lily didn't care. All she wanted in that moment, when Vin opened his mouth, exciting her with a skillful sweep of his tongue, was more of him. All thoughts of the reception, her family, and even no-show Thomas evaporating from her mind as the heat of her body connected with his and the late spring breeze swirled around them both.

Vin fueled her and made her grateful for the single free life she had. Sure, her sisters were happy, but did they have this type of freedom? These types of thrills or excitement? That only came from no commitments, from not being tied down.

Lily ignored the surprising lump in her throat that came with the normally thrilling thought of freedom and pushed it down as she focused on the gorgeous hunk of man under her hands. She let her fingers wander to feel his strong pecs, barely concealed under the fine cotton of his dress shirt, while breathing deeply, taking in his masculine scent. He was all sea and spice, the déjà vu of it just about drugging her as the memory of them both wet from the ocean and kissing under the docks came back to her mind.

Vin pulled her in tighter, and she ground her hips against him while he brought his large hands around to her behind and pulled her even closer. He took control, and she let him, liking the shift from what she was used to. Letting go, she pulled away slightly and let her head fall back while he took the hint, taking his kisses and moving from her lips downward, letting them trail to her jawline and her neck, playing special attention to her collarbone, where she was oh-so sensitive. The feeling he was giving her was incredible and unlike anything she'd ever experienced. This man didn't make her work for her pleasure but brought the pleasure to her. It was different, new, and she liked it.

Lily let go. Her hands wandered back over his chest and then went south over his abs. The urge to rip at the buttons of his shirt to see if he really was as hard as he felt was almost overwhelming. Lily sucked in a gasp and clenched her thighs together when Vin's hand came up and his fingers brushed over her already peaked nipples. *Holy hell.* This was going from zero to a hundred real quick, and she was loving it. She leaned forward and let her cheek brush against the gorgeous stubble she'd been eyeing earlier. It was satisfyingly as rough as she'd hoped it would be, and she let out a long breath as Vin smoothly took that clever hand and dipped it over the top of her dress, shifting her one shoulder strap. Suddenly it was bare skin against bare skin, and her knees practically buckled. All sorts of visions ran through her head as sparks flew, and Lily cursed the fact the she was in chiffon, the old bench no match for the fine material. Besides, by the sound of the slowing of the pounding overhead, she knew she'd have to return to the reception soon. Lily moaned and moved forward, arching her back and pushing her breasts farther into his palm.

"Tell me this is what you want." His deep voice rumbled over her eardrums and caressed her from the inside out almost as expertly as his hands.

Just then the wind kicked up, fluttering her dress high, bringing a sudden cool breeze to her thighs at the same time a cheer went up overhead. Lily blinked and looked up into Vin's eyes. Openmouthed, she extracted her hand from the groin area of his pants. *Okay, when did that happen?* And at the same time Vin hit her senses with that damned grin again as if he were reading her mind.

Lily blinked. What was she doing? This was her sister's day and she was supposed to be on the clock, not out rubbing on some guys—well, she'd just leave that right there. No matter, the fact remained that Lily didn't have time for clandestine trysts with hunky empanada cooks. She gave Vin a long look, then an embarrassed smile as she eased out of his embrace. "Sorry, I think we'd better stop here. I need to check on my sister and make sure everything is running smoothly."

He cleared his throat and looked at her. There was no anger and no hint of disappointment. Normally a guy with a hard-on like the one he was sporting wouldn't take this news so coolly. Still he did ask, "So they can't get on without you?"

"Usually not," she said dryly while smoothing her hair in place. She looked up at him with barely concealed surprise when he once again righted the strap on her dress. She silently nodded her thanks.

Lily took Vin's hand for balance and eased around him to head back up to the main hall of the VFW and the reception space. When he didn't follow, she turned back puzzled. "Are you coming?"

He laughed then and raised his brow. "Sadly, no."

She chuckled getting his joke. "Funny."

"Yeah, I try, but I think I'll give you a minute and follow when I'm more presentable. How about we keep in touch this time?" He looked sheepish as he pulled out his phone. "Um, is your number still the same?"

Lily pulled back and looked at him objectively. She'd seen this movie before. And with this passing year he'd only turned more handsome and way more self-assured than he needed to be. He'd let her down back then, and there was no reason to open herself up and give him a chance to do it again.

Vin gave her a smile as he seemed to scroll through his contacts ready to double-check her info. Lily shook her head. "Thanks for the food and the fun tonight. But I'll have to decline. How about we just leave this where it is. It was fun, meeting you again like this. And who knows, maybe we'll meet again in another year." Lily laughed, though she didn't miss the hollow feeling it left behind. "Despite what you overheard from my family this afternoon, I'm good just how I am."

Vin looked at her as if she'd suddenly grown two heads, and if it wouldn't have sent mixed signals she would have taken out her cell just to get a photo of his expression. "But you are a great cook," Lily added by way of masculine placation. "Really. I'll keep you in mind for possible future jobs. I'll get your info from Simon if anything comes up."

Vin gave his head a small shake, then rubbed his hand over his scalp before slipping his phone back in his pocket. "Why do I feel like we've been here before?"

She leaned into him then and gave him a quick kiss on the side of his cheek. "Because we have, but isn't that life?"

Chapter 3

Vin took another pull from his beer as he looked out onto the surf crashing against the rocks from the balcony of his apartment above his restaurant, Canela, on Rockaway Beach. Tonight, though, not even the sound of the waves could calm his nerves.

It had been a slow night at the restaurant, which wasn't so surprising given that it was a Tuesday night, but still, things should be starting to pick up since they were coming into the late spring season and the weather was warming. They'd even had a few days that hinted at summer being just around the corner. No, they weren't the fancy Hamptons but they were out of Manhattan, on the Island and just beachy enough to be considered a weekend destination.

Vin didn't want to waste his energy on worrying, but the mortgage was due on the first of the month and there was no denying that. Since he'd taken over the restaurant lease, along with his semi-silent part-ner friends, Aidan Walker and Carter Bain from the family, who'd had the space running as an old Italian restaurant for years, it seemed the first of the month kept coming quicker and quicker. The looming date and the responsibly of it constantly kept him on edge.

Vin shook his head as he brought his palm down sharply on the deck's ledge. Hell, maybe he shouldn't have taken on the restaurant at all. He was doing fine with his little food stand on the beach, which was open seasonally, and then taking on odd cooking and construction jobs during the off-season. He'd been making ends meet. It wasn't any sort of path to fame or expansive fortune, but it kept him, and back then his mom, comfortable enough, and that was enough. Vin pushed back on emotions he wasn't in the mood to wrestle with tonight, but still they wouldn't let him go. He knew—and how couldn't he know, since his mother was never shy about sharing her dreams for him—that she'd always hoped for more than their little stand and his selling waters at a dollar a pop up and down the beach. At times, yeah, sure, Vin felt like an idiot for letting Carter and Aidan fill his head with grand ideas about him being able to expand and do more. Carter with all his bullshit talk about the neighborhood being on the rise with gentrification. Although he could admit he may have been right there. He just didn't like the idea of it all being in his hands and his possibly letting them down. He'd been down that road before.

Still, Vin couldn't put all the blame on Aidan and Carter. No one had that kind of pull to make him do anything that he didn't think was the right thing to do. No, he knew the decision to open the restaurant was all on him. Him and his guilt over not making more of himself back when his mom was alive. She shouldn't have had to have died without seeing all her hard work materialize into something more permanent than a little stand that could blow away with the first gust of a storm. He should have given her something lasting. Solid and permanent. Been a son for her to be proud of when she was still alive.

Vin swallowed down the ever-present lump in his throat. The one that formed whenever thoughts of his mother, Sonia, and her quick passing entered his mind.

How was it he didn't see the signs of how sick she was? How much the backbreaking work of running the stand was taking a toll on her? He should have watched her more closely. Should have made sure she was seeing her doctor regularly, health insurance or not. He should have taken better care of her. They were all they'd had. Vin looked down at his clenched fists, then loosened them. He knew this sort of thinking was ridiculous and also knew if his mother were alive she'd take him to task for it. Yes, cancer took her away from him way too quickly and, yes, he'd barely had a chance to enjoy his final moments with her and say good-bye before she was gone. But he also knew she'd be the first to tell him not to question God's plan but to be grateful in all things. Vin let out a breath. Grateful. Yeah, that was a hard one. Here he was now with the restaurant she'd always talk about having, and the one person he wanted to share it with wasn't by his side. It was hard to be grateful about that.

Vin let out another breath harshly and forcefully pushed the thought away. The restaurant. That was it. He needed to keep his mind on the restaurant and business. Not the fact that his mother spent most of her days in the off season working in other people's kitchens and, when not doing that, she'd spent her on-season hours working to make something of their little stand while dreaming out loud of a place just like the one he had now. With this restaurant he would not let her down. With Canela he'd see her legacy of good food live on. And he'd also not let his friends down. He'd bust his ass to make sure Carter and Aidan made their money back with interest. No way would he be the one out of the three of them to fall.

After taking another swig of his beer, Vin pulled it away from his lips and let out a low sigh. He didn't know what had gotten into him tonight. It wasn't his usual first of the month money musings. It was something more, and he knew he had to shake it. He didn't like feeling powerless or out of control. He'd had enough of that in his life. He also didn't like the idea of his fate resting in the hands of others. He had to find a way to drum up new business. Vin turned and headed back into his apartment through the deck's double sliding doors. Pausing, he gave a brief whistle, and his lab, Dex, came bounding up the back deck stairs from where he was down on the sand. Dex was about to go into the apartment when Vin stopped him by holding up his hand. "Hold it right there," he said. "You're not bringing all that sand into the house; wipe your feet."

Dex looked up at him sheepishly and then hopped unsteadily on the mat before the entryway to the apartment's open-plan living room/bedroom. He looked up at Vin expectantly. Eyes wide and hopeful. At Vin's nod he leaped into the apartment. Vin shook his head and walked in behind the dog, clos-ing the sliders behind him. Shifting his head back and forth he tried to let go of some of the tension he felt creeping along his neck and spine. Ignoring the couch, and even the game on TV, Vin walked toward the kitchen to make something quick to eat.

Although he could have had leftovers from the day's restaurant specials, he wasn't in the mood. Opening his fridge and looking around, Vin furrowed his brows as he surveyed his many choices, still coming up empty. Just then a vision of full lips, smooth skin, and delicate shoulders came to his mind, and he flexed his fingers as if spontaneously his hands remembered the perfect feel of the fullness of her hips.

Shit.

Vin couldn't believe that he was still thinking about her despite her brusque brush-off. But there she was. Wham! Once again in the forefront of his mind, and here he was, hard and hungry and still fixated on her with no remedy for the situation. With yet another long sigh, as if on automatic pilot, he reached toward the back of the fridge and pulled out what he knew was premade filling for empanadas. Vin placed the filling on his prep island as he quickly pulled out flour and butter, plus a bowl to prepare an easy dough.

He'd never had a woman cut and run the way Lily Perry did, twice no less, just when things had the chance for some real momentum. Now here it was two weeks later and he still couldn't get her out of his mind. He'd planned to pursue her more when he'd gotten back to the reception, but when he'd returned, hard-on sufficiently dormant, she was wrapped up in her family. They'd indeed, as she'd feared, trapped her in a line dance, and though she protested by saying she hated line dances, she dipped, shimmied, and wobbled expertly with the best of them. Smiling and laughing gloriously, barely sparing him a glance for the rest of the evening.

Vin turned the fire to a medium-high flame as he filled the dough shells, his mind divided, partially on his cooking but mostly on her. Could he really blame her? It wasn't like he went after her when he'd had the chance after their encounter under the dock. Not the way Simon had gone after her sister. Vin snorted to himself. A partial laugh, partial smirk. And look where Simon was now. Chained. Sophie was a great girl and all, but come on. Everyone knew forever was a fallacy, and the headache on the way to learning that lesson was just too much of a pain in the ass.

Nah, chasing a girl like Lily was not for him at that time, just as it wasn't presently. Back then his mind was where his mind always was, half on the surf and the other half on his grind. He knew he wasn't in any mental state for commitment. That sort of thing wasn't for him anyway. It was one thing to commit with friends to a business venture but to put your heart into something more . . . No way. He'd never do that.

Although he'd inherited his mother's gift when it came to cooking he'd seriously feared he'd inherited his father's traits when it came to women. When not even the good love of a woman like his mother or the responsibility of taking care of a son could keep his father held down, well, Vincent had to wonder what hope there was for him. His mother, for all her love and positive reinforcement, could never deny the faint resemblances to his father when he'd go out and surf the most dangerous waves or do reckless things like zip around on his motorcycle in the rain. And she'd never stopped praying that there would be a woman who would make him want to actually settle down and slow down. He snorted. That was yet to happen. Of all the women he'd dated he'd not met one who'd been around longer than a season and the changing of weather patterns before he'd started to feel restless. He could almost see his mother now as she pull her lips together tight before opening her mouth and voicing her disapproval, not directly to him but to the pot of whatever she was cooking. "I swear, Vincent, it's at these times I think my angel is cursed by the devil. You have your father's same wandering spirit. A born heartbreaker is what you are." But when he'd start to protest, she shake her head and come at him with a spoon to taste whatever delectable sauce it was she had cooked up, silencing him all together. "No matter," she'd say. "You'll get caught soon enough. And it won't just be the girl's heart that's gets broken. I just hope I'm around to see it."

And then he'd protest and she'd wave a hand, shooing him away as he went on, his bike roaring as he was off to his latest conquest.

All of that reminiscing didn't matter. Canela was his first love now. All he had room for in his heart and head. Vin knew he needed to truly make a go of the restaurant and get on sure footing so that money, or lack of it, could stop being a stressor for him. He remembered what a stressor it was for his mother, raising him alone, and he'd never forgive himself for doing that to her, for spending so much of his life carefree and on his own terms that he didn't really stop to think of her needs.

Not wanting to let his mind go any deeper, Vin popped four empanadas into the fryer and instead let his mind wander back to Lily. He was hoping he'd run into her at the reception; he was glad he did despite the outcome of their encounter. She was just as hot as he remembered, no, even hotter. And it was clear that their time apart had done her very well. Not that he knew all that much about her then besides what they'd discussed that afternoon, and they sure as much didn't discuss much of anything lip-locked that evening. She must be nearing thirty; he knew she was younger than him but older than her sister. It was surprising, on one hand, and even refreshing how she didn't feel the need to settle down, but part of him, the practical part, wondered if it was all an act. He hadn't met one woman in the past few years who wasn't on the fast track to two and a half kids and a white picket fence as she chased down her biological clock running a relay, passing the baton with her career-ladder clock. Growing up with a single mother, he could admit it was a tough race.

But it wasn't his race. He wasn't chasing clocks, fences, or kids. At least not yet. And truth be told, he didn't think he ever would be. Presently, and for the foreseeable future, all he saw was his restaurant, building that in his mother's honor, and while his body held out, his surfboard and battling the waves. That was enough for him. Enough to keep him, if not happy, content for a good long while.

Vin took his empanadas out of the fryer and set them on a paper towel to dry. Frowning, he transferred them to a small plate, then opened another beer while heading over to the couch to flip on *SportsCenter* and the results of the game. Dex came sniffing around, all eyes and whines, but Vin headed him off with a chew toy tossed over to his bed. "Sorry, dude, I'm not in a sharing mood tonight."

Leaning back he made quick work of the small, hot pies but still wasn't satisfied. He let out a groan when images of Lily in that pretty semi-sheer dress came back to his mind. The way it fluttered up in the breeze and he caught glimpses of her smooth, curvy thighs. Just the thought had him going hard again. Damn! You'd think he was a teenager with no control over his own body the way she stirred him up.

But, man, was she hot. That gorgeous, soft brown skin of hers that reminded him of sugared cinnamon, and he could just about taste her on his tongue. Her lips. So pretty and pouty. Cute as hell even when she frowned. Little did she know that frown only served to tease him and made him want to kiss her all the more. Vin flexed his fists as his hands remembered the feel of her perfectly shaped ass under his palms. He let out a groan. Fuck. This was getting ridiculous.

Looking down at his empty plate with a frown, Vin suddenly was more than hungry. It was as if his hunger had turned to a longing. But a longing for what exactly? He shook his head. Even for him this type of thinking was a bit dramatic but with the dramatic thoughts and the deep hunger Vin knew that another batch of empanadas just wouldn't cut it. Ignoring the TV and the depressing score results from the New York teams, Vin picked up his phone and quickly scrolled through the contacts. There were plenty of women he could call to help his current urges. He'd be satisfied and so would she, but frustratingly there was only one contact on his list whom he really wanted to call and she'd made it clear that he might as well lose her number. Lily had told him in no uncertain terms that he was nothing more than a wedding reception playmate and if they were to get in touch, it would be business only. She was a woman who liked to be in charge, calling the shots, and wanted it no other way. And though he could admit that sexy boss ladyness was part of her appeal, it did nothing for his current situation. Should he call her, make up a business proposition that she'd clearly see through in a moment? Or just give up and wait it out until the next Perry wedding, which was sure to come soon?

Part of Vin knew that Lily was totally full of crap with all her talk. There was no way should could have been faking her responses to him. He'd felt her excitement, the way her body quivered ever so slightly as his tongue stroked hers, and unless she was the best actress ever she was just as heated as he was. Those were some hard-ass nipples he'd felt under the pads of his fingertips. Part of him knew a repeat would not be wholly frowned upon. He was sure of it.

So why didn't they just pick up where they'd left off and have something mutually satisfying for them both? Clearly the need for release wasn't one-sided. Vin shifted uncomfortably in his jeans, and with that, his decision was made. But he couldn't call her this late. This late, a call would definitely be considered a bootie call, and only a bootie call to a woman like Lily, even if it was just to pick up where they'd left off at her sister's wedding, would not be taken favorably. But despite making out twice, she wasn't the type you just rung up past eleven. No, with Lily a man had to have a plan. He'd wait another day or two and then tell her he'd been thinking of her. Maybe offer her a special dinner at his restaurant. Their date, whether she was up for strictly business or pleasure has been months in the making—the least he could do was put in a little effort.

Lily was exhausted as she flipped from the news to the sound of the late-night banter of the evening talk show host. But exhaustion aside, she opened her laptop to do a little research for her latest client. Owning her own business meant that nine-to-five was not a part of her vocabulary; she was a 24–7 type of operation. Not quite a one-woman show, her boutique event-planning organization also included her part-time assistant, Tori, running everything with her; the two of them had to fudge it and pretend to be big-time to hang with the sophisticated Manhattan firms that catered to the rich and famous.

Thankfully she was finally starting to wedge her name in with that set, and her latest client, Chelsea Carlyle, had hired her to put together the ultimate in graduation parties for her daughter, Christie. Normally Lily preferred to stick to corporate events and weddings, but with corporate downsizing and the economy, corporations weren't spending as much as they had in the past on events and increasingly, weddings were becoming intimate destination situations, so her New York specialized services weren't as in demand as she had hoped. Still she would not be defeated. Lily knew she had talent and she loved this business, so she'd find a way to make it work. Hence here she was putting together what was essentially a glorified kiddie party. No matter though, with the long reach of a socialite like Chelsea Carlyle it would do Lily a load of good if this party went off without a hitch and her business name would get a certain cache if it was uttered from the right side of Chelsea's mouth. There was always a birthday, and bar and bat mitzvahs came around every year, not to mention sweet sixteens and Quinceañeras.

Lily tightened her lips as she opened up a new program on her laptop to begin to storyboard some party ideas. But her brows drew together as her mind started to wander yet again to heated kisses, strong hands, and the feel of rough scruff as it rubbed against her bare cheek and down her décolletage. Lily gave her head a shake to clear it. *This won't do.* She'd been telling herself the words repeatedly in the two weeks since her wooded tryst with Vincent Caro.

After the wedding, she and Thomas had talked only briefly. He'd felt like there wasn't much of a need to offer up excuses as to why he couldn't come to the wedding since they weren't a couple like that. But he'd generously (his words) offered to pay for his uneaten meal. Lily told him to send the check to her sister as a wedding present and let him know she wouldn't be contacting him for future dates. It was no use getting bent out of shape about it. In all relationships someone eventually leaves. Even in those relationships where you're not really together. She figured in this case she'd get a jump on what was inevitable. It wasn't worth it to have a man on your arm if he was just weighing you down like an anchor, and Thomas was definitely turning into an anchor.

Besides, if he had been there she wouldn't have been able to have so much fun with Vin. That also wasn't turning out as it should have. She'd made a clean break from Vin after their little, okay, not-so-little encounter. So why was it he was still firmly taking up so much space in her mind? What was this preoccupation with Vincent Caro? Even if things went further with him to the point of finally going past hand-to-hand groping, Lily knew she couldn't, no, wouldn't get but so close. So why stress it so much?

She let out a frustrated sigh as her stomach growled. Great, just the thought of that tall, delicious hunk of man and Lily was hungry. Hungry and horny. She put her laptop aside on her bed and headed toward the kitchen. Opening her fridge she was almost blinded by the brightness of the light reflecting off the practically empty space.

"Shit," she murmured. How long had it been since she'd taken a visit to the grocery store? She'd been going from job to job almost nonstop, mostly having food on the run, and then on her nights off she'd been hightailing it out to the island to see her family. Guilted by her mom, and truth be told Mama Dee too, to not miss out on their weekly family dinners. All the Perry women, Mama Dee, though a Henton, took the Perry name in stride since taking the place at the other end of the table in the absence of their father. The gathering was large now with extra folding chairs with the sudden addition of male extensions in the form of the new brothers-in-law. To Lily though, the dinners were still bittersweet without her dad and though she knew she was angry she still missed him.

But as much as she wanted to be a no show she knew she couldn't have missed out on tonight's dinner, because Sophie and Simon were back and sharing tales and photos from their honeymoon in Hawaii. Not that she hadn't seen them all already on

Facebook, Instagram, Snapchat, and any other way her sister could poke the hell out of everyone with her wedded bliss. Lily reminded herself that Sophie was living the dream, and it was a dream that she had helped create by giving her the advice of forgoing the usual bridal registry and instead having guests help pay for certain extras on their honeymoon. Both Sophie and Simon's social media accounts were filled with likes and hearts from people who were happy to see them getting massages by the pool or zip-lining through the lush terrain of their generosity.

Coming away from the fridge with nothing more than limp celery stalks and suspiciously dated hummus, Lily dumped both in the trash and headed back to the bedroom to work.

She clicked a few keys and made a couple of notes in her leather-bound planner. She knew what she really wanted, and that was to work out the restlessness she was having in the nether regions of her body. For that she really wanted the body of one Vincent Caro. Lily pulled the hem of her T-shirt down, bringing it lower over her hips, while pulling up on the throw at her feet so that it came up over her bare legs. Suddenly chilled, she knew what would warm her, and felt nothing but frustration. After picking up her phone, she scrolled through until she once again found Vin's never-really-deleted number. She let her eyes glance over the fours and the sevens but stopped herself before the number seeped any deeper into her memory banks. Vexed, she put the phone back down with a sigh.

There was no way she could call him after the way she'd left things. Walking away like she was all big and bad and had not a care in the world. Of course she had a care, and he had the upper hand, which he'd used, once again, to let her know that he gave not two craps about their encounter by making no effort to get in touch with her. Yet again. Lily twisted her lips with frustration.

What did it matter? Especially with a guy like him. She knew he was best left forgotten, and besides, someone else would be along soon enough. Someone always came along. If not for anything special, at least for taking care of the momentary urges. And that was all that mattered. Lily wasn't looking for anything long term, because, unlike her sisters, she knew there was no such thing. Better to hold on to what you could really hold on to, and that was yourself.

Lily fiddled with her work a moment longer when Mama Dee came to her mind. Her grandmother had been so thrilled seeing Sophie and Simon's honeymoon pictures along with the proofs from the wedding that night. But still her mother couldn't help pointing out that Lily was the only one of her daughters alone, dateless, and therefore worthy of that matronly distinction at the wedding. She completely left their youngest sister, Violet, off since she was still in college. If the poor girl knew what Lily knew, she'd stay out of state where it was safe.

"What are we going to do with you?" her mother, Renée, had said by way of supposedly easygoing dinner conversation. It felt like echoes of Uncle Gene all over again.

Lily trained her mother with a sharp glare in the middle of the dining room as silence grew over the suddenly not-so-happy family gathering. All eyes had turned to the two of them, waiting for some big confrontation. For a moment she had imagined her brothers-in-law getting their popcorn ready, since this was quickly turning into a weekly thing. "What do you mean do with me, Mom? I was under the impression I didn't need doing at all."

Her mother had waved a hand. "Oh, honey, don't go getting up in arms, now, and don't be so dramatic and sensitive. I'm just saying you're almost the last of my girls and you're the oldest one. I would've thought you'd have snagged someone by now. I mean, it's not like there is anything wrong with you. You're beautiful. A bit strong-willed, Lord knows where you got that from." That last bit she murmured under her breath, since she knew exactly where Lily got her strong personality. "You could learn to bend a little bit, at least until you get someone to lean a little in your direction. Relationships take give-and-take, you know."

Lily had felt her temperature rise and her cheeks flame as her mother continued, seemingly oblivious to her daughter's anger.

"I'm just saying I hate seeing you here with all of us together and then you go and get in that old jalopy of yours and head toward the city alone, at night. It doesn't seem right. You could stay here. Your room is always waiting."

Lily had let out a breath as she struggled to keep her control. It was baffling. Her mother had more nerve than any one person should. She was the most controlling person Lily knew, and she managed their family with an iron fist. Hell, she'd managed her father right out of his place at the table, she had. Her fist was so strong. Lily remembered the massive shouting matches her mother and father used to have, though most of the shouting was one-sided as her mother would explode over some minor infraction or another and take her feelings out on her father. For a while Lily, being the oldest, tried to be the fixer. She worked hard at keeping her sisters quiet, doing little things to distract her mother and steer her mother's anger away from her father and toward herself. It was as if Lily saw the writing on the wall before either one of them did. He father had called Lily their glue.

Forgiving her mother for her outbursts, he'd explain to Lily when she'd asked why he took her tirades, that love meant bending a bit and seeing past the surface to inside the other person. He'd told Lily he saw inside her mother and knew her deep down where it counted. What a load of bull. It turned out he'd seen inside quite a few other women in the Rockaways and the neighboring counties, and no amount of glue Lily was trying to spread around her home was holding that together.

But still, in that moment, a grown Lily had looked around the table and, feeling like a silly child, wished she could go back to the days when her father was still there and when she still believed in men like him, or men like the one he'd pretended to be. Those who accepted women despite their crankiness and flaws. Their outbursts and mental meltdowns. The ones who gave women a soft space to land instead of the hard concrete that the outside world offered.

Back then if her father was sitting in his usual spot and her mother's ire was directed her way, he'd be there to give Lily that assurance, that bit of help that he'd always give when her mother came down on her for being flighty or daydreaming or just being her own strong willed self.

Lily knew what he would say, and the memory of it made her smile. "Oh, Renée," he'd ease out in that slow drawl of his, which was more south of the border than any place north of DC. "You let the girl be. She knows what she's doing with herself. Don't you worry about Lily, she's got it all together." Then he'd give Lily a serious pat on the hand, his eyes getting a hint of a misty glaze about them. "It will be a sad day when I have to hand you over to another to love, because he surely won't care for you as much as I do, baby girl."

Lily had inwardly sighed. Her father wasn't there, and for all his talk of love and seeing deep inside, he'd left her mother for some woman who was about as deep as a birdbath. Silicone enhanced breasts and an over exaggerated bottom to match, and the kicker was she wasn't more than ten years Lily's senior. Hell, her picture still graced their high school cabinet, under the cheer trophies. Lily was devastated the day her father moved out. But still he returned for each of his daughter's weddings, Little Miss Cheer now gone and a new woman clinging to his arm at each gathering. And through it all, her mother put on a brave face while her frown lines deepened. Lily watched her grow more and more bitter as each year passed. Lily had snorted to herself then. Really she should thank her parents. From them she learned that nothing was forever and only heartbreak was guaranteed. Love? Well, that was for dreamers, and when it came to relationships she was done being one of those.

Lily had looked back at her mother, ready to give her prepared speech about her work and being perfectly happy, when a voice came from the end of the table. "Oh, Renée, let the girl be. Give it a rest.

She knows what she's all about." Lily let out a much-needed breath. It was Mama Dee speaking the words she longed to hear from her father. Lily turned and gave her grandmother a smile.

Mama Dee looked over at Lily's mom. "Now, you know I want to see all the girls settled and happy, and it'll do my heart good, before I go, to know that they will be taken care of, but these are modern times. They have partners now, and the taking care works both ways. Lily will be fine. She's a smart women, and she's taking care of herself. Besides, I believe when she finds the right one everything will work out according to plan. And if Mr. Right doesn't come along, his loss." And with that declaration Mama Dee turned and gave Lily a smile that was a touch more chilling than reassuring.

"Before you go?" Lily had said. "Why must you go talking like that, Mama Dee? You know you ain't going nowhere."

But like her father, Mama Dee had reached over and put her hand over Lily's. Her touch was cool and not at all comforting but forced Lily to meet her eyes and not look away. "Oh, honey, we all going some-time and by right, and if I'm lucky my time will be well before all of you." She'd smiled then and waved her hand, clearly trying to lighten the mood. "So of course I want to get my groove on at weddings for all my girls before I go. I just have you and Violet to go, and I'm gonna do my best with taking my meds and keeping these old hips well lubricated so they are in dancing shape for when that time comes." Mama Dee had then done a little shimmy in her chair that had everyone giggling.

But Lily couldn't find her smile, and remembering

her grandmother's shimmy now as she tried to focus on the laptop keys and on the Carlyle graduation party gave Lily pause. Why was it that her family couldn't understand that she was living her life as she felt she needed? Why was her mother so concerned about her being alone and needing a man? Was it that she really felt so disconnected now that Daddy had moved on? She more than anyone should be proud of her only daughter who had broken free and didn't fall for the "marriage is the only way to happiness" load of bullcrap.

Lily shook her head. This was not where she needed her mind to be, and it frustrated her to no end. She needed to work, not be worried about her mother and her cutting remarks or the fact that maybe she was making those cutting remarks because she was feeling lonely and possibly scared for her daughter and her future. She also didn't need the added guilt from Mama Dee with buzzkill talk about her mortality. Who could let that slide? Talk about good cop, bad cop. Between the two of them they were about to send her over the edge.

Lily remembered kissing Mama Dee's cool, soft cheek, and her final words as she had left the house. "Don't you pay your mama no mind, baby. You got this. Everything you do is gonna be a success. And one day I will see you walk down that aisle, and I'll be grinning from ear to ear. Trust me, someone is going to catch you, and it's going to be quite the party."

She'd shaken her head at Mama Dee and, with a wave of the hand, told her to stop all that talk, that she had plenty of work to do before she even considered marriage. She'd sooner see her name on some

top business list before she saw herself walking down
a church aisle.

With a frustrated sigh Lily put her mind back on
her work as she tapped the keys and started surfing
the Internet looking for some inspiration. During her
party search she happened across a strange article:
"Woman Weds Oneself in the Ultimate Act of Self-
Love." Accompanying the article was a picture of a
beautiful woman of forty-five, maybe fifty, with a
wide-open smile; smooth, clear skin; and an updo.
She was dressed in a white wedding dress and a veil
and surrounded by a ten-person female wedding
party at some sort of alter.

Lily read the short article quickly and at the end
was longing for more details. Could this woman
really have wed herself? The article said there was a
ceremony, guests and family present to cheer her on
as she made a commitment to honor herself in love,
care, and devotion.

Her mouth hanging open, Lily read the article
again. She was both shocked and excited, her mind
racing. Could this be a new budding business opportunity? How many women did she know who were
ready to have their dream wedding but were missing
that one important little component? The groom.

Also, how many of these women were just like
her. Fine with their lives as they were but the world
seemed to think they were some sort of charity
cases—on the shelf, as it were—just because they
hadn't yet walked down the aisle into the waiting
arms of some man. No one gave a woman the credit
that men got for the freedom singledom afforded
them. The freedom to come and go as you pleased,
to consider only yourself when it came to meals (so

what if she currently had nothing in her fridge?), the freedom to vacation in any way the winds took her, not to mention the sexual freedom that singledom afforded her or any single women. No, these things were touted as pluses only for bachelors, never for women happy and single in their thirties and forties. Lily grinned. It was as if this article had opened her eyes to a whole new world of celebrations, and she was almost giddy with the possibilities of it.

But still, the article itself seemed almost blasphemous. Just by her upbringing and society being what it is, Lily couldn't help but think, who would do such a thing and what would others think about this person? It seemed so ridiculous and almost, dare she say, selfish. Just thinking of something so freeing and fabulous as being selfish made her want to kick her own ass. But she knew how people were, and women were most critical of their own kind. She could practically hear the criticism even before the invites went out. A wedding could be expensive, and she was sure most people would think, hell, a person could just spend the money on a nice rejuvenation vacation and keep it moving. Maybe the whole venture was an awful idea. Lily sighed, suddenly feeling deflated, and her balloon hadn't even gotten off the ground.

And just to put a pin good and well in the already fragile idea, Lily decided to scroll through the comments section, expecting the worse. A few people were kind, giving the woman a thumbs-up for being so brave, but for the most part the comments were scathing, with folks skewering the woman for being just what Lily embarrassingly thought at first glance, selfish. They called her self-indulgent, an attention seeker, and desperate. *Desperate.* Ouch. That was the worst one of all.

The word cut Lily to her core as she thought of Uncle Gene and his prying questions wedding after wedding after wedding. "When is it going to be your turn to get married?" he'd say like an undertrained parrot. With his har-har laugh and a stupid point with his finger gun. Yeah, he'd say it was all innocent banter, but she knew it wasn't. She knew all the cutting remarks and Aunt Ruby making judgy eyes along with cousin Nikki as her hype girl. The three of them didn't come out and say it, but they didn't work hard to hide that they felt there was something quite desperate about her no matter how much she declared the opposite.

Lily looked again at the picture of the woman from the article. She was beautiful. No, not your conventional angular, skinny model beautiful, but she was still beautiful nonetheless. Brown skin, glossy hair—and that smile of hers was captivating. She was a person anyone would want to know or want to be around. And in that moment looking at the picture, Lily wanted to be around her; Lily wanted to know her. Lily did know her. Lily was her.

The realization of the bond with this woman she didn't know and never met hit Lily like a sucker punch to the gut. Lily looked at the woman's bright smile, her flawless skin, and her sparking eyes and knew the woman was leaps and bounds ahead of her. She was where, for all her talk, Lily wanted to be. Lily wanted to express that type of inner strength, to say, "Fuck it! I love myself, I'm worthy to receive love, and that is a truth that is good enough for me to celebrate. I don't need any man to be the validator in order to make it true."

Suddenly, the image of her mother came to mind and how much more bitter she'd become since her father had left them. Did his walking away from the marriage somehow make her any less worthy of love? Hell, no. She then thought of Mama Dee, who'd found her true love after going through her fair share of frogs along the way. Was she any less loveable during the highs and the lows? Of course not. And for all the talk of dancing at Lily's wedding? She'd get her dance on, all right. Lily would make sure of it.

Excited, Lily shifted from her laptop to her cell and quickly tapped out a message to her assistant, Tori.

We need to start making plans; we have a wedding.

Already used to the crazy schedule, Tori seemed to be sleeping with her phone surgically attached to her fingers.

Great! Who's the client?
Me!

Lily was met with nothing but three dots for about a minute and a half. She could almost imagine Tori looking at the screen openmouthed. Finally Tori came back with a reply.

And the groom?
Also me.

This time the silence was much longer, and Lily couldn't help but giggle. Poor Tori probably didn't know what to say. It was fine. Tori was an excellent assistant, and Lily was sure that by morning she'd have her head back on straight. Feeling slightly nervous, but ultimately great about her decision, Lily was once again full of energy and ready to get back on track with work. She now had another project to go all in on, adding her wedding to the mix, but still there was a question of Vincent Caro. Like a bad earworm, he was back on her mind and the stirrings were back in her belly and, dammit, farther below. She was still hungry, that problem nagging at her, brewing up another momentary lapse of reason as she fired off a quick e-mail to Tori telling her to set up a meeting for her with a hot, new potential caterer for her wedding.

Chapter 4

Vin was excited. Okay, excited was pushing it. He didn't do excited. But still he was moderately charged over the fact that he was meeting a potential client this morning for an in-house event. A wedding, of all things. Now, that thought had his charge draining a bit.

Normally the idea of hosting an in-house event didn't appeal, and especially a wedding, since dealing with a bride had the potential to be a huge pain in the ass, not to mention the fact that Vin liked total control and he knew that when it came to brides they were all about the control. But money was money, and right now that was his true bottom line. He'd find his way to deal with the rest. The thought of hosting a wedding gave Vin pause as thoughts of Lily once again came to his mind. Somehow yesterday slipped away from him and though she was at the forefront of his mind for most of the day, things got crazy with a freezer malfunction that he thankfully caught early or it could have been disastrous, and then he got into it with his seafood supplier. By the time he had a moment to breathe it was eleven p.m. and once again he had not called her and he was back in the booty call hours. Vin was starting to think that maybe he had an avoidance or dare he think confidence problem when it came to Miss Perry. Vin quickly pushed that thought aside as the feel of her in his arms came back to him. Oh he had a problem alright and it was one he needed to fix and quick. Right after he sealed the deal on this wedding job.

About this job, Vin didn't know if he should blame or thank his friend and in this case not-so-silent partner Carter for this job, since he was sure it came from the local magazine feature Carter had finagled. The one that labeled him the "Bad Boy of the Beach." It was short on food substance but long on atmosphere about the beach and descriptors about his physique. He didn't much like the piece, but Carter thought it was just the type of feature Canela needed.

Vin didn't get it. Just because he cooked and rode a motorcycle and happened to be a minority, he was labeled a bad boy. Breaking freaking news. But he knew that everyone had to have an angle, so he guessed he had to work this one and use what he had to get what he needed. And what he needed was yet another way to clear his costs for the month and come out in the black.

With the gentrification of the old neighborhood and the prime beachside location, he could admit they were lucky as hell to be in the position they were in. He also knew he couldn't let his ego get in the way and blow this opportunity. With the peak season jumping off to a slow start he'd do whatever it took to get this wedding gig.

Vin and his sous chef, Manny, were just finishing

unloading their haul from the local farmers market out of his delivery van when he heard a car pull up. Shit, he hoped it wasn't his new clients. If it was, they were fifteen minutes early and Vin had wanted to run in and at least change his T-shirt before they met.

But the closer the car came, the more he questioned if it was his clients. Vin eyed the old Buick suspiciously as it lumbered up the hill toward Canela's driveway. No, this couldn't be his clients. Not with a car like that. Besides, there were two women in the front, and Vin was under the impression he was meeting a couple today. He looked closer, his eyes squinting against the glare of the sun, when suddenly his heart did an annoying skip-jump thing as he recognized Lily Perry in the driver's seat. Yes! She'd come to him. Even before he'd gotten a chance to call and set a formal date. But crap, she was here fifteen minutes before he was due to meet with clients. Vin let out a breath. No matter. He'd do whatever it took to hold her there while he dealt with the clients today. Maybe he'd have Manny whip up something for her and her friend. Anything she wanted to not let her out of his grasp this time without firm plans to meet again.

The car chugged to a stop, and he watched as Lily cut the engine but the car still labored on. Jeeze, Vin thought, she had some trouble there. He attempted to play it cool as he handed the last box to Manny and walked toward Lily and her noisy car.

She opened her door before he could assist, and the first thing that Vin noticed was the curve of her calf, then her shapely ankles as she stepped out onto the gravel drive in her sexy black pumps. The rest of her followed in what should've been a perfectly

professional, slim black skirt and demure pink blouse
that nipped in at her slim waist and then fanned out
across her hips. But there was nothing demure about
it, because the way the fabric gently skimmed her
luscious curves immediately brought to Vin's mind
all sorts of erotic fantasies. He knew he had to play it
cool, but for the life of him all he wanted to do was
stride up to her, take her in his arms, and pull that
sexy body hard against his own, then kiss her until
her lips were just as pink as that pretty little blouse.

But of course that wouldn't do, because despite
being labeled a bad boy or whatever it was they had
tagged him, he wasn't some type of Neanderthal.
Besides, just as she was getting out of the car the passenger door opened and out came another young
woman, maybe four or five years younger than Lily.
She was pretty with clear, sepia-toned skin and tor-
toiseshell glasses that accented eyes that seemed to
see everything all at once. She was coming around
to the front of the car at the same time that Manny
was coming out the restaurant side door. Vin could
see Manny's female radar detector pinging from
where he was standing and shot him a quick look.

Vin was just about to greet Lily when she cut him
off at the pass by opening her mouth first. She was all
business, giving off not a hint to the fact that the last
time they'd seen each other they were so close that a
person could barely wedge a hand between the two of
them. No, now here was Lily sticking out her hand as
if she was about to negotiate a deal on new tires for
that old boat she was calling a car. Vin couldn't help
but be taken aback and looked at her hand as if he
didn't know what to do with it. Was she for real? Vin
gave himself a mental shake. Of course she was. This

was Lily—*Take control, Perry!*—so he stuck out his hand and shook hers.

"So good to see you again," she said, her honey voice light and clear as she looked up, taking in the façade of his restaurant with a critical eye. For some reason, in that moment, Vin felt the need to stick his chest out and possibly defend his little square of the island.

"So this is your place," she said, turning away from the restaurant's signage and now looking over the drive and the surrounding areas critically. She gave a nod and smiled at him. "I have to say, it is nice. Though the access and the parking situation could use a bit of help. I'm sure you're already aware of it. That aside, your location and proximity to the beach can't be denied."

She then turned to the younger woman. "Tori, please make a note that parking and the valet situation will need to be attended to."

The young woman whom he now knew to be Tori gave a nod and then quickly started tapping on her phone.

Lily looked up at Vin, catching his confusion, and gave a laugh. "I'm sorry, I'm getting ahead of myself, but then again I always seem to do that. How about we go inside?"

Go inside and do what? He did say he wanted to keep her there, but what was she talking about? Maybe she had plans for some sort of event? That was her business, of course. That had to be it. He'd explain to her that he had other clients coming but if she could wait he'd be happy to talk to her. He didn't know much about his incoming clients; the late-night e-mail from a Miss Shelton didn't say much, but it did imply they were short on time and would be checking out other venues.

Still, Vin felt his mood start to rise. Actually, this could all work out for the best. If Lily wanted to use his place for an event that she was planning, he didn't need to come off like some schoolboy with a crush chasing after her by calling on her for a date. This would be a perfect cover and he'd have a ready-made excuse to see her, be in touch with her, get to know her better, no groveling necessary. This must be his lucky day; things could not work out any better if he'd planned it himself. Vin gave Lily what he hoped was an easygoing smile. "That sounds great. Please come in, and welcome to Canela."

She walked in as if she owned the place, or at least was thinking of leasing it. He watched as her eyes scanned quickly, taking in all Canela had to offer. He caught her assessing the rustic décor and felt silly that he was hanging on her every inflection, waiting to catch some sort of glimmer of her approval. When she gave a slight smile to his choice of the modern chandelier over the bar, the one he had rescued from a salvage yard and restored himself, he couldn't help but swell with pride. But when she frowned as she ran her hand over the old barstools and then came toward the same style wheelbarrow chairs and table with a frown, making yet another note to her assistant to call some sort of chair rental company, he couldn't stop himself from stepping in.

"Listen, Lily, I'm really happy to see you again, you and your—"

Lily spoke up then. "Oh, I'm sorry. This is really rude of me. I was just so excited to see your restaurant. Please meet my assistant, Tori. Tori handles all my day-to-day and is integral to my operations." She then turned toward Manny, who was still taking everything in as if there wasn't some serious prep to do for tonight's dinner service. With a bright smile she stuck out her hand. "Lily Perry, so nice to meet you."

Manny ran a hand quickly down the side of his jeans and then shook Lily's. "Manny Esposito, sous chef and right-hand man around here. Nice to meet you." He gave her a grin before unleashing one of his panty dropper smiles in Tori's direction. "Nice to meet you too, Tori."

Vin let out a low growl. This could get sticky real quick if he let it. Nobody could work a room like Manny did, and nobody could tangle a web with the ladies like Manny. Manny was a genius in the kitchen, almost as good as Vin, which wasn't easy for him to admit. And when he had Manny out front and put him behind the bar, suddenly mixed drinks were the call of the hour and he was getting just as many numbers as he was serving up the sweet beverages, each one specially named for the woman he was serving. Yeah, Manny was full of it, all right, but he was also a great employee and a good friend. But this was potential business, and not just potential business for him, something with the possibility for more. He couldn't let Manny's proclivity for the ladies mess up his situation.

"Listen, Lily, it's great to see you and I hope you've got a little bit of time because—" Vin quickly looked at his watch and then back up into her eyes, and for a moment he was dumbstruck. Damn, she was pretty. Her eyes all big and brown and lashy. Was that even a word? Lashy? Never mind, it fit the look of her captivating dark eyes and the way they were framed by her dark, sooty lashes. Suddenly the time came back to him. Shit, he needed to get on with it. "I'd really like to talk with you about whatever event you have coming up, but I have clients coming in about two minutes. So, if you don't mind, can I let Manny set you and Tori up with some drinks and appetizers and then we can get to it right after I finish with these clients who are coming to talk about their wedding?"

He watched as those pretty brown eyes shadowed with confusion. "Oh, I didn't know you did so many weddings that you'd have another booked at the same time as me."

Now it was his turn to be confused. "What do you mean at the same time as you?" he asked.

Lily laughed and then looked toward her assistant. "Didn't you give him my name?"

Tori looked at her, puzzled. "No, I didn't give him your name. I booked it under mine and the LP Agency. You know we don't give client names until they are booked."

Now it was Vin's turn to be confused, but then understanding dawned. "So you're LP?" He grinned as it all came together. "Hey, I'm sorry. Please come in and look around. Take all the time you need." Vin was suddenly having a hard time containing his excitement and caught himself rocking on the balls of his feet. He caught her cock a brow and knew he needed to chill.

"So you want to book my place for one of your clients? Have a seat and let's get down to discussing the details, and I can let you know what sort of services I can offer." He watched as Lily and her assistant exchanged another look as they headed toward the table. Okay, he could do this. He'd gotten back on track. Now to keep things professional for the meeting, and then afterward he would let Lily know plainly that he'd like to discuss getting together about something a lot more personal. Or maybe he'd hold out. Feel her out a bit and wait for their next meeting. He'd be sure there was a next meeting.

Vin got the women seated and asked Manny to please bring them some refreshments while he grabbed a notepad. Once they were situated, he tried his best to focus on the business at hand and not the fact that Lily was less than two feet away, looking so alluring and smelling once again like that delicious scent of honey mixed with spring rain. Vin cleared his throat and looked at her. "So what day are you looking at?"

She reached into her bag and pulled out a pretty leather binder, flipping to the calendar section. Her long fingers, the nails tipped in a soft pink polish, drummed on the page that held the month of August. "How about the fourth Saturday in August? It will be right before Labor Day, so we won't run into everyone's big plans but still have a nice turnout."

He checked his calendar, and though he hated to close the restaurant on a Saturday, especially during high summer, if her clients had the money to back it, then he could do it.

"A Saturday at the end of August is my high season and that'll cost a lot, closing the restaurant during that time. Your clients will need to have long pockets. Now, if they do, that is something we can work out. But if they wait for the weekend after Labor Day I can cut the cost by twenty percent. I know it's not the best business deal on my part, but it's something that might work for you."

He watched as Lily's brows came together, and she bit her bottom lip. He could tell she was calculating things. Running over the cost in her head and weighing her client's day in her mind.

Finally she spoke, looking him in the eye. "Well, that does make a lot of sense, and I appreciate your making the offer." She paused. Her eyes glinted as she tipped her tongue out for a brief moment. Finally she nodded. "I think that could be an option."

Vin smiled then. She gave Tori a nod, and once again Tori started tapping on her phone. "Do you need to call your clients to set up a time when they can come and see the space and possibly confirm the date?"

Lily waved her hand. "It's not necessary. The date is fine. Let's confirm it."

Vin cocked his head. She was confident, he'd give her that. He just hoped that without the client's approval his holding the date didn't backfire on her. Vin decided to give her some sort of out just in case things happened to fall apart. He wrote the date down on his legal pad and then looked up at her. "Great, we have the date, and please, if anything does come up within the next week or two just let me know. It's no problem to work something else out."

His mind returned to their time by the little shack in the woods two weeks prior. She was so lush and so delicious, he couldn't wait to ask her out and pick up where they'd left off. He hoped more than anything that her choosing his restaurant to book this job meant that she felt the same way. But first he had to get back to business and finish up. "Now, if you can give me the name of the bride," Vin said, pen poised.

It was then that Lily smiled at him brightly, and his heart betrayed him by doing an annoying flip-skip right before she started to speak. Her honey-cream voice hit his eardrums clear and smooth. "The bride's name is Lily Perry."

Lily watched as the color rose on Vin's tanned cheeks. He blinked and then blinked again, the expression so comical with its shock she almost laughed out loud. She knew she should've been put out by his reaction, by his assumption that she was there for someone else, but honestly she expected it. When you were throwing a wedding for yourself, you had to be prepared for this type of thing. She watched his nostrils flare and his grip tighten on his pen. His next words came out through clinched teeth. "And the name of the groom?"

And that was when it hit her that he thought she was marrying someone else. He thought she was marrying someone else when she was just making out with him not two weeks earlier. She didn't know whether to laugh or be completely pissed off by his lack of faith in her morality. Come on. She definitely wasn't the type to be a cheater once she did make the decision to settle down. But once again her gaze went to his tight jaw and his even tighter hold on his pen. She looked back up into his eyes.

Oh God, this was total and complete jealousy. His reaction over what he thought he knew was jealousy and anger. Not only did he think she was a cheater, he probably also thought she was a total and complete bitch. One who was getting married and had chosen his place to rub it in his face.

At that so off-base thought, Lily couldn't help the laughter as it bubbled up in her chest. She threw her head back then and enjoyed the moment of confusion. But when she looked back at Vin, he wasn't laughing at all, and her laughter only served to egg him on all the more. "I don't see what's so funny here, Lily. Taking into account our recent circumstances and all." His words held a steely tone, so much so that she was sure she should have been shaking in her boots. But for the life of her, just thinking about it made her want to laugh even more. She chuckled and had to reach for a napkin to wipe at the tears gathering in the corners of her eyes.

"You don't understand, and I'm sorry, that's my fault," she squeaked out.

Vin pushed back his chair, scraping against the wooden floor with a screech. "I understand that you are probably certifiable and I don't know if I want to do business with you, closing my restaurant down on a Saturday so you can make a mockery of marriage. This is my business and I take it seriously. You can't even stop laughing when you tell me about it. Sorry, but you can find another venue. Suddenly I don't think you can afford me." He started to get up, and Lily reached out, clamping her hand tightly on his wrist.

She looked up at him, her eyes now wide, her expression more solemn—or at least she was trying her best at making it so. "Please let me explain," she said, trying hard to hold a straight face while Vin glared down at her.

"The name of the groom is also Lily Perry." And

with that, Vin blinked and his mouth flew open. Lily couldn't help but burst out in laughter once more.

She really needed to get it together. Lily cleared her throat and tried to pull herself upright, dabbing at her eyes as she looked at Vin working hard to bring a semi-seriousness to her countenance. "Please sit down and let me explain things to you." With a nod in Tori's direction she was handed her iPad and clicked open a new screen.

Vin was still giving her the serious and skeptical side eye, but she knew she had to win him over because this was the beginning of launching her mission to show everyone that she was fine just the way she was, and this was the launch of a brand-new arm of her business. But for that to happen, Vin and his restaurant was an integral part of pulling the whole thing off. Lily pulled up the article on the woman who married herself and showed Vin the screen. She watched as his dark brows furrowed, his midnight eyes quickly scanning the article. He reached out with his expressive but blunt fingers, lightly touching the screen to bring in the article, and once he was done he looked at her with the same critical eye and gave a shrug.

"Okay, so you've got a woman here clearly in need of some attention or lacking something in her life, so she decides to throw a wedding party for herself and instead of making it say . . ." Vin's eyes went skyward for a moment before he trained them back on Lily. "Say, a birthday party like some grand fortieth blowout, she decides to turn it into a media spectacle. And now you're telling me that you want to do the same thing, here in my place?" He let out a long, soft sigh and shook his head. "Woman, I had you all wrong."

Lily felt the heat of anger rise faster than she could tamp it back down. Who the hell was he to judge her or the woman in the article so quickly and to be so ungodly and frustratingly dismissive? He had a lot of nerve. She snatched the iPad from his hands and shoved it into her bag. Lily pushed her chair back, making a loud noise against the floor as she got up.

She towered over Vin in a fit. "And it looks like I had you pegged just right when I said good-bye to you last year. You're nothing but a small-minded townie who thinks of women in one of two ways— either in the kitchen or on their backs, but never as being accomplished in their own right. Back then I was good for a quick afternoon and nothing more, but for you to see me or any other woman for that matter as being successful and something beyond chasing after a man, well, you and your small mind can't even handle it. I'm great just as I am, just as the woman in this article is. Women like her and women like me don't need ridiculous pieces of paper like a marriage license and the validation of the government and another person to cosign on our worthiness. We're good just as we are."

Lily watched his brows draw together, and his nostrils flare. His mouth started to open, but she didn't want to hear whatever was about to come out. Screw him and his cute, rustic beachside restaurant. She'd have her day, and she'd have it in a better place than the dive she was standing in. She was doing him a favor anyway by helping to put his place on the map. But there was no way she needed to patronize some sort of chauvinistic asshole. She turned to walk away when she felt his hand on her arm, stopping her in her tracks.

Lily looked down at his big hand and slowly over to his face. "I'd move that hand if I were you. That is, if you don't want to lose it." Her tone was low and steady despite her agitation, the monster in her head quaking. But Vin immediately let her go, looking up at her with his eyes wide.

"Listen, I'm sorry," he said. The straightforwardness, clarity, and—she couldn't tell but she suspected—sincerity of the apology gave her quick pause.

Lily was skeptical. "Sorry for what? Sorry for your stupid assumptions, or are you sorry because I'm walking out the door with my business?"

Vin looked down for a moment, then his eyes came up, meeting hers as he started to stand. She would've preferred that he just stayed seated. Standing brought his body way too close to hers and brought back memories of their last encounter and the real reason she chose his restaurant. "Would you hate me all the more if I told you honestly that I was sorry for both?"

Lily let his answer and his deliciously masculine scent roll over her for a moment or three. She knew she wasn't walking out anytime soon. Not when he was so close and she had come so far. She pretended to mull things over when in truth her answer was set as soon as he'd apologized. And it was sealed when he stood and she'd gotten another whiff of him. Lily cocked her head, then tipped her tongue over her top lip for a second, and finally raised her left brow. "No, Vin, I won't hate you, at least not anymore. How about we just let this little moment go and continue on with our business?"

He smiled that smile that she remembered from the wedding, and she let her mind go to the first time she saw it on the beach. That damn smile was her kryptonite. It hyped her up like sunshine after too many cloudy days, and she was starting to think he knew it. When she let out a low breath he walked around her and went for her chair, putting his hand out to offer for her to sit once again. "Thank you. Now let's get down to work and you tell me more about this wedding you plan on having. What can I do to make your day perfect, Miss Perry? Your wish is my command."

Chapter 5

"Your wish is my command." Vin's words were echoing in Lily's head as she and Tori merged onto the highway heading back to the city. He'd said them lightly, supposedly coming out all sweet and innocent, but the implication of the words held so much more.

"So that went well," Tori said from the passenger seat, bringing Lily out of her musings.

Lily shot her a quick glance before turning back toward traffic. "You think so?"

"Of course not. That was an absolute disaster." The high-pitched tone of Tori's voice was completely out of character and had Lily swiveling her head quickly back in her assistant's direction.

"What are you talking about? It went fine. We have our date set and we have a venue set on the first day of planning. I say we're way ahead of the game. Not to mention we got in some tasty appetizers. The afternoon was a complete win." Once again she looked back at traffic, then did a quick check of her gauges as she said a silent prayer that the car would hold up as she continued on. She felt a little hint of niggling discomfort. Maybe Tori had a point. Part of her felt she shouldn't have been quite so impulsive when it came to planning this wedding. Her car was barely chugging along, and though a smarter, less sentimental women would just let it go, she wasn't prepared to do that. So her only option was getting it repaired, which meant putting further strains on her funds.

Yeah, she knew what Tori was talking about, but she didn't want to face it. Facing their almost disastrous meeting would make what she was embarking on too real and, for at least the ride home, she wanted to live in la-la land.

"Oh, come on, Lil. I know I'm just your assistant, but being that it's now after five o'clock, I'm going to put it out there and tell it like it is. You could have warned me that we were heading into the lion's den over there."

For a moment, Lily's eyes went skyward. "Tori, it's not all that bad. We've dealt with difficult vendors before, and Vin is new and eager, but with me as a client this should be a piece of cake."

"It's the *you as a client* that I'm worried about, not to mention the eager. Yes, he's eager, all right. I just wished you would have given me a heads-up that you and he were, well, acquainted. The fact that you were holding a wedding for yourself just about sent him into a fit, and it was worse when he thought you were marrying someone else. The poor guy looked completely blindsided. In the future I would just prefer to know a little bit more about how to handle the situation."

Lily let out a sigh. Okay, so Tori didn't have it

wrong. Lily hadn't prepared her and she should have, and really she would have if she had known how to prepare herself. She was flying by the seat of her pants and, if truth be told, though she laughed everything off and put on a great air of confidence, the whole thing had her unnerved. Seeing Vin, then hearing his tone of disapproval, had her practically wanting to back out of the whole married-to-herself situation all the way. If she couldn't convince him of what she was doing, then how did she expect her family to get it and jump on board?

Part of her told herself she was doing the right thing, but the other part told her she was about to make herself a total farce, the laughingstock of Long Island. And this went for both personally and professionally. If she was going to pull this off and make it a viable part of her business, she had to get a handle on herself.

Lily quickly glanced over at Tori, who was looking at her phone, tapping and scrolling as usual, her brows pulled tightly together, her expression one of total consternation. "Do you think I'm making a huge mistake?" The words came from Lily low and quiet.

Tori looked up at her boss, her eyes softening, her brow smoothing out. She gave Lily a half smile and shook her head. "What do I know?" the younger woman said. "Who knows, you could be making a mistake, but for the record I don't think you are. Despite this afternoon's little hiccups, in the time I've worked with you I've never known you to doubt yourself when it comes to business and I've never known you to take a wrong step." Tori's smile grew more reassuring. "Hey, I have total faith and complete confidence in you, and I'm sure that you're doing the right thing. As long as it feels right for you, I say go for it. Besides, I think what you're doing is fantastic, and if what you said to Vincent Caro back there is truly what you believe in your heart about a woman being enough without the cosign of a man, then I'm all for it. We'll make this the biggest event of the year and in the process put your name on the map."

Lily let out a groan as she thought about the idea of solidifying her status in such a way. It wasn't as if she was doing anything as outlandish as a sex tape, but she knew her family and the splash she'd be making. She sighed. A sex tape would possibly be less scandalous. Lily slowed, pumping the brakes as the usual evening traffic started to back up before them. Maybe she should hit the brakes on this whole situation? Echoing her feelings, she said them out loud. "I don't know, maybe I should just slow this whole thing down. It's not like I gave it a lot of think-through time. It seemed so carefree and fun the other night, so wrong that it just had to be so right. But one look in Vin's eyes and everything seemed to waiver."

"Come on now, Lily. Like I said, I've never known you to waiver, and you can't let one guy and his small-mindedness take you off your vision. That's just ridiculous. Besides, his location, for all of its rusticity and quaint charm, is still a great spot. Not to mention the fact that his reviews as a chef are phenomenal. He's hot, and I don't mean just as a dude du jour. But I mean he's getting quite the reputation for his location and fierce cooking." Tori cocked her head to the side a little bit. "And my research is telling me he's also getting press for his bad-boy good looks. Not that you don't already know that, but

I'm just saying, you need to have this celebration and you need to have it with him." Tori raised a brow and lowered the treble in her voice. "Now, if there's another reason you don't think you'll be able to work with Vin Caro, then maybe it is a mistake."

Lily raised a brow back, getting the challenge in Tori's voice. She turned and focused back on the traffic. "Of course I'll be able to work with Vin. We have a merest of histories, but you know me when it comes to business. There won't be any problems."

Lily was focused on the SUV in front of her but could still hear the smile in Tori's voice when she spoke. "Great! Then it's a win all the way around."

Lily nodded but inwardly frowned as she considered Tori's words. She knew she had a gem when she found Tori straight out of school. The girl wasn't around just for filing. She was a whiz when it came to marketing and had a wonderful eye when it came to style and design, but she really had something when it came to finding the right angle. And at the moment, Lily needed all the angles she could get if she planned on taking her business to the next level instead of staying stagnant. There was nothing sadder and no quicker way to bankruptcy in this fast-paced New York events business than becoming predictable.

She gave herself a confidence boosting nod just as traffic started to pick up again. "You're absolutely right, and this is just like the gut feeling that I had last night. This is a win, or at least it will be, and I'll just have to go for it. Sure, there will be more people who won't understand it, like Vin didn't, but in time he'll see that it is not just good for me but an excellent opportunity for him."

"And this looks to be a good opportunity for the

two of you to possibly get a little closer," Tori said slyly.

Lily let out a slow breath as she tried to squelch the immediate tingle that the idea of being closer to Vin brought on. "I don't know about that. It's probably best to not mix business and pleasure together in this case. Smarter to keep things professional." Lily hoped she sounded convincing to Tori, because in that moment she sure as hell didn't sound convincing to herself. She realized that she was screwing up royally. What sort of an example was she being as a boss to Tori, acting like a giddy girl crushing on a hot guy? "Besides," she added, trying to bring lightness to her voice, "I'm an engaged woman now, so I'm no longer on the market."

Tori shook her head and leaned over, reaching for her boss's ring finger on her left hand. She playfully tapped it before she leaned back in her seat. "Well, I don't see no rings on your magic finger, and you know what they say: If you like it, then you'd better put a ring on it."

It was Lily's turn to shake her head. "All right, Ms. Smarty, I wouldn't go daring me if I were you. Just say the word, because it's no skin off my teeth when it comes to treating myself right."

As traffic really opened up, Lily lost herself for a moment in the speed and thoughts of her big day at the beachside restaurant, all the most important necessities taken care of by Vincent "Your wish is my command" Caro.

Of all the ridiculous things. . . . It was getting to be late afternoon and he was still considering his meeting with Lily as he prepped for the evening crowd. What he had gotten himself into? Was securing a little time with Lily Perry really worth the inevitable aggravation that was sure to come? Seriously getting married to yourself? The woman had now proven herself to be a complete nutter. Sure she may be good-looking—hell, may tip the scale over to the totally hot column—and she was constantly in his thoughts since they had that encounter at her sister's wedding, but was going in on this job, one that his gut told him was sure to send his life into a tailspin, really worth the money? *Of course it was, dummy.*

Vin shook his head as the answer came to him quicker than he could get the thought fully out of his head. But marrying herself? He just didn't get it. What was she trying to prove? The only women he'd ever heard of who got married without a groom were nuns, and even they came strutting hard with the Jesus groom card. This deal he had a hard time wrapping his head around. Vin let out yet another growl as he surveyed the vegetables Manny had prepped for the night's specials while he trimmed and marinated the beef.

"You gonna go on like that all night, boss?" Manny said from over his shoulder.

Vin eyed him with a hard stare. "Go on like what?"

"Go on with the growls and the sighs like some bear in need of Pepto."

"I wouldn't start with me if I were you, Manny. You may be good at what you do and you may be my friend, but just because I need you here in the kitchen doesn't mean I won't pop you one right quick."

The shorter Manny only laughed, throwing his head back as if it was the funniest thing he'd heard in a while. The sound infuriated Vin all the more, and he just shook his head as he decided the beef could use some pounding to soften it up a bit. At his taking out the mallet and pounding the beef, Manny laughed even harder before walking over to pat Vin on the back. "Man, you've got it bad. This I thought I'd never see. Wish I put some money on it. Then again, maybe not. I probably would have lost. Vincent Caro whipped just like that."

Vin shot him another look. "Like I said, you are really pushing it."

"Pushing what?"

Vin's eyes went skyward. So the gang was all there. Vin let out a breath as two of his waitstaff came in—Felix and his cousin, Terry, who was better known as Punchy on account of his physique growing up. It wasn't the nicest of nicknames but hey, those type of things stuck in town. It was just how it was. It was Felix who chimed in first. "What's going on? Manny at it again?" he asked with his usual jovial laugh.

Manny started to open his mouth when Vin gave him an elbow right into his side. "I wouldn't if I were you," he said ominously. He guessed something in his tone let Manny know that he meant it, since Manny looked at the cousins and just shook his head, a smile still playing on the corner of his mouth. "Nothing. Just giving the boss the business."

"Yeah," Vin added. "But I persuaded him to stop and be a good little employee if he knows what's good for him."

"Oh, I know it's good for me, all right. The question is, do you know?"

Vin let out one last growl and directed the guys to start setting up in the dining area. They had a bit of time but really he just wanted the heat of the attention off of him. He needed time to process the whole encounter with Lily.

Soon the other staff came in. Their waitress, Tracy, came in quietly. She was a single mother whom Vin knew from the neighborhood and who didn't mind the hours because she had her mom watching her six-year-old son during the dinner shift. She was followed by their other sous chef, Ricky, whom Vin suspected had been falling for her, because his offered rides had gotten more frequent. Though he didn't fail to notice a few side glances that went her way from Paunchy. Vin smiled to himself. At times running the restaurant, he felt like the head counselor at a summer camp in charge of a bunch of overgrown CIT's. At least tonight the restaurant was more than half booked with reservations, so Vin was expecting a busy evening between bookings and drop-ins. Therefore he had no more time to worry about Lily Perry and her outrageous plans for her wedding for one.

Vin ran upstairs for a quick shower and change of clothes, and he was back down in fifteen minutes, ready to face the busy evening ahead. Lily Perry with her luscious curves, determined eyes, and crazy ideas would just have to wait until the dinner shift was over. And when it was, he'd deal with her but good.

Chapter 6

Vin felt a lot more clearheaded when he came back ashore the following morning. After wedging his surfboard down in the sand, he turned back toward the surf, inhaled, and took in the beautiful vision of the sun breaking through on the horizon. Leaning back, he unzipped the top of his wetsuit, bringing his arms out, exposing his chest and letting the warmth hit his body. He felt his skin pebble a bit but still welcomed the feeling. Summer was a little ways away, but he could feel the anticipation of it in the air and it buoyed his spirits even though it brought on a bit of melancholy, since he knew tranquil mornings like this would quickly fade and be few and far between.

Vin's lips twisted when thoughts of Lily Perry entered his mind. He looked down the beach toward the old docks and remembered their encounter there. It was brief and sweet but one he'd never forgotten. It made that dock damned near impossible to look on without thinking about her, which baffled him. There had been plenty of other faceless women before Lily and since their time under the dock, but somehow it was Lily that had stuck. And now here she was, back again in his life and turning it on its head. It seemed she was everything he didn't need but still, for some confounded reason, he couldn't deny he was attracted to her.

Vin shook his head to clear it. He knew he had to do something to remedy the situation, but what? Maybe it was the fact that he had never slept with her. Everything between Lily Perry and him had been left undone. Maybe that was her thing. Try a man to distraction, then leave him hanging. It was an old game to play in order to get attention and one he thought would never work on him, but now that he'd seen the tactic up close he couldn't deny its effectiveness. Vin felt his eyes go narrow. Lily Perry was good. Real good. She was a shark. A shark disguised as a pretty little angelfish.

Vin also knew he could handle her. And certain parts of him wanted to handle her just right. But after their last meeting he knew that would take time— time and a little bit of patience to win her over. He thought it was nuts, her crazy ceremony to celebrate her union with herself or whatever the hell it was. It seemed like a bunch of new age hipster mumbo jumbo to him. Just a reason to spend a lot of money. But if she was spending the money in his spot and it was flowing his way, he wouldn't be a fool and turn it down. She may be nuts, but he sure as hell wasn't. The customer was always right, and he'd do his best to make sure that this particular one left satisfied. In any and every way.

The sun rose completely and reflected off the shimmering waves, the vision catching in his eyes.

Vin squinted and put his hand up. The hour was growing late and he needed to get on with the day. It was time to prep for what he hoped would be a busy weekend crowd. But first he had some boards to repair for his kids who would be by for their lessons from the Boys Club come Monday. Vin picked up his board to head back toward the restaurant and his apartment.

On the way to his place, he passed his stand, giving it a quick lap to make sure that nothing had been tampered with in the past couple of days. He made a mental note to get on with hiring yet another person since his time would soon be divided even more once the stand opened for the summer months. The thought of opening the stand and bringing on a new hire to help run it didn't bring him any joy. Even though the restaurant was his main priority, he didn't want to neglect his first love. Before his mom passed, he'd enjoyed being out with the people and spending most of his time front and center on the beach. His stand afforded him that. Nothing more than an eight-by-twelve setup with a small four-burner grill, it was all he needed to do quick handheld tacos and keep them coming for the patrons on the beach. The stand is what kept him and his mom going when times were rough. It was hard facing the fact that she was gone. Part of the reason he kept his stand open over the past summer was in her honor. Vin knew she'd be so upset if he just let it go. Despite the hard work, he couldn't deny that she was never happier than when cooking by his side and serving the people with the sun shining on her face. Something about seeing it there now. Old and worn but somehow still sturdy, strong and beautiful made him feel like she was there with him. The sun rising on her face.

After one last look, a quick kiss to his two fingers, and a tap to the little wooden sign that donned her name, SONIA'S, Vin continued his walk back, heading up the wooden plank stairs that separated the beach from the street, and was surprised when he saw Simon waiting with his arms folded.

"What in the world got you up and out so early? You're a newlywed. Shouldn't you be in bed with your bride somewhere?" Vin asked.

"I know, right? There's really no way I should be up this early," Simon answered. "But as it turns out, my lovely bride is back to her morning gym routine, and since she's leaving me cold and hanging, I decided to get up and go for a run myself. I knew that I'd find you out here. I want to thank you for the surf lessons and for coming through at the reception with the food. It was a big hit."

Vin brushed off Simon's praise with a shake of his head. "You don't have to thank me for the lessons. It's not like you didn't pay for them." He kept heading toward the back of Canela. "And as for the food, it was my gift to you. I was happy to do it."

"Well, Sophie was quite impressed with me when she saw my skills out in Hawaii. We both had a great time, and I was able to teach her a few things. Thank you."

"You're welcome," Vin said. "But I hope you're not going to give it up now that the honeymoon is over. I want to see you back out there. Don't let your skills become stagnant. I still have my lessons with the kids, and you could help me to stay current. Besides, with the way things are going and your getting married, I may end up being the only old dude left catching any waves."

Simon laughed and shook his head. "Yeah, I doubt that I or anyone will be calling you old by any stretch. And as for me coming out again, I'll try to get out there when I can, and I'll think about the kids. You're doing good work." Simon smiled then. That silly secret grin that too many of his friends had nowadays. "Though I have to admit, married life isn't the worst thing to happen to a guy," Simon said.

Vin seriously doubted that. At least in the long haul. The idea of having to actually answer to someone constantly in your day-to-day life seemed like *the* worst thing to happen to a guy. What man needed the aggravation in his life? Not to mention the constant pressure and responsibility? No, that thing was fine for some but definitely not for him. He liked his life as it was; he made all the decisions. If there was a mistake, he would be the one ultimately on the hook for it. And the one to ultimately suffer for it. Who needed the hassle of having another person to take care of? To worry about? To possibly let down? He saw from his own mother how disappointed she was in the way things turned out with his father. Sure she tried to hide it but in her quiet moments it was there and Vin knew he had the DNA to be just that type of disappointment to the woman in his life, if he ever went so far as to let one in. Shaking the maudlin thoughts off though, Vin turned to Simon. "You want to come in for some coffee? I haven't had mine yet."

Simon nodded. "Sure, I can have a quick cup. Guess I've got about another half an hour before Sophie is done and I need to be heading home."

Vin snorted but bit back his quick retort to Simon

about already being tied to the old ball and chain. Instead he just let his friend in and went up the back stairs to his apartment to get started on a pot of coffee.

A few minutes later, after Vin had quickly showered, getting rid of the salt water and sand that still clung to him and changed into casual loose fitting jeans and a tee, the two men started chatting and Simon brought up Vin's food again. "I wanted to thank you once again for your gift. Your food was such a hit at the reception. Just a small taste of empanadas had folks' tongues wagging. The restaurant must be doing great."

Vin shrugged. "It's going okay. A little slower than I'd hoped, but when I think about it, it's probably going at the exact right pace for a person just starting out. But you know how it goes. I need this to really take off. Restaurants can be risky. But, hey, I should be thanking you. My doing you that favor got me another job." Vin raised his coffee cup in his friend's direction by way of mock cheer.

Simon smiled and nodded. "That's great, man. Is it a catering job? You cooking for someone else's wedding?"

Vin frowned and a twinge of worry begin to twist at him low in the gut. Could it really be that Simon didn't know? What if his whole extended family didn't know? Vin paused. Lily's scheme seemed crazy to him and he supposed it would be too many others. He wouldn't put it past her not telling her family. Dammit, *he should have just kept his mouth shut*, Vin thought. He suddenly felt torn. What had Lily gotten herself into with this one, and why had she included him when, judging by Simon's wide-eyed and clueless look, she hadn't even said anything to her own family? "Shit, man, I probably shouldn't have opened my big mouth."

Simon's brows came together and his lips thinned as he pulled his coffee cup away from his lips picking up on Vin's apprehension. "Okay, well, now you've got to tell me. If you're just talking empanadas, it can't be all that serious, can it?"

Vin's brows went skyward and he tilted his head. "I don't know. That depends on how seriously your new in-laws take another wedding in the family."

Simon's brows went skyward then he cocked his head. "Okay, no more joking around. Spill it. What the hell is going on? I'm just getting into this family but I know they don't play when it comes to secrets and letting new guys in."

"Well you don't have to worry about anything on that front," Vin mumbled."

"Come again?"

After a deep sigh and a shake of his head, Vin let it out. "Well, it's like this. Your new sister-in-law, Lily, she's hired me to lease out my restaurant for the Saturday after Labor Day to host a wedding."

Simon grinned. "Well, what are you doing getting all bent out of shape about that? Lily is an event coordinator." He took another sip of his coffee before speaking again. "And I'm really happy to see you two, if not rekindling what you started, at least coming together in a professional capacity. She can be very good for your business." Simon leaned back. "What were you getting me all worked up about? I didn't have you pegged as one for theatrics. I thought that was my department, being an actor an all."

Vin let out a breath. He wasn't handling this

well at all. But then again he shouldn't be put in this situation. "I don't think you get it, Simon," Vin said. "She didn't hire me for just another client's wedding. She hired me to cater and host her wedding."

"Her wedding?!" It was almost comical the way that Simon practically choked on his coffee. Almost. "How the hell is it Lily is getting married? I didn't even know she was seeing anybody that seriously. And that one dude she was seeing, what's his name? Thomas? He was a no-show for my wedding, so how is it she's now suddenly getting married? Besides according to Sophie they were half on the outs anyway so no big loss." Simon frowned. "I don't know how the family will react to this."

Part of Vin wanted to hang out on the Thomas part of the conversation. No, it wasn't his business and no, he shouldn't care less, but still, he wanted to know more about what type of guy Lily usually went for and what type of idiot didn't show for a date with her. His mind paused. Could it be the same type that didn't call her back after having a mind blowing make out session with her? Yeah, so he was an ass. At least he could admit it to himself.

Vin swallowed, getting back to his friend and the subject at hand. He didn't want to be the one to deliver the odd news, but Simon was asking the questions and unfortunately he was stuck being the deliveryman. "Yeah, that's the stickiness of it all. The person she's getting married to, well, is herself."

Simon put his coffee cup down, slowly sucked in a breath, and let it out looking Vin straight in the eye. He then burst out laughing. The laughter went on for a good thirty seconds, making Vin feel uncomfortable, and he thought of how Lily must have felt when he laughed. Finally he stopped his laughter and looked at Vin again, seemingly shocked that his friend wasn't joining him in the joke. Simon's face went deadpan while his brows knit together. "Okay, enough of this. Please tell me you are shitting me."

"Shitting you? Sorry, man, I wish I was."

Simon let out a wry snort then a sigh. "Yeah man, me too."

It was another night of family torture. But Lily was taking it in stride, because tonight her mom had made her favorite roast beef and Mama Dee had dusted off her apron and whipped up a pecan pie. Lily didn't know what had gotten into the two women, since as of late they weren't doing any of her old faves or her sisters', having forgone their girls' dishes for whatever the new sons-in-law liked. Although there was still favor paid to Sylvie since she was pregnant and now Ma was sure to throw in glazed cauliflower each Sunday just for her. Sylvie was always an odd one when it came to her food taste. Why couldn't she crave mac and cheese or something sweet like a normal person. No matter, after the day Lily had she was thanking her lucky stars for the comforting treat and already mentally preparing her to-go bags.

She had planned on dropping her married-to-myself bombshell at dinner, but the food was so good that she didn't want to risk mucking up her prime eating time. Maybe after dessert. Or maybe not. Maybe she'd just phone this one in. Literally. Lily was getting over an awful day, having met with Chelsea Carlyle to go over plans for the graduation party for her daughter, and the woman who seemed like she'd be a bit of a stickler turned out to be a monumental piece of work.

Lily had pulled out all the stops with what she thought was a terrific theme of *Back to the Future* meets *The Matrix*, since the birthday girl herself had admitted to being a sci-fi buff. But clearly Chelsea was not impressed and scoffed at the idea. She wanted a traditional party that screamed Park Avenue money, heavy on the elegance, and to top it off she wanted her daughter done up as a modern-day princess, something reminiscent of a sweet sixteen ball or possibly a cotillion as opposed to sending the girl off to film school as the hip young adult she was. Lily knew that if Christie had been at the meeting and seen some of the ideas she would've loved them, but the fact remained that, although it was Christie's party, she was not the client since she was not cutting the checks. So Lily would have to find a way to bridge the gap and please both mother and daughter in this endeavor. No matter, she'd make it work and bring together the mother's traditional sensibilities while making the younger woman happy.

Lily was deep in thought trying to come up with other ideas but also considering if she would have another piece of roast beef or just dive into the pie when Sophie piped up. Her sweet, high voice was filled with innocence but laced with something dark lurking underneath the surface. "Mom, everything tastes so delicious. I'm going to have to take some of this roast home even though I know that Lily may have my head if I take too much for Simon and myself." She shot her older sister a slick side eye.

Lily gave her an equally sly look back. "Don't

worry, I'll share. Just don't get too greedy with it; you know it's my favorite."

"Is it now?" Sophie asked. "From what I hear, seems that you found a new favorite."

Lily froze mid-chew. She knew her sister and she knew her well. Sophie was up to something. She had that "I've got some dirt on you and I'm gonna spill it" face on. The same one she had when she told their mom that Audrey was the one who dented the car when they'd only just gotten their licenses and that Violet was cutting her after-lunch chemistry class. And it was the very same look Sophie had when, after overhearing Lily on the phone with a friend, she spilled the beans that Lily had switched her major and dropped out of prelaw, deciding to go into marketing. Sophie was a notorious snitch, and all the sisters knew it. If you had a secret you didn't dare share it with Sophie. Now she was ride or die for the sisters no matter what. She was the first person you'd call if you needed backup in a fight, but if you didn't want your tea spilled, you definitely kept the cup away from Miz Sophie.

Lily narrowed her eyes and looked at her sister, her voice filled with warning. "I'm sure I don't know what you're talking about, Soph." She leaned over and cut a nice hunk of pecan pie, and with one last warning glance in Sophie's direction she took a bite and began to chew.

But Sophie being Sophie and her mother being her mother, one could not be deterred and the other one had already picked up on the scent. "What are you two girls talking about over there?" her mother asked, looking hard back and forth between the two sisters.

"It's nothing, Ma," Lily said.

"Well, it doesn't look like nothing," Mama Dee chimed in from her seat on the other side of the table. "I know you, Sophie, and you look like you're about ready to burst over there. Why don't you get yourself a piece of this pie and fill that mouth of yours so it has something to do besides spilling your sister's business."

Sophie gave a slight, exasperated huff. But at the look she got from Mama Dee she quickly changed her frown to a smile and proceeded with cutting pieces of pie for herself and Simon. It was then that Lily caught the fact that Simon was looking down, his eyes not meeting hers, and she couldn't help but know the truth. Shit, the jig was up. They knew. That was definite. Vin must've told Simon and Simon must've told Sophie. There was no getting out of this now. It was only a matter of time. If Sophie didn't spill the beans tonight, she'd be on the horn with one of her sisters by tomorrow, and either way the family would know the whole deal in no time.

Lily looked down at her pie, suddenly not hungry for it anymore. Damn, but it was pecan pie. She made a note to get it over with and get her appetite back. There were some things one just powered though and pecan pie was one of those things. And with that thought Lily sucked in a deep breath, looked around the table, and let it out. "So I've got a bit of good news," she said, hoping her voice exposed none of her nervousness.

Mama Dee's eyes widened expectantly while her mother's narrowed with skepticism. "Oh really, what is it?" her mother asked.

Lily forced a smile. "Mom, you don't have to look

like I'm about to kick your dog. This is good news. The family has another wedding coming up."

With that declaration her mother blinked and looked around the table as if to see if all her kids were accounted for. Mama Dee gave a cheerful clap and a yelp. "That's fantastic. You know how I love a good wedding."

It was then that her mother chimed in again. "Well, that is good news. But where is the groom? I'm assuming that you and Thomas are on better footing than you were during Sophie's wedding. He should have been with you tonight. I would have made him his favorite dish. " Her mother's eyes brightened then she looked at Lily, a question in her eyes. "What is his favorite dish anyway? I know it's not modern but you really should brush up on your kitchen skills Lily."

Lily held back on an eye roll. "You know cooking is not my area of expertise Ma. And what Thomas likes to eat and doesn't is irrelevant to this conversation. We're not currently together. "

Her mother frowned deeply. "So you're telling me it's Violet getting married? I'm going to kill that girl. She's got to finish getting her degree first and she knows it. Now, I do want all my girls to settle down, but you know how I feel about getting your education."

"Yeah, about the same as getting our skills in the kitchen," Lily mumbled.

"Don't be a smart ass, Miz Lily," her mother countered back quickly. Lily sucked in a breath and briefly closed her eyes then opened them again. She was being a smart ass and needed to get a handle on it if she was getting any of her family on board with her plan. She looked from her now simmering with anger mother to the other concerned and confused faces around the table. She knew she shouldn't care but she loved them and she did want to get them on board. It was time to clear up the confusion. Lily looked her mother in the eye. "No, Mom, it's not Violet. It is me."

Her mother's frown deepened and she let out a weary sigh. "Okay, now you've lost me Lily. You just said that you and Thomas weren't seeing each other. So now what? Have you worked things out and decided to make a go at marriage?" Her mouth then formed the shape of an O as another option hit her. "Wait, did you break up because you were seeing someone else? I can't believe you kept a person you were so serious with a secret from us." She waved a hand. "No matter. As long as I still think this person could have had the decency to at least come with you as you made the announcement to your family tonight. I mean, it is only right, don't you think so, Mama Dee?"

Mama Dee tilted her head and looked at Lily quizzically. "That I do, but I also don't think that's the whole crux of the story, now, is it, Lily?"

Lily swallowed. Leave it to Mama Dee to get right to it and to know she wasn't sharing all the facts. She let out a short sigh, then looked at her grandmother first and then at her mother. "No, that's not all of it. I'm not marrying Thomas."

Her mother raised a brow. "So we gathered. Thanks for getting that out. Now, please tell us, if you're not marrying Thomas, then who are you marrying? I swear, I can't keep track of you, Lily. You flit from one guy to the next and to the next, never lasting more than a season in any relationship and now you talk about getting married. Marriage takes commitment, girl. It's serious, not something you jump into lightly or play with. You can't make a commitment to someone and then move on as if you're switching to the latest fashion. How can you expect to be a good wife? Tell me who is crazy enough to take you on?"

"Me," Lily said, her voice low and hushed. But when she spoke again it was louder, clearer. "It's me, Mom. I'm marrying myself."

Renée Perry shook her head, and Lily watched as her mother's lips quirked up into a smile that held no humor. "If that don't just beat anything. Lily Perry, have you gone and completely lost your mind? What the hell are you talking about marrying yourself? Is this some sort of joke or just your way of acting out? If so, get over it, because you are way too old to play games to get attention. Now get the silliness out of your head; go on, get yourself another piece of pie and let's talk about your wedding when it's time to really have a wedding worth talking about." Her mother gave her body a little shake as if physically pushing Lily's news aside. "And just when I thought this day couldn't get any worse. I swear, child, you are just like your father. Always gotta be the star of the show. We're still barely over Sophie's day. Can't we just bask in that for a while?"

Lily felt the heat in her body threaten to boil over with her mother's quick and rude dismissal. She should have known that her mother was going to laugh her off. Her mom was just like those commenters on the article she'd seen, accusing the bride of being desperate or somehow unhinged or worst just attention seeking. But her mother's dismissal only served to fuel her and make her that more determined to have her wedding. Not to mention the comparison to her father. Lily looked around the table at her family's confused expressions and let out a breath before speaking. "I'm just telling you to let you know because more than anything I'd like to have my family with me, supporting me, as I make this commitment to myself. But if you're not there, I'll fully understand. My celebration is happening either way, because right now I do feel like celebrating." She looked pointedly at her mom. "No, I don't have a man in my life right now, at least not one I'm seeing seriously, and you know I'm cool with that. It doesn't bring me down or keep me up at night. I'm happy. I'm carefree, and I love myself and my own company. And my coming to that realization thrills me to no end." Lily smiled even though her mother didn't smile back. Just continued to stare at her with both condemnation and confusion. No matter. She wouldn't be held back. "September ninth will be my wedding day. It's all arranged; I'm having the ceremony out on the beach. The reception will follow at Simon's friend's restaurant Canela." She looked at her sisters then and gave them a wink. "Dress is semiformal, and I insist that shoes not be dyed to match."

Her mother stared her down. "Well then, maybe you should call up your dad and see about getting a two-for-one, or should I call it one in a half deal?"

It was Lily's turn now to look confused. "What are you talking about, Mom?"

Her mother let out a weary sigh, all her cool pretense evaporating on her slow breath. "What I'm talking about is the fact that it seems your father done went and got himself engaged to his latest chippie. So maybe you all could get in and have a ceremony together."

Lily quickly sucked in air as she struggled to get all the life-preserving oxygen she could. How could he do this? How could he finally end the dream of their family once and for all?

With that declaration from her mom, Lily was clear out of words. All she could do was look at her mother and mouth an apology. She then got up, grabbed a napkin, and cut herself a to-go piece of pecan pie before making her way to the door.

Chapter 7

It was Sunday afternoon, but just barely, when Lily's phone rang. "I feel like going shopping." Mama Dee's voice was light and matter of fact.

"And you're telling me this because . . ." Lily said teasingly. She was still in a huff over the horrendous disaster after her wedding announcement but knew it would do no good showing any of that huffiness toward Mama Dee. Besides, they played this little game twice monthly. Mama Dee would call her up for their usual Sunday hangout and shopping trip to either the big-box store, where Mama Dee stocked up on food for the house for the rest of the month, or the local Walmart, or if Lily could persuade her the fancy mall with the Neiman's over on the south side. She left it up to Mama Dee. Half the fun was the surprise.

Lily's sisters never quite got the allure of their twice-monthly trips. They all seemed to think that Lily was being so kind, taking their grandmother out and spending the afternoon with her as if it were some sort of hardship. But Lily truly loved the time she spent with her grandmother. An afternoon with

Mama Dee was never dull. The older woman was quick-witted and at times downright bawdy. Lily found her easy to talk to, and she usually left her company feeling somehow lighter than when the day began. Mama Dee had a way of making the issues that were weighted on her mind seem trivial and not worth the stress.

"Girl, don't go playing those games with me. I can't believe you're not already on your way. I've been out of church for a full half hour. What is it?" she admonished, then whispered, "Don't tell me you got some man up there in your fancy city apartment? Wait." Mama Dee lowered her voice as if she had hit the nail on the head. "Do you have some man up there? If so, I'll let you alone to get back to whatever and we can go out next week. I don't want to be an interrupter."

Lily thought she felt her eyes roll on their own. "No, Mama Dee, I don't have some man here. And there is no 'whatever' going on. I thought I made it clear at dinner that I was fine as I was."

"Sweetie, you made nothing clear at dinner, but we can get to that when we go out. Now, are you on your way or what?"

"Yes, ma'am. I'm actually walking out the door now," Lily said, grabbing her purse and car keys. "I should be to you within the hour." She heard Mama Dee snort.

"Within the hour . . . sure. You know how traffic is on Sunday, especially out here. I won't go holding my breath. At my age you don't play with things like that."

"Now who's the one being dramatic?" Lily said as she made her way down to the underground garage in her building. She was so lucky to have her space. The landlord of the high-rise where she rented her old Brooklyn condo was actually an old friend of the family, so he cut her an amazing deal. Honestly, she had a feeling that back in the day he'd had his heart put through its paces by Mama Dee. He never failed to ask about her, and she never spilled the tea on him, but Lily got a great deal on her apartment and her parking spot was thrown in, which by Brooklyn standards should have at least run her the cost of a spare kidney. Without the parking spot there was no other way she'd ever be able to have a car anywhere near the city. Her friends and even her family thought she was crazy for holding on to the old Buick that her father had passed on to her. But she liked the freedom it afforded her to travel back and forth between home and her family without having to rely on mass transportation. Besides, her father didn't leave her or any of them much of anything else when he hit the road so, she didn't know, maybe she was keeping the car out of some sort of misplaced maudlin attachment or maybe it was out of spite, but still she held on to it as well as her spot. As Lily unlocked the car door she gave a silent prayer that the old girl would hold up just a little longer. She's gotten attached to old Bitsy. "Listen, I'm getting in the car now; let me hang up to get to you that much faster."

"Okay, baby, drive carefully," Mama Dee said. "I'll see you soon. I can put together some sandwiches if you'd like for the road?"

Lily shook her head. "No thanks, Mama Dee. We're hitting the stores. It's not like we're driving down south. And you eat light if you going to get anything out. How about we go to the mall today?

We can stop at the Cheesecake Factory and have lunch?" She knew she wasn't being aboveboard, but she really didn't want to hang out at the Walmart this afternoon, so she figured she'd dangle the idea of cheesecake in front of her grandmother as a way of a bribe.

"Now you know you're not playing fair, child, but if you twist my arm I could be persuaded into having some of that fried macaroni and cheese that they serve."

Lily cranked up the car and backed out of her spot, having put the phone on speaker. "All right, I'll get it for you as long as you promise not to tell Mom about it."

"Darling, you know I never spill any secrets between the two of us. See you soon. Bye."

Lily hung up and spent her time on the road thinking of how grateful she was for the precious time she had with Mama Dee. It really meant so much to her, but she couldn't help the moments of worry that came over her when she thought about Mama Dee's declining health. She knew that her grandmother would scoff if she were to bring it up with her, but the fact still remained that two years prior she had given all of them a scare when quite suddenly the vibrant woman fell ill with a minor heart attack. The thought of it still gave Lily a chill. As if any heart attack could ever be considered minor. But thank goodness it wasn't major, and her grandmother had received quick and very good medical attention. Her blockages were cleared and stents were put in.

Still, Mama Dee was changed. Lily saw the small differences. How Mama Dee's normally quick pace had slowed; how she was so careful now with all her movements. Careful when cooking and prepping so as not to cut herself because of the blood thinners. Careful watching her food. Although she talked about the fried macaroni and cheese, Lily knew that she would let her grandmother have only a small taste, because the high-fat food was not on her diet. No, Mama Dee was all talk; she had to take care of herself, and Lily helped to make sure that she did.

And as much as their outings helped Lily, she hoped they helped Mama Dee too. Giving her a certain amount of respite from Renée's all-seeing eye. For the most part the two women got along, but Lily knew that in a way these outings were a necessary form of therapy for Mama Dee, finding freedom from Lily's mom, who'd barely cut Mama Dee any slack when it came to her health and her diet. Renée was usually there with her medication before Mama Dee could even get it herself. She watched what Mama Dee ate like a hawk, and when it came down to Mama Dee's antics of going on bus rides to the casino or to see friends or on weekend shopping trips, well, her mother tried to put a stop to that also. Lily had to think that although it was all done out of love, it was still slightly crazy making.

Lily's mind flittered from the relationship between her mother and grandmother and wandered over to her upcoming ceremony and the fact that she needed to get in next week to meet with Vin. The thought brought an instant tenseness to her shoulder blades and at the same time, in a weird juxtaposition, a tingling in her breasts.

If that didn't just beat all, she thought. What was she supposed to do with the roller coaster of emotions that just the thought of him put her through?

How was she supposed to plan a specular party while she was in the midst of a hormonal firestorm? And what was she doing feeling this way anyway? She should know good and well to have a firm hand on her emotions if she couldn't or wouldn't get a firm hand on Vin. The thought of taking him in hand once again had her smiling against her will, if there was any such thing. But the man really was delicious. She had to give herself props for not jumping his bones during the meeting the other day. He was just that tempting with his strong and silent good looks, and then his sexy skill in the kitchen . . . The man was the full package, and it was clear he knew it.

Quicker than she expected, Lily was pulling up to her old family house. Traffic turned out to be lighter than normal, which was good because, after the talk about macaroni and cheese balls, Lily's stomach was talking back to her and she could use a little something to eat. Lily started to open her door and was halfway out when she caught sight of Mama Dee hurrying out the front door.

Mama Dee gave her head a quick shake as she came toward the car. "I wouldn't go inside there if I were you."

Lily's brows knit together. "Why in the world not? Honestly, I need to go and pee before we get back on the road. "

Mama Dee got into the passenger seat and slammed the door shut. "Well, you can go in and pee at your own risk. Your mama is on a warpath today, and she is just waiting to give you an earful about this wedding/commitment ceremony/whatever you want to call this shindig you're having. She's been on the phone with Ruby for half the morning getting herself in a right rile up. You, child, have become the talk of the Rockaways."

Lily groaned, letting her head fall back against the headrest. She turned toward her grandmother and looked her in the eyes. "I can only imagine what Aunt Ruby is saying. I'm sure she's egging Mom on with talk about me not being able to hold down a man or some such crap. And she's only making it worse by bringing up Nikki and her ever-so-perfect soldier-boy fiancé."

Mama Dee nodded. "Well, it seems that's about the size of it, and don't go hatin' on Nikki. You two are first cousins. You need to support each other."

At that declaration Lily shot her grandmother a look. Mama Dee knew that Nikki was damn near insufferable with her overly plucked and plasticized behind.

Mama Dee continued, "Don't give me that look, and I don't have to explain it no further to you about your mama. You've got the gist of it. So are you gonna go in, or are you going to crank this baby up and get us going? There is a gas station right down around the corner, or you can hold it until we get to the mall, your choice."

Lily's eyes swept from her grandmother toward the old Cape Cod–style house. As she was looking she saw the curtains in the front room flutter open and knew her mother was peering through to look at them, waiting for Lily to get out of the car and step inside. She could practically feel her simmering anger through the window, across the sidewalk, and into the car. Lily swallowed. "You know, I think I'm going to hold it for a little bit."

Mama Dee looked from Lily over to the house and

then back at her again. "Good to know that, even with
this commitment wedding to yourself, or whatever it
is, you haven't completely lost your senses. Smart
move. Come on, girl, let's go. I'm hungry."

Lily gave her head a shake and cranked up the car.
It rumbled to life with the low horse cough and then
an insistent sputter. Lily ran her hand lovingly across
the steering wheel and put on what she hoped was
a confident smile. "Let's blow this popsicle stand,
girlie," she said brightly.

Her grandmother smiled, taking some of the heavy
weight off her chest with the twinkle in her eyes.
"Let's do this. Maybe along the way I can convince
you to drive a little farther north and we can hit up
some slot machines. I just got my social security
check, and it's burning a hole in my pocket."

Lily laughed as she pulled away from the curb.
"Don't tempt me, lady; I just may be in a gambling
mood."

Forty-five minutes later they were seated at the
Cheesecake Factory and had just given the waitress
their orders. Mama Dee took a sip of her ice tea and
then put it down regally before training her keen eyes
on Lily. "Okay, darling, we're seated. I should be
happy and have my mac and cheese balls soon. Why
don't you explain to me what the deal is with this
whole marriage-to-yourself ceremony that you plan
on doing? Why this and why now?"

Lily looked at her grandmother and let out a short
sigh. She knew this question would be coming, and
honestly she should've prepared better to answer it.

When she ran over how it would go, she saw herself spewing out all the right answers. *Because I'm confident in myself,* she thought she would say. *Because I'm happy where I am in life and I don't need a man to make me whole and to fulfill me.* That one sounded like it would come off so well. *Because I want to celebrate me; I love me and I want the world to know it.* That one seemed a little bit shaky, but it sounded good enough.

But as she sat looking her grandmother straight in the eyes, none of her prepared answers seemed quite right. They didn't seem quite right because she didn't know if she really believed them down deep in her heart. They were all true in their own ways, but were they really the reason she was doing it? Could she really tell Mama Dee that she chose to do it partially in a fit of anger because she was tired of answering the same "When are you getting married?" question and the ceremony seemed like an inspired thing to do but with further thought she was faltering?

No, she really couldn't tell her that. That would send her grandmother into a tizzy worrying about her, and she didn't need to have that type of worry added to her conscience.

Mama Dee reached across the table and took Lily's hands in her own. Up until that moment, when Mama Dee stilled them, Lily didn't even know her hands were shaking. She blinked, doing her best to push back the tears fighting to be unleashed.

"Babe, you are ready to cry. You haven't done anything wrong. If you want to have this party for yourself, and if you want to tell the world that you love yourself, then go ahead and do it. Hell, you should love yourself. You know the old saying—If you don't love yourself, then nobody else will. But let me just caution you right there. Somebody always loves you and always has." Mama Dee squeezed her hands tightly. "Despite what you think of this crazy family of yours, we're here for you. We love you unconditionally. I love you unconditionally, and even that tight-lipped, steel-backed mama of yours loves you unconditionally. I never want you to feel like you're fighting this fight called life out here by yourself." Mama Dee's words, her declaration of love, had Lily choking back a quick sob. She knew her grandmother loved her, but she also knew that one day her grandmother would leave her, and she wanted to make her happy. She wanted her to have the day to see her walk down the aisle. She also wanted Mama Dee to have peace and know she'd be fine. But she didn't want to tell her the truth—that she was afraid if she waited for the right man to come along, Mama Dee would never have that happy day to see her walk down the aisle. Lily pushed out a weak smile, moving her hands so they were over her grandmother's, and gave her a squeeze. "Well, then, I know I have all I need. But I still want to have my wedding while I'm looking good and of an age where I can get away with wearing white. There are those sketchy years where no matter what anyone says, the color is just not appropriate."

Mama Dee smiled back. "Nonsense. I reckon you can wear white at eighty if you want." Just then, the waitress came over with their appetizers. The poor girl looked a little stunned and embarrassed as she took them in, holding hands, eyes all red-rimmed from crying. It was clear that she wasn't sure what to do with the two women in front of her who were clearly deep in thought and conversation. "Um, excuse me," she said. "Can I put these down?"

Mama Dee looked up at her and grinned. "Well, you'd better before I snatch them out of your hands. I'm so hungry, bring 'em to me," she said with laughter in her voice.

Lily and Mama Dee started to eat with quiet ease. Lily hoped she could convince Mama Dee with her next words. "Really, I'm doing this because I want everyone to see that I am truly happy with the way things are in my life. I'm tired of the questions and everyone asking me about settling down. Nothing in me wants to settle."

That got a grin out of Mama Dee, and Lily continued. "I'm happy with just being myself. I'm happy making my own decisions for myself. My business is picking up and going well. I have some really good friends. I am able to travel and come and go as I please. What do I need a man mucking that up for?"

"Well, amen to that," Mama Dee said with a quick nod. "But why do you have to have a whole ceremony to do it, is my question."

Lily's eyes narrowed. "Does it embarrass you so much? Does it embarrass the family? Is that why you're asking?"

"No, child. Me? Nothing embarrasses me. If you wanna run naked through the neighborhood, you know me. I'll find a way to convince the neighbors it is the latest fashion and join in. But you know your mama, she likes to keep up appearances. So yeah, it does embarrass her a little bit. But don't you worry. I'll bring her around. Besides, I've been looking into things on the Internet."

Lily's brows went up. "Mama Dee, you realize you

and the Internet don't get along so well, right?" Lily tried to squelch down the immediate thread of panic she felt when Mama Dee brought up the Internet, but it was hard. The last time Mama Dee got on the Internet, she ended up opening quite a few dating accounts and took it upon herself to snap some rather provocative pictures for her profile. Lily's mother still hadn't gotten over the shock of all the illicit phone calls to the house—so much so, they had to change their number.

"Don't you worry, I wasn't surfing no place I wasn't supposed to," Mama Dee said with a shake of her head. "But I did find out that this married-to-yourself deal might actually be something. Looks like you are about to get in on the ground floor of a hot, new trend. This might be a really good business venture for you."

Lily nodded at Mama Dee, feeling suddenly more buoyant. "That's what I was thinking too. It could be fantastic if I can spin it the right way. If I can pull this off and convince others of what a fabulous time it can be. Hey, you never know, I may find a whole new niche market."

Mama Dee grinned, not bothering to hide her pride. "I always knew you were the smartest one of the bunch," she said, then looked at Lily sternly. "Though, if you quote me on that part, I'll lie on a stack of Bibles. I don't need your sisters looking at me all sideways at the next dinner."

Lily laughed. "Don't worry, that'll stay between you and me. Just like you don't need them looking sideways, I don't need my sisters any more jealous of me than they already are. And speaking of jealous, the added bonus of all this is that I could drive my sisters crazy by putting them through the whole bridesmaid nightmare they've all put me through. I'm going to pick out some shoes for them that are gonna pinch the hell out of their feet."

Mama Dee raised her brow and looked at Lily with a knowing glance. "*Hmph*, that sounds great, but there I was thinking that the added bonus was the fact that you get to spend so much time with that delicious-looking empanada man. You are using his place for the venue, right?"

Lily sputtered and choked on a piece of fried macaroni. She quickly reached for her water glass. Mama Dee was always seeing way too much. And the nerve tagging Vin, the empanada man, not to mention that she totally peeped Lily's hole card and the fact that she was low key definitely looking forward to spending time with said empanada man with the midnight eyes.

When Lily quit her coughing her grandmother was shaking her head and smiling. "Oh, honey, I need to teach you a lot better."

Lily frowned. "What are you talking about now, Mama Dee?"

"Your poker face is for crap. You might be well versed and quite convincing when it comes to spouting off about how much you don't need a man to complete you or whatever. But I can tell you one thing, from what I'm seeing over here, you definitely wouldn't turn down that man."

And with that comment, Lily shook her head and prayed for the waitress to come with the rest of their food so that they could eat more and talk a whole lot less.

Chapter 8

Vin was determined to make damn sure that he was better prepared for Lily Perry's next visit. He may have been caught completely off guard during the last meeting, but this time he was prepped and ready to roll.

The restaurant was closed, so he was by himself. Normally he'd be happy for the opportunity to get a little alone time with a beautiful woman, but for some reason, and if his annoying fidgetiness was any indication, he was actually missing Manny's presence as a buffer. The thought had him inwardly cringing. God, did he really have it that bad?

Vin grunted at the blasphemous thought and gave a quick glance to what he had prepared for Lily for brunch. Though she'd said she was just stopping by for a quick chat and look around in order to take photos and get more décor and layout ideas, he'd prepared a tasting menu that featured some of his favorite dishes: camarones en salsa verde, filete de pescado, and his seafood paella, not to mention a few of the empanadas she'd enjoyed at the wedding. He

suddenly got a knot of dread when he wondered if
she even liked seafood. What if she had a problem
with shellfish? Shrimp, fish, and paella—what a
rookie move. He was so off his game. This was something he should have checked. Damn it.

Vin let out a long breath. He knew what the
problem was. It wasn't so much that he was nervous
because he was attracted to her and just the thought
of her had him stiffening like a schoolboy, though
that didn't make things any easier. No, it was that he
hoped she'd be so enamored with his place and his
food that she'd get past his judgy attitude at their last
meeting and forgive him for his reaction, or over-
reaction as it were, to her whole wedding-to-herself
announcement. That she'd see that it wasn't a big deal
and he was over it and understood. Not that any of
that was true, because he wasn't over it and he still
didn't understand why she was doing what she was
doing, despite his trying. No matter what angle he
used to approach it, the whole thing didn't make a bit
of sense to him.

Lily was a perfectly intelligent and vibrant, not to
mention hot as shit, woman. What was she doing
sticking her neck out and possibly opening herself
up to this type of public scrutiny? Had she been so
screwed over by men that this was the outcome? Vin's
stomach suddenly twisted over on itself. Knotted up,
as his own involvement in her screw-ation hit him.
He shook his head against the thought. No way. There
was no way he was putting that on himself. So he'd
never pursued her after they'd gotten hot and heavy
that day on the beach. It wasn't like she'd ever come
looking for him. Shouldn't the screw turn both ways?
Especially with a modern woman like her.

Besides, Lily had said so herself. This was her choice. Her situation.

She'd said she was fine. That she was happy and secure and perfectly content with herself and her life. Why shouldn't he take her word for it? Vin snorted as he remembered the passionate abandon with which she'd kissed him at Simon and Sophie's reception. The way she'd opened up and broken loose. Drinking him in like a woman lost in the desert hitching a ride from a water truck. She sure didn't seem like she had it all together.

And it was with that thought that Vin heard Little Miss Together lumber up his drive once again in that loud-ass car of hers. From the sound of it, he wondered if the car would find its way back down. But quickly he stirred his sauce and lowered the flame, then wiped his hands on a dish towel before removing his apron and stepping out of the restaurant's kitchen just as she stepped through Canela's doors.

Vin sucked in a breath as he steeled his resolve and took in the image of Lily on this late spring morning. Despite her dark sunglasses, she looked like rays of bohemian sunshine in a flowing, white peasant blouse with billowy sleeves and lace accents. Its low V-neck showed off her full breasts just enough to stir his blood. Down below she wore black leggings that hugged her every curve and showed off her long legs to perfection. When she did remove her glasses and shook out her soft brown curls, she just about took his breath away. "So you ready to work this out?"

Hell, he was ready to work anything, no strike that, everything out with her. Anytime, anyplace.

But to answer, Vin grinned at her as he strode forward, finally coming to a stop right before her. "Like I said at our last meeting, your wish is my command."

Lily walked into Canela and blinked rapidly against the darkness as her eyes tried to adjust. For the first time she felt that maybe it was too dark in Vin's restaurant to hold a wedding. But then she remembered she was still wearing her sunglasses and eased them off, bringing the full force of Vincent Caro into focus as he strode toward her. No, it wasn't too dark. As a matter of fact the lighting in here was just perfect. Giving her brain a kick, Lily knew she was just making excuses. She'd come there partly to gain ideas and firm up her plans, but she knew the other part of her, the part that she most feared and often denied, was there to look for a way out. And there he was standing before her. Flashing like a well-muscled neon sign. WAY OUT!

Damn, Vin was a lot to take in. And all just right in his well-worn jeans and black tee. On his feet he wore well-worn, though not grimy by any means, basketball sneakers. Nothing about him said he was putting on airs or had anything to hide. The whole outfit, with its perfect casual flare, hanging in all the right ways on his toned body, had her mind immediately jumping off her commitment ceremony and onto the nonexistent honeymoon she would not be having. Lily fought against the nerve to fan herself and inwardly murmured, "Be cool."

She smiled up at him. "You and your promises

about wishes. I would be careful about what I said if I were you. Fair warning, I can be a pretty demanding client."

With that comment, Vin smiled. Those gorgeously scruffy cheeks spread just enough to show his beautiful white teeth, the canines flashing a slight point that had parts of her body tingling that really shouldn't at the moment.

"That's what I'm hoping for," was his only reply. That and a quirk of his brow.

Lily's mind quickly fluttered backward to their first meeting and the first time she'd seen his smile full-on. He'd seemed so dark and broody against the backdrop of the beach and sun and all the people happily going about their lives. She didn't know, something about him when he was going about his business and working that little taco stand gave off a serious "don't mess with me" air. But when he'd finally been persuaded to come out, thanks to Simon, and their eyes met and the full force of his smile hit her, well, it was like a car getting a jump-start the way he revved her up. It made her feel supercharged, as if she could take on anything, but at the same time it scared her, bringing out a recklessness she didn't know she had. Lily felt a frown pull at her brows with the thought. That recklessness was yet another reason she should, if not rethink her commitment ceremony, at least reconsider having it here, with him.

Lily inhaled deeply and, as the enticing aromas of sweet, savory, and spicy hit her senses, told herself not to be too hasty. With her mind almost firmly and solely on her ceremony, Lily brought business back into focus and leveled Vin with her gaze. "It smells great. But I thought you were closed today."

"I am," Vin said as he walked her farther into the

restaurant. "But I thought I'd prepare a little something for you. That way we can discuss what you'd like for the menu, talk more in depth, and I could learn your tastes."

A smiled quirked at the corner of Lily's lips. She knew he was just being professional and doing what he should as a vendor, but she couldn't help it. Something about the way he'd said that he wanted to know her tastes made her hope for more. It was stupid and she knew it. She was his client, nothing more. She looked at his full lips surrounded by that delicious hint of beard and remembered the slight scratchy feel of it. Hell, this wasn't going to be as easy as she thought.

She didn't know why, maybe it was her being the client for once or maybe it was a case of his being the vendor, but she didn't know what to expect or do with herself. Lily felt suddenly fidgety. In any other case, she'd have things down pat and do her usual tight-ship situation. However, now that all the balls were in her court, all she felt she could do was duck and dodge. She looked at Vin and blinked, taking in his confused expression. She felt foolish and didn't blame him for being bewildered. She was supposed to be taking the lead. Hell, it was her wedding; she should be taking the lead in all ways. Lily cleared her throat. "That sounds great, and honestly I am kind of hungry. But do you mind if I take a few pictures first?"

He nodded. "Of course not."

Lily reached into her bag and took out her phone, then took quick snaps of the room from all angles. She frowned as she started to look at things objectively and really take in the venue with a more critical eye. It would take a bit of work to turn the place into the wedding location of her dreams. But really, what about this was her dream anyway? In her dream, she was walking down a rose-petal path with the sky and ocean as its backdrop. She was heading confidently toward the strong, waiting arms of the faceless man who was as eager to be joined with her as she was to be joined to him. Lily almost laughed at the silly thought, since, in all her years of dating and premature mating, she'd yet to come close to meeting a man to fill the faceless void.

She continued snapping while Vin leaned by the bar and watched her. "So, how married are you to those stools?"

He frowned but quickly eased. "I'm not all that. You can change what you like as long as it's set back to rights when you're done."

She smiled, relieved that he'd acquiesced so easily. It was then that she noticed the photo in the center of the bar. The pretty woman with the young boy, their matching eyes and smiles undeniable in the little shack she knew to be his on the beach. "Is that your mother?"

Lily couldn't mistake the immediate tension that zinged the air as Vin straightened. His voice came out hoarse and rough. "Yes. It is."

"She's beautiful."

"Yes, she was."

Lily frowned. Oh hell, she didn't mean to hit on a sore spot. The last thing she wanted to do was cause him pain. Also, she definitely didn't want to add anymore tension to their already tense situation. "I'm sorry," she said sincerely, hoping he could feel that she meant it. "Hey, I can see the resemblance in the eyes. You have a lot of her features."

Vin didn't turn to look at the photo. Only stayed turned her way. Frowning, not quite connecting.

"Yeah, I guess." He cleared his throat. "Listen, I think we should eat. How about I show you the kitchen and we plate it up."

"Great." So that was it. Door slammed firmly shut on the subject of his mother. Sharp, but she could respect his need for privacy. Besides he hardly knew her. Lily smiled. "Lead the way."

With her smile, Lily noticed Vin ease up on the tightly wound tension in his stance. "Come on, follow me."

Not the worst part of any day, Lily thought as she followed Vin, taking a moment to further admire his amazing physique. Wide shoulders, corded arms, that sexily tapered waist, not to mention—but since she was there she was totally going to mention it—that ass that was museum sculpture worthy. How did he do it? The guy must work out every day. Around food all the time and he still looks like he looks. "Do you work out a lot?" Lily had murmured her question before she had a chance to think about it and pull it back behind her tongue.

Vin stopped right before hitting the kitchen door, turned, and looked back at her. His movements so quick that she couldn't bring her eyes up from his behind fast enough to not get caught. By the time her eyes met his, his were shimmering with mirth.

"It's just, well, uh . . ." Lily stuttered, trying to find an explanation for being caught staring. And judging by the look Vin was giving her, it didn't seem like he was going to give her an out. "Working around food all the time must be really tempting. I don't know if I could handle it."

His grin was playful and accompanied by a long up and down. The look was heated enough to pleasantly warm each body part his eyes caressed. "Thanks for noticing. Not that you have anything to worry about in that department."

Lily fought not to blush under his praise, and as for the look, she guessed he gave as good as he got.

Vin continued, "And as for exercise, I'm not that big on anything formal. I may or may not do a little something in the gym every once in a while. But I mostly get my exercise out on the water."

When Lily's brows pulled together, he explained. "I surf as much as I can during the season. When it's not the season is when I hit the gym." Lily was grateful to follow him and head into the kitchen.

"Ah, gotcha," she said as she took in how organized, not to mention clean, Vin's kitchen was. It was a true testament to his work ethic. She knew from the reception and the small sampling she'd had of his empanadas that he was a good chef, but the kitchen showed just how much he cared about his business and his customers. It also showed an exceptional respect for his food. Following him to the stove, she was almost overwhelmed by the full impact of the aromas hitting her. Lily inhaled deeply. "Still, I don't know if I'd be as disciplined as you." She waved a hand over the food. "Like I said, the temptation would be too much. I'd have to live in the gym."

He leaned in just a hairbreadth closer to her, hitting her with the full force of the darkness of his eyes and the huskiness of his voice. He was close. So very close that all she had to do was lean forward and she'd have him. Lily swallowed and took a step back. Warring with herself over what, she didn't know.

She expected Vin to follow suit, take the cue and step back too. Break the sexually charged tension in the air. But instead he leaned in even farther. "Believe me, there are many more things to be tempted by than food."

Before Lily could reply, his lips were on hers, full and firm, taking control just as she'd hoped he would from the moment she'd walked in the door, although oddly she hadn't known it was what she wanted at the time. But further checking off the yes boxes in her mind, Lily opened her mouth to suck in a much needed breath, and let out a low moan of pleasure as Vin filled the space with his tongue, stroking hers in a way that sent pulses throughout her entire body. He pulled her toward him, and she melted in, her softness against his hardness, and she matched him, every curve fitting to his bend. It just felt right. Almost too right. The thrill of it caused her heart to speed up, and she thought she could feel his race to keep up with her. But that made no sense. Of course this had to be just a kiss to him, she thought to herself. Just something to pass the time, a little fun for the night with someone of the opposite sex. It was the only thing that made sense. And it was the way she should be thinking of it too.

Lily let Vin and that tongue of his have its way a few seconds more and indulged herself in the headiness of the moment before reaching her hands up between the two of them and gently pushing at his practically unyielding chest. Coming away, she looked him in the eyes, trying hard to gain focus and clarity. Finally she spoke. "Now that we've gotten that out of the way and cleared the air, you think we can get back to business?"

Chapter 9

Vin stepped back and cleared his throat, trying hard to control both his passion and his simmering anger. How many times would he be overcome and pulled in by this woman only to get blindsided and be completely shut down again? He was quickly turning into the definition of an idiot. Shit!

He leveled Lily with what he hoped was an emotionless look as he did as she bade and got down to business. If business was what she wanted, then business was what she'd get. If she could turn on a dime after a kiss like that then more power to her. He swallowed back a growl. Screw it. She had it right anyway. His head, the thinking one, knew after their beach encounter that she was nothing but trouble for him, and he was definitely trouble for her. She'd stirred up a heated kind of passion that he had a hard time controlling and a level of emotion that he definitely didn't want in any part of his life. That was precisely why he'd never pursued her. He never came up against these kind of dangerous feelings with any other woman. With anyone else it was easy to move on. Get in and get out. Figuratively and at times literally. And Vin never had any trouble with spelling things out from the get-go so no hard feelings got in the way of a good time.

Too bad he wasn't smart enough currently to hold on to that same thinking. If he'd had any sense, he would have sent the empanadas on to Simon's wedding via his delivery guy and been done with it. But no, he had to go and get all gussied up in a tight-assed suit and go sniffing around for trouble. As if he didn't know it, trouble was just what he'd gotten.

No matter, the fact still remained he needed the job and the money, if not the recognition from it. Vin forced a smile and cleared his throat. He could do this. Lily Perry may be a player, but he'd invented the game. "Well, now that your taste buds have been suitably wetted, um, no, I mean tempted." He watched her eyes shift in confusion. *Fuck. Did I really just say wetted? Game, where are you when I need you?* Vin let out a slow breath. Way to go with the words. Just feed the woman, Vin, and move on.

They had been eating silently for eight minutes, although it felt more like twenty-eight. Vin knew there wasn't anything wrong with his food, or at least he was almost certain there wasn't anything wrong with it, so he could only blame the uncomfortable silence on his crossing the line with the kiss. He looked toward the large sliding doors he'd had installed at the back of the restaurant to take advantage of the beach-front location and ocean view. Though it was overcast earlier, the sun had come out and was shining brightly. "Would you like to take our food outside to eat on the patio? That way you can see what it would be like if you choose to have guests dine out there," he asked in an attempt at breaking the uncomfortable silence.

Lily looked up at him in an almost surprised sort of way as if she'd forgotten he was sitting across from her. Something else he'd never experienced before. Way to make an impression. "No, this is fine here," she said. "Though the deck looks lovely. I think we should find a way to utilize it. How many people can it accommodate?"

Vin turned toward the deck, then back to her. "One hundred comfortably, and the dining room one fifty, seated."

She seemed to ease a bit as she nodded. "That's plenty of space for my needs. Probably more, since I'd like to keep this an intimate family gathering. She took a bite of her shrimp. He was glad to see a hint of satisfaction bloom at the edge of her mouth.

"Are you liking the shrimp?" he asked, and was immediately annoyed since he'd never showed any hint of doubt in his abilities in the kitchen before.

She nodded as her reply.

Shit, maybe it was the kiss. He had gone too far. She hadn't given him any more feedback but the cool brush-off. Vin cleared his throat. "Um, listen, about the kiss. I hope it was okay." Damn it, now she was making him just as doubtful about his kissing skills as she was with his food? What the hell?

Once again all he got was a nod as she took another mouthful of food.

Vin let out a long breath as he searched for patience. What was with her? He'd never seen a woman so hot and cold in such a short span of time. Frustrated, he pushed back in his chair. "Listen," he started, maybe with just a little too much force behind his voice, just as she was going for an empanada. Her eyes widened, and he cooled his tone before continuing. "I'm sorry but you were the one who came on to me first, not once but twice." For the life of him, Vin didn't get why he was explaining himself to this woman. He'd never had to do so before, but he was rambling on like some kid in junior high trying to get out of, or was it into, detention? When Lily only raised a brow, he continued. "I just thought, hey, maybe we could kick it. Do business while engaging in a little pleasure, but you've gotta give me something to go on here. Your mixed signals are starting to drive me crazy."

She stared at him long and hard. The silence ticked off between them for what felt like infinite beats until finally his heart took a dip when she reached down for the napkin in her lap and placed it by her plate. "Thank you for the lovely meal, but you're right." Lily said as she started to get up from her chair.

Dejection hit him like a physical blow. Shit. He'd blown it, his chance at her not to mention a paying job. Way to go.

She looked at him as she rose, and in that moment his mind clicked fast, suddenly thinking he'd do anything to get her to stay. Make any promise not to see her walk out the door. "But hey," Vin started again, "maybe I was too quick. We can work something out. Just bu—"

But she held up a hand, cutting him off and shaking her head. "No. You had it just right. I have been sending mixed signals, but I thought you understood." Lily then shocked him by leaning over, her sweet scent replacing that of the food. Her beautiful face suddenly right in front of his. Close. So very close. And then she kissed him. Full on. Her lips now the aggressor. She was the one in control. As if on autopilot, like he was heading toward his true north Vin reached for her. His hands pulled her down onto his lap as he drew her further into him, taking her luscious mouth harder against his own while her body connected perfectly with his. As duel emotions of both excitement and fear coursed through his body Vin did his best to devour as much of her as he could in whatever time she would give him. In that moment, Vin wanted her all. He wanted to taste, touch even smell as much as he could of her. He was instantly hard, with every nerve in his body on edge and pointing in her direction. Damn, Lily Perry was a brain-wrecking, flighty mystery, and more than anything, he wanted to figure her out.

When she finally pulled back, momentarily unfusing her lips from his to grab a breath of air, she looked up at him with bright eyes that seemed to hold just as many questions as his own treacherous head. Or maybe not, because only a second later she grinned and the look she gave him changed to one of a devilish mirth. Vin frowned and squeezed at her full hip. "Are you just screwing with me woman? Is this whole thing all a game to you?" He knew he should be playing it cool, but in that moment, as hard and as amped as he was, he just didn't have it in him.

Lily shifted to get up and he reluctantly released her, the coolness hitting his lap almost as bracing as a splash of cold water. Vin watched as she eased back into her seat and took a delicate sip of the wine he'd put out before answering him with a sly smile on her face. "Oh, don't look so serious. It's not that deep. I felt like kissing you, so I did. Just like you felt like kissing me earlier. It's not a big deal. We're two adults here with no ties. I see no reason why we can't do what we want."

What the ever-loving hell? Could it be that the woman was truly certifiable or was she just that cold? Vin tried to wrap his head around what she was proposing. Anyone else would have literally jumped on the delectable opportunity before them. Hell, maybe he was the one who was nuts to even be warring with this in his mind. But there it was. He was looking her in those fire-filled brown eyes and, for the life of him, he couldn't figure her out. And more than anything, at that moment, he wanted to understand her. Hell, if he was being truthful he may have even wanted to understand her, figure out what made her tick in that moment even more than he wanted to get her in his bed. Now he knew she was going crazy. He had to get a hold of himself. By way of no reply, Vin shook his head and got up to clear the plates. "Maybe we should just focus and talk about this ceremony you plan on having."

Lily rose with him, gathering her own dish before he could reach it. "You mean wedding?" she challenged.

He raised a brow. "Wedding. Sorry. I stand corrected." He started off toward the kitchen with the plates without looking back but somehow knowing she'd follow. Her dander was up. She'd definitely follow.

"Why do I get the feeling you didn't make a mistake back there? I could hear the derision in your voice," Lily said once they were in the kitchen.

He took her plate from her hand and placed it in the sink with the others, quickly running some water over them before looking back at her. *Just keep it cool, Vin*. She was the client, not just some kissing partner. Or was she the kissing client? This freaking woman had him all over the place. "Of course it was a mistake. I said I was sorry, didn't I? Not that it seems to matter what I call it. Ceremony, wedding, mad party for one. I don't see the difference."

With that Lily threw up her hands in frustration and turned to head back for the dining room. "Of course you wouldn't."

Vin closed his eyes for a moment and hung his head. Fuck, he'd gone too far. Went and showed his hand. What was his problem? He never went off like that and never showed his emotions in such a way. Lily hit the double doors quicker than he thought, leaving him practically with a door in the face as he followed her back out into the dining room. "I'm sorry, I shouldn't have said that. It was wrong of me. But what do you mean, of course I wouldn't? Are you implying I'm dense?"

"Who's implying? Maybe I'm flat-out saying it. I thought at least you, Mr. No Call, would get what I was doing here."

Vin paused, his mind clicking fast, then nodded in satisfaction as puzzle pieces started to fit together.

"What are you suddenly looking so smug about?"

He shrugged. "I'm starting to get it now. So all this is really over the fact that I didn't look you up or call you back after we made out those months ago. The hot and cold. The ceremony. Tell me, if I sincerely apologize, can we just start over and you call all this crazy off."

She pulled back and snorted a laugh. "You really are a piece of work. Tell me, that ego ever get too heavy for you to carry? Do you really think I'm doing all this, taking the time, the expense, just to get validation from you or any man?" She shook her head and raked her eyes over his body in a way that made him feel like she'd quickly undressed him and then redressed him after not liking what she'd seen underneath. "It's sad that you can't get your head around the fact that I'm having a celebration just for me. That I think I'm good enough just how I am." She started to turn away but then looked back at him. "Or, that in the time we've been apart, I've some-how been pining and scheming over you. Trust there have been men before you and there will be men after you. "

Vin felt that muscle in his jaw start to tick.

Lily challenged him with a hard stare. "There is no part of me that needs the validation or the participation of a man."

Ire up, Vin let out a snort, which only served to piss her off all the more.

"What the hell is that about?"

"What is what about?" Vin asked.

"That snort," she lashed back.

"Seriously? You give me that grand speech and ask about my snort?"

"What part of my question makes you think I'm not serious?"

"Fine. It's just there are certain parts of you that I'm sure would definitely do well with the participation of a man. I've felt them." Vin cocked his head to the side and held his stance.

To that Lily just narrowed her eyes and did that superior-look-down-her-nose thing she did so well. "Oh, please. Don't flatter your sex so much." She let her eyes travel low so they hit him dead on the groin. "Nearly anything can be bought. And I can do perfectly well, if not better, on my own."

He raised a brow. "Now *that* I'd like to see."

He watched the anger rise in her cheeks again and her nostrils flare at the same time a crack of thunder broke overhead. They both turned to look at the deck, surprised to see that where there was sun, just minutes before, had now turned shadowed and dark. Lily reached for her bag. "I'm sure you would. Though this has been real . . . stimulating. We'll have to continue it another time."

Vin was shocked. After all that, she still wanted to use his place for her ceremony. As if reading his mind, she reached into her bag and handed him a check. "Here's your deposit to secure my date. See, don't think I'm as petty as all that. I said I'd book your place and I stand by my word. But as to my earlier thoughts, I'm thinking you're right, maybe we should keep things all business. I don't think you can handle mixing the two, and right now your space is more valuable to me than anything else."

Vin felt his hands involuntarily twitch right along with the muscle in his jaw. In that moment he didn't know what he was itching to do. Shake her or pull her in to him and work her body until she was a puddle at his feet. "Trust and believe me, Lily, my space is not the most valuable asset I have."

She laughed. "That may be true, but right now it's all I'm interested in. I'll have my assistant e-mail you to set up our next appointment in order to firm up more details."

And with that she was gone. Just as the thunder cracked again and the sky opened up.

Chapter 10

Shit! Lily banged on the old Buick's steering wheel when the car just coughed and sputtered but once again refused to turn over and start. Why now, after her big speech and grand exit from Vin and his restaurant? And why when it was pouring cats, dogs, and maybe an assorted pig or goat for good measure? Lily tried the ignition once again to no avail. She was screwed. She reached for her cell and considered calling for a tow, but the expense would probably be more than the car was worth. Maybe her mom was right and it was time to give the old thing up.

The thought of it brought a wave of sadness down on Lily. She didn't get much from her dad, but somehow, even though he wasn't living at home with them anymore, she felt a strange connection to him through her car. Her car felt like home to her. It would be hard to give up. She considered calling her dad and asking him to come and give her a jump. She knew he would but also knew he'd probably agree with her mother and say it was time to let the car go. He had no problem with letting old things go. For her it wasn't so easy.

She quickly dialed her sister Sylvie. She hated to bother Sylvie, pregnant as she was, but she was not too far, and when the rain lessened she could come pick Lily up or have her husband, George, do it. George was always fiddling with cars anyway. He'd help her out. Sylvie's phone went straight to voice mail, so Lily left a message and settled in to wait. Of all the places and times to break down. Lily turned to look back at the restaurant and cursed when she saw Vin running her way with an umbrella in hand. The rain was pounding down in sideways sheet so even with the umbrella his T-shirt was getting wet and quickly sticking to his broad chest in a ridiculously delicious way. Lily watched for about three seconds too long as he tapped on the car's window. With a huff Lily reached over to open the passenger door and let him inside.

Vin opened the door but didn't get in, bringing with him a rush of wind and rain.

"Hey, what are you doing out here?" she yelled.

"That is what I'm here to ask you. The car won't start?"

She shot him a look. "Obviously."

He opened his mouth to say something, but she saw the words die in the back of his mind. No matter, she heard the unspoken words anyway without his even uttering them: "But I thought you didn't need anybody." Funny how fast things can come around to bite you in the ass. Just then lightning flashed and she jumped. He looked at her and slammed the passenger door shut, then ran around to her side of the car, pulling her door open and reaching out his hand.

"Come on back in. We'll call it a truce while you wait out this storm."

Lily shook her head. "I'm fine right here. I called for someone to pick me up. It should be here soon." She shivered against the sudden cold.

He took her hand and pulled her up and out toward him. "So you'll wait inside with a cup of tea or coffee. Don't be so stubborn."

Lily let out a breath, reaching back for her bag before racing back inside with Vin.

"Are you always so forceful?" she asked as he pushed the dark cup of coffee toward her.

He had come in and gone up to his apartment area, where he'd changed into casual, low-slung sweatpants and a loose cotton tee. Lily decided as he shrugged that it didn't matter what the man was wearing, if anything at all. He was totally hot.

He took a sip from his cup after adding a liberal amount of sugar and cream and then answered her. "I normally don't have to be."

Lily snorted. "That figures."

Vin raised a brow as he came around the bar to sit on the stool next to her. "What figures?"

She thought about how she should answer and then decided, what the hell. She had nothing to lose with Vin, since she wasn't looking for anything to gain. "Well, look at you. You're built like a muscle truck." When he frowned she added, "In the best of ways, believe me. So I'd think that men would give you a wide-enough berth and probably respect on sight, and women, well, I'm sure most drop panties without much effort on your part."

To that Vin voiced an almost incoherent snort into his next sip of coffee. "Yeah, most."

Lily couldn't help but laugh. "And that's what I like about you and about this." She did a back and forth with her hands between the two of them. "I get that about you, and I don't blame you or think it's in any way bad. I admire it, just like I admire the space you have here. I'm also highly attracted to it." She watched as he pulled up straighter and leaned in a little closer to her. Lily got up, taking her coffee with her, and eased toward the large wall of windows at the back of the restaurant, giving herself some much needed space. The rain was still pounding and it made it difficult to see past the deck and beyond to the Atlantic. But she focused first on the rain, then farther out to the faded wood of the deck, then farther to the deserted beach, and finally farther into the void of the ocean. It was peaceful, and she wondered if Vin knew how lucky he was to have this spot. For a moment, an idea flashed before her. Maybe she could propose this spot to the Carlyles for the graduation party. Cancelling the other location would be a hassle but it could be done, and a beach party complete with party bus transport could be just the thing. She was about to run it by Vin when she felt him come up behind her, and a part of her expected him to reach around her waist and pull her in toward him. But he didn't. Instead he stood by her side. "It's amazing, isn't it?"

Lily nodded. "It really is. Hey, I was just thinking— how would you feel about hosting another party here? Say two hundred fifty for a graduation beach party? If I can sell the concept, I have a client who will pay top dollar for your premium night rate." Vin looked at her skeptically. She knew he was weighing the cost of dealing with her against the money. She also knew the money would win out. He nodded.

"Sure, if you can swing it. I'm new so I need all the business I can get."

Lily grinned, pleased with the idea and excited to get to work on the new concept. "That's great. Thanks so much. I have to come up with concept boards and see if I can sell my client on it, but I'll work fast and get back to you right away. It's just that you're so close to the city, yet it's like we're on another planet. I'm sure I can make this work."

They were silent for a few long moments before she turned and looked at his profile. His high forehead and strong, sloping nose. Those lips were her major kryptonite. "Is this why you stayed here? I know you grew up on the island. Most who stay, and never find work elsewhere, have a pretty compelling reason. I mean, even before you got this spot you could have worked anywhere. Your food is delicious. Your talent is undeniable."

Seeming to not hear the compliment, Vin stared out into the void of the sea a moment longer before turning her way, his eyes dark, full and wide with a sense of something she couldn't quite put her finger on. Part of it looked like loss, but then she could swear it was longing. He shrugged. "I guess for the surf. The water is my true love. You can't get that in the city also I like a little breathing room. We don't get all that much out here but I enjoy what little we've got." Changing subjects he flipped on a dime. "Besides, I thought you were talking about why we get along so well. You left me hanging back there."

Lily shook her head. Deflection received. "Okay,

I got you." She thought a moment, then put down her coffee and folded her arms as she looked him in the eyes. "I like that we can kick it and be honest. I want to work with you because I see talent in you and your space is great. Also, I checked you out and you're on the rise for sure. I want in on that. I'm like you, just getting in on the rising part of my business and I need to keep that momentum going. I think business wise we could be good for each other. As for the other part, if you're not seriously attached to anyone, I wouldn't mind kicking it, no strings attached, but if you're going to go all judgmental on me and my choices, that I can't deal with."

It was Vin's turn to fold his arms as he stared at her. She watched as the muscles in his forearms became like tight cord and his chest rose and fell. She couldn't deny how sexy he was and she also couldn't deny for all her outward confidence and bravado she couldn't deny what she hoped his answer to her would be. "But answer me this," Vin started. "What if I want something more than just to kick it?"

Lily raised her eyes and looked at him harder. Trying her best to read him like a master poker player. Could he really be serious? His gaze never wavered. The only sign she detected was a slight flaring of his nostrils. "Do you? Want to do more than kick it?" she asked.

He looked at her a little longer, then blinked. She had him. "No," he said. Giving it to her straight. His voice low but strong and steady. "But don't take that no as any form of a lack of interest in you. As you can plainly see, I'm highly interested. I just don't want either of us to go into this, business or personal, playing any games."

Lily let out a slow breath. She didn't know if it was from relief or sadness. To placate herself in the moment her mind decided it was the former though her heart said the latter. She smiled just as the rain began to let up. "Good. Then I think this has truly not been a wasted morning."

"No, it definitely hasn't," Vin said as he stepped forward and wrapped an arm around her waist. "Now, how would you like to finish out the afternoon?"

Lily grinned as she pushed all niggling thoughts aside, telling herself she was about to have the best of both worlds. His lips were all she wanted as she looked at him greedily, relishing the hard feel of him, happily running her hands along his strong back, Lily let her hands roam to his bottom and she pulled him closer into her center. They were so deep into each other that neither heard the restaurant door open. At the sound of Sylvie's voice, they jumped apart like teenagers caught making out in a basement. Sylvie had her hand over her amply curved belly, her eyes held quite a bit of mirth as she cleared her throat. "Well, your message said you needed a ride, but it looks to me like you've got that firmly covered. Thanks for wasting my time, sis."

Chapter 11

Lily had never been so embarrassed. No strike that. She had, but that was a different type of embarrassment than losing your lunch in front of the entire third-grade class after being dared to eat an entire sleeve of Oreos faster than Jimmy Resetti. On second thought, maybe it wasn't. Sylvie had arrived to pick up Lily from the restaurant with George, and as it turned out it was all for nothing because the car started like a champ—well, that is, if the champ was an eighty-year-old with emphysema, but still it started.

Not wanting to form an awkward foursome, and despite her pregnant sister saying she could eat, an embarrassed Lily turned down Vin's offer for drinks and food for the group and instead sent her sister and brother-in-law on their way, successfully dodging Sylvie's questioning eyes and long looks with excuses about a late appointment in the city. Sylvie was only mildly placated by the fact that Vin wouldn't let them leave without a couple of plates to go. Explaining to Lily that no one ever left his restaurant

hungry. The man was a charmer and Sylvie was in
the bag taste testing and half in love with him before
they'd pulled out of their parking space. But now here
she was, less than a week later, and she was facing
her sister again. This time she had backup.

Lily went to the bridal shop for a quick try-on.
There was a dress that she just couldn't get out of her
mind. It was silly, really, that she'd been thinking
about it for so long with no plans for a wedding or
potential groom, even back when Audrey was getting
married. So Lily figured, why not try it? She'd invited her best friend, Bobbi, to be her critical eye and
tell her if she was crazy to even think she could pull
off the open-back, sexy-style dress. Normally she
didn't shy away from the sexier cuts, but this dress,
while being sexy, also had a certain amount of sweetness and a delicateness to it that put Lily on the fence.

Lily felt weird not having her sisters with her. But
with all the mixed feelings about her having the
ceremony—great, now saying *wedding* even sounded
odd in her own ears—Vin was rubbing off on her; she
didn't want to invite further trouble and doubt in
these early planning stages.

She was holding up a pretty blush-colored bridesmaid dress when in walked Sylvie along with Audrey.
"Now, you know that color washes me out, so just put
it back. Also, would a sleeved dress be the death of
you? And don't forget about you know who," she said
pointing toward her belly.

Lily shook her head and rolled her eyes before she
turned to Bobbi. "Was this you?"

Bobbi held up her hands. "Don't even look in my direction."

"Oh, stop placing blame, girl," Mama Dee said, marching into the shop behind Sylvie, along with Sophie and Peggy. "Did you really think you could make an appointment to try on a wedding dress in this town and I wouldn't hear about it?"

Lily growled and walked forward to kiss her grandmother on the cheek. "I should have known."

Mama Dee gave her a sharp eye. "Yes, you should have. You know I've got connections."

"Yeah, you and the mafia."

Mama Dee took a seat in the grand chair and looked up at Lily smugly. "As long as you all remember it. I see all."

Suddenly the room grew hushed, and it was as if all the girls were thinking for a moment to some such indiscretion they needed to cover their tracks on. The bell over the shop door jingled, breaking the spell, and in walked Lily's mom, shocking Lily all the more. Lily looked toward Mama Dee, who gave her a smug smile in return for her questioning look. She didn't expect the overwhelming flood of emotion at seeing her mother in this setting, but still it came. She'd been feeling so guilty about their last encounter and how it all ended. She should have been stronger, been there for her mother, who though she'd always seemed so stoic had to be reeling from her father's news.

"No need to look so shocked, dear," Lily's mom said. "I may not fully get it, but you're my daughter and I'm here to support you whether you're marrying yourself or a goat."

Lily frowned. "Thanks, Ma. I'm sure there's a compliment in there somewhere."

Her mother looked her in the eyes. "There's an 'I love you' in there too if you care to look for it. Now come on, let's see about getting you a dress."

She moved in and hugged her mother close, whispering in her ear, "I'm sorry. Are you okay?"

Her mother pulled back and tucked a finger under Lily's chin. "I'm just fine, honey. Don't you worry about me. This is your day. Now let's get to shopping."

Lily didn't understand it but was thankful to have her family with her. She decided to save the special dress she'd been eyeing for last and instead tortured her sisters for a while by having them try on some particularly hideous bridesmaid dresses. Threatening Sophie by seriously considering a horrible puce-colored number. The look on her face when she tried on the stacked heels and tried to walk in them was priceless. In the end Lily let them know that she had a vision to see them all in shades of ivory with her and they could choose whatever they wanted to wear that suited them best—dress pants, whatever. To this news Violet whooped it up over FaceTime and let Lily know she was going to rock it.

Finally it was time for Lily to put on the dress she'd been dreaming of. She knew she would love it but didn't expect to love it as much as she did through her family's eyes. The fine bias-cut fabric skimmed over her body just so and draped in all the right places, accentuating the curves of her hip. The halter exposed her shoulders, which she liked to show off. The back was, yes, low but not so much that it was indecent, and at the small of her back there were organza flowers that mimicked the one at her neck. The dress was the perfect amount of understated elegance.

That one look in her mother's and grandmother's shining eyes made Lily know she had to have it. "Now, don't you two get to crying. It's just a silly dress," Lily said.

"On someone else it may be. But on you, it's so much more," her mother said. "Baby, you were made for that dress."

Lily looked to her sisters, and even Sophie was quiet. Hell, the dress was worth it just for that. She looked to Sylvie, who nodded, then Peggy, who gave her a thumbs-up as she turned her phone around and saw Violet's smiling face. "Woman, you'd better get that dress and then invite every ex you ever had to the ceremony. They'll be knocking one another over trying to get to you."

Lily shook her head. "Thanks, Vi, but this is not about getting back at any exes."

"Then where's the fun in it?" Violet yelled from the screen. "You can't waste a day looking that good on just us."

Lily glanced over at Mama Dee, who was looking at her with an appreciative but slightly wistful gaze. "Trust me, any day with you all won't be wasted." She smiled. "Now you get off the phone. I'll put some things on hold for you to try when you get home from school."

Violet groaned. "Please don't. I've got this. I've had my eye on a banging white jumpsuit for a while now, and this will be just the excuse I need to wear it." She hung up and left them all in silence for a moment as Mrs. Benning, the shop's owner, came over. "So, Lily, what do you think? Is this dress all you hoped it would be?"

"It is," Lily said, turning to get one more look at herself in the three-way mirror. With her family as her backdrop she could already see her photos and sadly, for all her bravado, see what was missing. Maybe she should hold off and try on a few more dresses before making a final decision. But then Mama Dee smiled and met her eyes before speaking up. "Yep, that's the one, Cora. Order one up on my account. She'll need some alterations, but I know you'll have everything done perfectly and in time for her big day."

Lily turned and looked at her grandmother while blinking back tears.

"Girl, don't you dare start," Mama Dee admonished. "We may be loud, irreverent, and a bit out of hand, but we're not ones to cry in the middle of the afternoon over silly dresses."

Lily sniffled loudly as Peggy handed her a tissue. "Aren't we just the type, Mama Dee?"

Chapter 12

Lily sat in her small downtown office space, which was more of a glorified closet really. A subdivision of a subdivision of an office space, but it gave her a cool New York address and the cache she needed to project an air of legitimacy in the events game. It had a small window that afforded her a glimmer of the Hudson River and the Freedom Tower. The view always bolstered her spirits, but this afternoon she was distracted from the view as she flipped over the invitation to the party at 202 Park for Crystalline Entertainment's new artist's launch, and once again thought about just trashing it. When she'd finagled the invite, thanks to her connection with Eva Ward, through Thomas she'd been thrilled. Of course she'd have been more thrilled to get the contract for the party herself, but she could understand that Ward Group would go with their tried-and-true event planners. She was still small in the grand scheme of things, but she was well on her way to building her client list. Which was why she couldn't skip going to the party, even with the possibility of running into Thomas.

Lily held the invite in one hand and her cell in the other. Not that she was really weighing her options. She knew what she was going to do as soon as she picked up the phone. But that didn't stop her from being nervous; what if he got the wrong idea? Worse yet, what if he got the right idea? Just as she was having that thought, her phone vibrated in her hand and she jumped, dropping the invitation and flipping the phone between her hands like a hot potato. Righting it and swiping at the screen, she tried to calm her voice.

"Lily Perry," she said by way of greeting.

"Vincent Caro. Now that we have that out of the way, why do you sound so breathless? Did I catch you at an inconvenient time?"

Shit. Of course it was him. He would be the one to have some sort of crazed mental telepathy and be able to catch her thinking of him from across waterways and bridges. She forced a smile to her voice. "Of course not. Well, I mean yes; I'm working, of course, but I can spare a minute." Lily looked at her ceiling. "Spare a minute. What the hell?" She let out a frustrated breath. "What can I help you with, Vin?"

"Well . . ." It was then that she caught a bit of hesitation in his voice and for a moment wondered if he was just as apprehensive as she was. "I was calling to see if you'd gotten in touch with your client. I'd been thinking about your party idea. I know the date is soon, so I'd have to get to planning and putting in any special requests with my suppliers."

She nodded, slightly disappointed that it was purely a work call. "I have, and as a matter of fact I was going to call you. My client really liked the idea and is just about ready to give the go-ahead, though she'd like a quick walk through next week to finalize plans. Is that all right with you?"

"Of course," he said in a way he probably thought was light and easy, but she could catch the tension threaded in his tone.

"Don't worry, it's not a test. She'll love your place. And it will be fine." Lily was about to let him know about the Crystalline event and see if he wanted to tag along. She wanted to go at it delicately so that he didn't confuse it with actually being some type of date, but Vin spoke up first.

"I'm not worried. It's just that I don't like the idea of having to jump through hoops for the business."

"I understand. Believe me, I really do. But you won't be jumping alone." She took a breath and decided to take her chance. "Speaking of hoops, I was wondering if you'd like to go to a thing with me."

"A thing?" Lily could hear the question as well as the humor as it seeped into his voice.

She knew she suddenly sounded all of fourteen and told herself to get it together. To not goofily picture him walking and talking, loose and carefree in his second-skin tee and ass-hugging jeans, while she clumsily asked him to go with her to a party that her ex would be attending so essentially she didn't look pathetic. Oh God, she did look pathetic. The more she thought about it, the more it was below her. "You know what, that's okay. It was just a work thing. I'm not working the event, but I thought it would be good to check out the competition, as well as a way for both of us to possibly get some new ideas for the grad party and maybe my wedding."

"Where and when is this event?" he asked, surprising her.

"It's next week. Tuesday night. At a club, Distro on the West Side, for Crystalline Entertainment."

"I'll be there."

Lily couldn't help but smile. That was easy. "Thank you so much. I know it's tough with the restaurant. Can you pre-prep and get someone to cover for you?"

"No, you don't get it. I'll be there. One of my boys, who is a silent partner in the restaurant, is engaged to Eva Ward, who's running it. I was invited. I hadn't planned to go, but now I guess I will."

"That's great." Lily tried to keep her enthusiasm to a low simmer. "Then I guess I'll see you there?"

"I could pick you up," he said easily, as if offering to pick her up was the most normal thing.

Lily looked at her phone for a moment, dumbfounded. She hadn't been picked up for a date in . . . she didn't know how long. Did people actually do that anymore in this day of online and over-the-phone hookups? Not that this was a date or a hookup, but still. "I wouldn't want to put you through any trouble," she said. "I could just call an Uber and meet you there."

"Is that what you do with all your dates?" he asked, throwing her into a tailspin.

"But this is not a date. This is just two colleagues meeting to exchange ideas and get some inspiration."

There was a long pause before he finally spoke. "I've never heard it put quite that way. But fine. It's not a date. I'll meet you there. Expect the inspiration to begin around seven."

Lily swallowed, then uncrossed and recrossed her legs. Inspired. She really walked into that one. "Goodbye, Vincent."

"Till Tuesday, Lily."

"If not before, Vin."

"I just don't know. A beach party? And a Mexican one at that? Out in Queens, of all places." Lily took one look at the pursed lips and skeptical eyes of Chelsea Carlyle and knew she had to find another way. They were meeting in the Carlyle apartment, a Classic Six off Fifth Avenue that was beautifully decorated in a sleek, modern style with views of Central Park that were Instagram worthy.

Christie had just gotten in from school. The pretty young blonde seemed to be right on the edge of adulthood and playing with the fine line of kid and young adult. She was still in her private school uniform consisting of a plaid pleated skirt, the required kneesocks she'd nixed, and the coveted crested blazer was a no show too. Instead she was using a white, men's collared shirt with the sleeves rolled as her outerwear, and underneath she sported an ironic T-shirt that said IRONIC T-SHIRT, which made Lily feel ancient. And judging by the way she was quick texting, Lily could tell she was either bored with the whole idea of a party or not as into the beach theme as Lily'd hoped she would be. But as Lily looked at Christie a little closer she could see that, though Christie worked hard at putting on an over-it attitude, she wasn't as far off from her ultrapolished mother as she pretended to be. One, her backpack was designer and the price of a month of Lily's rent. Two, the same went for the chunky black shoes she was wearing. And three, she may not care about image or money but it didn't stop her from wearing the monster rock earring studs that her parents, no doubt, gifted her with or blinging out her cell phone case in a diamond skull pattern to match.

Lily decided to switch tactics as she flipped the screen on her iPad, pulling up a chart. "Ladies, I've done my research for this year's graduation season and for Christie's class in particular. So far, in your month alone, there will be six parties in the Paris salon and four in the Versailles room. Now just a few blocks away at the more modern West Hotel, there are eight parties booked in their Club West." She looked at Christie. "I'm sure you're invited to many of them and are exhausted over picking out yet another little black dress to wear to each."

"Now in contrast . . ." Lily flipped the screen to the slideshow of the surfers catching waves and brought the images up of Vin's restaurant—the view taken from the beach of the patio with its casual bohemian feel. Chelsea finally placed her phone next to her and leaned forward. "If you move your party to a destination like this, have a killer deejay, and keep it loose, you'll be a trailblazer. You and your friends can cut loose, have some fun. Shoes can even be optional." Lily turned to Chelsea. "And yes, though it may be in Queens, technically it's Long Island, and you'll be right on the cutting edge of discovering a hot, new chef who is just starting to get press." She flipped to the feature of Vin, and his photo came up. He had his arms folded across his chest, and he was leaning on his motorcycle in front of Canela looking more like a bouncer than a restaurateur. But he was still hot, and the photo had both mother and daughter sitting straighter and moving in.

"And that's the owner?" Chelsea asked, leaning in.

Lily almost snorted. Not like she hadn't been there when looking at the hunk of walking sex that was Vincent Caro.

"It is. I have to say, he's a bit"—Lily paused for effect—"cautious about doing this sort of party. You know how temperamental creatives can be. But I have a persuasive connection through a mutual friend, so he's willing to consider it." Lily hoped she wasn't laying it on too thick, but if she could just get Chelsea thinking she was getting a hot commodity that was exclusive, even to her set, then maybe she'd win her over.

Chelsea swiped the screen, quickly glancing at the article. She then went back to Vin's photo and let out a husky breath before looking back at Lily. "Book him. Uh, I mean, yes. Book his place. Can . . . whatever it's called. You're right, we should stand out from the rest of this season's parties." She turned to Christie, realizing she hadn't considered her daughter. She put a French-manicured hand on Christie's thigh. "You think this is best, don't you, honey? You know Daddy and I want to make you happy." She rolled her eyes and chuckled. "And you know we don't want another disaster like the year of your bat mitzvah season." She turned back to Lily to explain. "I tell you, each party was more of the same, practically down to the entertainment."

Christie picked up her phone as if bored again but then looked at Vin's photo briefly before sweeping Lily with her eyes. She gave a shrug. "It's fine, Mother. Whatever you want."

Lily didn't know whether to cheer or be annoyed. No matter, she had the job and that was the bottom line.

Exiting the Carlyles' building, Lily shot Vin a quick text. Clients said yes. Sight unseen. We're a go!

She stared at her phone for a few beats, hoping he'd see it right away. Silly, he was probably busy, but just as she was about to cross over toward Madison Avenue her phone pinged and she stopped to look down.

Great! We'll have something to celebrate on Tuesday. You are fantastic!

Lily fought the urge to blush.

Nothing fantastic about me. You practically sell yourself.

She frowned as she waited for his response. Sell yourself? What was that? Lily stared at the phone 'till it pinged.

Sell myself? Now that's comforting. Till Tuesday, Lil.

She rolled her eyes at her own ridiculousness. Till Tuesday, V.

Chapter 13

As Lily paced back and forth in front of Club Distro she cursed herself for both her punctuality and choice of footwear. She was early as per her usual, and Vin still had fifteen minutes before their appointed meeting time. She stopped pacing and once again checked the time on her phone. Twelve minutes. When she looked up, some of the people on line to get in the club were eyeing her as if she was some sort of sad case. Okay, maybe the pacing had to stop. Though her outfit was in no way overtly over-the-top sexy, at least not in her eyes, one did not pace back and forth in a drapey black minidress that hung off the shoulder while wearing what could definitely be thought of as questionable heels this close to New York's West Side Highway. It just wasn't done.

She checked her phone again and let out a sigh. Ten minutes. Maybe she should just meet him inside. She was on the list and, as she'd pointed out multiple times, this was work. It was not a date, so she didn't have to desperately wait for him outside like it was one. She'd just text him and let him know where she was.

Lily was focused shooting off her text so she hardly heard the motorcycle pull up in front of her until it was right there. "What the hell!" she yelled, jumping back.

Vin took off his helmet and met her eyes. "I'm sorry. I didn't mean to scare you. I just saw you as I was pulling onto the street and, well, maybe I hit the gas a little too hard."

Lily raised a brow. "You think?"

Vin laughed, and Lily couldn't help but smile before taking him in on his bike. And it was a lot to take in. A lot of good to take in. Lily let her eyes wander. Black leather boots; great-fitting dark jeans that, though not as worn as what she was used to seeing him in, fit well; and a finely knit black tee that hugged him perfectly. His shirts did not look like any typical T-shirts she'd seen on a man, and Lily was starting to think that Vin may have them knitted right on his body; they showed him off so well.

Vin cleared his throat. "Would you like help taking that picture?"

Lily met his eyes. "Very funny." But then Vin's eyes raked over her and everything went all warm. She knew she had planned to say something else but for the moment forgot what that statement may have been.

"You're looking great, Lil. I'm thinking I may not be worthy to walk in with you." He reached behind him and patted the back of his bike. "I did bring a jacket to jazz myself up a bit." The compliment brought her back to earth.

"Oh, please. Thanks, but I'm not all that and you're fine. These are entertainment people. It's not so formal." By way of proving her point a sprinter van pulled up and a group of young women teamed out, followed by an up-and-coming hip-hop artist who was wearing a bright green Adidas sweatsuit. Paparazzi seemed to jump out of nowhere, and candid pictures were taken before the group slid into the club.

"See what I mean?" Lily said. "Now, where are you going to park this thing so we can go inside?"

Vin looked up and down the block, then back at her. "Just give me two minutes."

Lily watched as Vin did a quick turn and slipped into a spot that most New Yorkers could only pass and dream about. He slipped on his jacket and jogged back over to her all in what may have been a minute and a half. "Ready?"

Lily gave him a nod. "Wow, if I wasn't totally un-coordinated and deathly afraid of killing myself, I would trade my Buick in for a motorcycle. Slipping into a spot like that is the stuff of legends."

They turned to head into the club, and as they did Lily didn't miss the out-and-out envious looks she got from some of the women in line. It could have been because Lily and Vin bypassed the line and went straight to the bouncer, giving their names, but these side-eye looks were clearly due to rooted jealousy and to the fact that Vin had casually slipped a hand onto her lower back as he steered her toward the door. Good thing this wasn't a date, or she would read more into it than there was.

This wasn't Lily's first visit to Club Distro. She was immediately impressed by the way the normally dark and slightly seedy club had been transformed into a sleeker, more modern space with the use of cleverly designed lighted cubes on the tables and the intricate spotlighting. The cool look went along with the vibe of the smooth hip-hop that was being pumped through the club's invisible speakers.

Though Lily liked the room's décor, she couldn't help scoping out the problems with the space and the party. As usual, there were huddled groups of people, in some cases very close together, in the rectangular banquettes, but there were hardly any people on the dance floor. Not to mention that, though there were waiters sailing around with trays piled high with some gourmet treats, the bar was by far where the action was. It looked as if the people were at least three deep, and for a space that size, that should not be happening. Lily thought that if it were her, she would have come up with a signature cocktail and had that on half the food trays. Especially since this was more of a drinking than eating crowd.

"Earth to Lily."

Lily looked over and up at Vin. "I'm sorry, I was just taking the lay of the land," she said loudly, trying to be heard over the music.

He nodded and then leaned in close to her ear, the feeling of his breath on her giving her an immediate thrill. "See anything you like?"

"Don't answer that. Trust me, it's a trap."

Lily grinned as she turned from Vin and looked toward the handsome man with the teasing warning. She immediately recognized him as Aidan Walker, television exec and fiancé of Eva Ward. "Thanks. I think I know not to fall into his trap."

"You know you're wrong for that," Vin said as a word of warning to his friend.

Aidan came over and slapped Vin's hand, giving him daps. "You know I'm just messing with you, man. Somebody needs to." He turned to Lily. "You must be Lily. I'm Aiden. Nice to finally meet you."

Lily couldn't help the confused look that she knew crossed her visage. "Finally? Nice to know I've been spoken of. I hope all good things." She gave Vin a glance, which Aidan no doubt caught.

"Yes, Eva's spoken of you highly." He looked around. "You didn't hear it from me but, with the way she speaks of you, I'm sure your touch could have helped this party."

Lily smiled at the compliment as she glanced around the room. "The space is lovely and everyone seems to be enjoying themselves. Whomever Eva used is doing a great job."

Aidan tilted his head. "Well said and so diplomatic. I'll be sure to keep you in mind for things at the station. If I go to one more dull meet and greet where the food is about as bland as the vision for the casting, I may lose it."

Lily laughed. "Thank you for that, and I totally understand. Please call on me anytime. Where is Eva? I'm sure she's busy, but I'd love to thank her for the invite."

Aidan pointed to a flight of stairs. "She's up in the VIP making sure that the talent doesn't have too much fun tonight, at least not until all interviews are given and paparazzi cleared. Come on and follow me."

On the way up, Lily pointed to the row of lights and elegant vases with single orchids in each that ran the length of the bar. "That would look great in your place," she directed to Vin. "Or at least something similar for the bar area. If you don't mind, I'd like to have my lighting guy come and check it out."

She got a small grunt as a reply from Vin's side of the conversation.

"Is there an answer somewhere mixed in with that grunt?"

He gave her a sideways look. "Why do I feel like I've agreed to a total overhaul of my place when it comes to your wedding?"

Lily gave him an easy pat on the chest, silently taking note of his hard pecs and coming up with a fine mental picture, before continuing up the stairs. "Now, don't go getting all sulky on me. It's not going to be that bad, and I promise to put it all back the way that I found it, if not better. By the time I'm through, you'll be better than you started."

Vin's telling brow raised again. "Why do I feel like you're not just talking about my restaurant?"

Lily shook her head. "Don't go reading into that too much. I'm definitely talking about the restaurant."

They were cleared into the VIP easily. The area was large and opulently appointed with tufted leather couches, and large leather ottomans served as both coffee tables and chaises for the perfect backdrop to the artfully arranged model/actresses. Of course, with her luck, one of the first people Lily saw was Thomas. He was standing off to the side in his usual dark gray suit, custom tailored so it fit his tall, slim frame perfectly. He had a full week's worth of them in his immaculately organized closet. She was surprised, because against his usual grain, he had opted to go tieless. As usual, the collar of his pristine white shirt was perfectly creased and his cuffs showed just enough at the edge of his jacket to show off his silver monogramed cufflinks. He was talking to another dark-suited guy, and they both shared the same starched, analytical look that let Lily know the other guy probably worked in Crystalline's marketing or finance department with Thomas.

Lily's eyes clicked with Thomas's at the same time one of the club's servers came over to him and his companion with a couple of drinks. The pretty brunette said something to the men and added a discreet pat to Thomas's chest that would no doubt help her tip later. Or maybe not, Lily thought, when a petite brunette with hair down to her waist in a barely there white stretch slip dress sidled up to Thomas soon after. Lily held back a frown, originating either from the fact that Thomas had just casually wrapped an arm around the brunette's waist and let his hand linger at her ample behind or from the fact that he took his other hand and raised his glass in Lily's direction. It didn't matter which reason. Both told her he'd moved on, probably long before as she should have.

Brushing off the eyeball encounter with Thomas, Lily focused on Vin, trying to have a little fun as they got some of their business taken care of. It didn't matter who Thomas was with now or who he'd be going home with. She knew that her relationship with him hadn't been heading to anything permanent, and even if it had, would she have been happy with their relationship? Despite having her feelings hurt at being so easily rejected, Lily knew she didn't feel a bit of passion for Thomas, and passion was what she wanted and also what she feared.

She cleared her throat and smiled as Aidan turned back to both of them with an easygoing smile and offered them champagne from a passing server. Lily took her glass happily, but Vin looked at the flute and then up at Aidan as if he'd grown an extra head.

"Can you bring my friend a beer, please?"

"Thanks," Vin said, and Aidan shrugged as the pretty server headed off to get the beer.

"It's not like you're hard to figure out. You have your basics. You like what you like and you want what you want. That's it."

Vin frowned. "You make me sound really boring."

Aidan cocked his head. "You are not boring, my friend. More like steady." He turned to Lily. "Don't you think of Vin as the steady sort?"

She turned to Vin and gave him a glance. Handsome, yes, with his close-shaved head, beautifully trimmed beard, strong profile, and dark, mysterious eyes. He was also large and solid. A definite tangible presence in the club, where it seemed everyone wanted to see and be seen, but somehow Vin was just there. Quietly assured in his own being. There was nothing flashy or ostentatious about him; he couldn't help but stand out by just being him. He looked back at her, playfully shrugging his shoulders and posing, causing her to laugh. "You're ridiculous," Lily said as she took a sip of her champagne.

"And you should take a picture, it lasts longer." He grinned, clearly fine with her lingering perusal.

Lily shook her head and turned back to Aidan, surprised to see that Eva was now by his side. They were looking at her and Vin with smiles. Lily shook off the silly tingly feeling and once again told herself this was all business. She gave Eva a warm smile and came forward to greet her in a casual hug. "It's so good to see you again. Thank you for the invite. The space looks great."

Eva smiled but rolled her eyes slightly. "Whew, this day has been one disaster after another. But I'm so glad you came. Trust me, I will be calling you for our next event."

"Thank you for thinking of me. But I will say from the outside it all looks like it's flowing wonderfully."

"Thank goodness for looks," Eva said, then turned to Vin. "And we sure could have used your skills in the kitchen. The caterer is a disaster."

Vin pulled a face. "Yes, but I don't really cater. I do have a restaurant to run. Remember?"

"Of course," Eva said. "It's just hard to go from grand to bland after tasting your food. Maybe we can work something out for our wedding."

Aidan turned as he gave her a sweet look and pulled her in close. "Are you dropping the hint that you're finally ready to marry me?"

Eva blinked. After her disastrous national TV wedding fiasco, no one could blame her for being gun-shy. But the color rose high on her cheeks. "I'm not doing any such thing. Just talking in hypotheticals. Don't go getting ahead of yourself."

Aidan leaned in and affectionately nuzzled at her neck. "How can I not when it comes to you?"

They were so cute together and clearly in sync. Lily inwardly pushed back at the slight pull of longing that threatened to enter her heart while Eva shook her head. "I've got to go work, and here comes your other Musketeer." She turned Lily's way. "I'm sorry to leave you with the lions, Lily, but I have to mingle and make sure everyone is all right, and also get the talent ready for the show." She gave Aidan a quick kiss just as another guy walked over. He too was good looking, a bit more polished than Aidan or

Vin with his sharp pinstripe suit, perfectly knotted geometric print tie, and shiny wing tips. He gave Eva a warm hug as she passed.

"So what are you bums up to while the rest of us work for a living?" the guy said upon reaching the group, causing both Vin and Aidan to groan.

"Don't start, I work plenty hard," Aidan stated. "Just because you choose to make the station your life doesn't mean I have to hang with you until after nine."

The man shrugged. "Hey, some of us aren't gifted with being born into a corner office. A man's gotta do what a man's gotta do." It was then that he seemed to notice that Lily was on the fringe of the group. "Oh, I'm so sorry. Where are my manners? Carter Bain, producer and VP at WBC."

Lily put out her hand and Carter took it, looking straight into her eyes. She almost laughed at the way he was trying so quickly to pull some serious game.

"Do you handle all your introductions with all those stats?" Aidan asked from Carter's side.

Carter didn't look his way but continued to stare at Lily. "I do when the person I'm being introduced to is clearly someone worthy of knowing and getting to know."

Oh, really. This was getting funny. Lily smiled. "Lily Perry. I run my own events planning agency. I was invited by Eva."

Vin stepped forward and gently removed her hand from Carter's while giving him a hard look. "And escorted by me," Vin added.

She looked up at him. "Was I?"

Vin frowned down at her. "Well, weren't you? I could be at my own place taking care of customers, but you called me asking me to come and see the setup here."

Lily felt her cheeks immediately heat. "Well, I'm sorry if I've inconvenienced you, but if I remember correctly you said you were coming anyway."

Vin looked clearly annoyed. "I said I was thinking about it."

Carter stepped forward and leaned in toward Vin. "Yo, bro, that's not how this is done."

But Vin ignored him, still focused on Lily. "If I recall correctly, you had to have me here to see about candles for your kooky wedding."

She heard both Aidan and Carter intake a breath and looked at them wide eyed. Carter leaned forward again and mumbled out the side of his mouth. "Yeah, dude. Definitely not how it's done."

Lily let out a breath, then smoothed her hair by way of calming her nerves. "Don't worry, gentleman. This is perfectly normal for Vin and me. We only have a business arrangement. You see, I'm renting out Canela and using Vin's services for a couple of events. One is my wedding reception, and Vin has clear ideas about it that he can't quite keep to himself. If you'll excuse me, I think I'll go freshen up." She started to walk away but remembered she hadn't answered Aidan's question, so she turned back. "To answer your question of whether I think he's steady. No. He's yet to show me he's anything more than temperamental and at times immature and unreasonable." She put on a bright smile and shrugged. "But hey, he can cook."

Vin's voice was a low growl beside her. "It's a good thing that's all you hired me for."

Chapter 14

Vin watched Lily walk away as he tried to wrap a tight band around his anger. She was all strutting through the crowd on curves, long legs and screw you, attitude. In that moment he wanted nothing more but to pick her up, throw her on the back of his bike, and take her somewhere, anywhere, where he could make love to her until all that attitude dissolved into nothing but a mass of flesh and feelings underneath him.

Vin knew he'd crossed the line. That he should have done his normal play-it-cool thing with her, but for the life of him he couldn't. She had him doing all sorts of stupid shit that was completely not in his nature or his character. He didn't get emotional and show his cards when it came to women. Hell, when it came to women he didn't have any cards to hide anyway. He was straight up. He wanted them, they wanted him. There was some form of mutual acceptance of getting it on to have a good time until the good time gave out. Cool. Cut and dry. Nothing messy. It was all clean and easy. So why was everything so jumbled when it came to Lily Perry?

He watched her head back toward the steps and then pause for a moment. His eyes shifted to see if she would get held up. He saw some suit with another suit eyeing her harder than they should, and for another moment he thought about, once again, making a fool of himself as he took in the way the suit on the right was staring her down.

"What the hell was all of that about?" Carter asked from Vin's side, pulling him back from making another mistake. Vin turned his anger in another direction. "What the hell was what? It was your fault with all your fucking hand holding and weak-ass game. You're lucky I was so gentle and didn't break your hand."

"Damn!" Carter and Aidan said in unison.

"I think I need a stiffer drink," Aidan muffled.

"Never thought I'd see the day," Carter said.

Eva came back to join the group. "Hey, the entertainment's going to start soon. Lil C is about to perform his just-released hit." She took quick stock of the expressions on the guys' faces and frowned. "What's going on here, and you never thought you'd see what?" she asked, not missing a thing after being in Aidan's life for the past year and learning the cues of the three old friends. Their server take out came with his beer and headed off in the same direction Lily had gone. Vin couldn't help but look for her. It seemed that The Suit had made his way over to her and had her engaged in conversation. Vin sucked in a breath and turned back to his friends, two of which he was considering cutting out of his life if they kept up the ragging.

"Don't listen to anything they say, Eva. Obviously I didn't get the Bust on Vin Day memo."

When Eva frowned, Aidan laughed. "Don't look like that, babe. We're just teasing. It's nice to see our boy here get hot under the collar for a woman." He directed his comment back to Vin. "Too bad she's engaged, though. You picked the wrong one there."

Vin took a pull from his beer. "Too bad she's certifiable and throwing a wedding so she can marry herself. So, yeah, I definitely picked the wrong one."

At the shocked expression on his friends' faces, Vin knew he'd hit the mark. "See, a nutjob, not to mention the fact that she doesn't want anything more from me than business, and if it's for pleasure, she's made it clear it won't go further than that."

"Hold up, hold up!" Carter made a big show of spinning around and holding his fist to his mouth before he came in close to Vin. "She doesn't want anything further? And the only person she wants to marry is herself?" He patted Vin on his back. "Man, how is she not the perfect woman?" He turned quickly to Eva then. "No offense, E. But you're like my sister. And I give you all the gold stars for putting up with Aidan."

Eva nodded, then frowned. "None taken. I guess."

Just then the DJ made an announcement and Lil C made his entry on the downstairs center stage. Most of the crowd quickly gathered around him. Those up in the VIP made their way to the outer-edge railings so they could view the performance.

"Well, she may seem perfect, but trust me," Vin yelled over the rumbling beats and hum of the crowd, "that woman is nothing but headaches and trouble. Definitely not what I need. I'll do this party she's got planned, then this wedding to herself to get some notoriety and make some bucks for the business, but after that I'm out. The quicker I'm done with Lily Perry, the better."

He looked back at Eva, who was not paying attention to them anymore. Her eyes were trained on the direction Lily had walked. "I find it so strange that she's throwing a wedding to herself."

Vin nodded. "See, you're with me. That's what I said. Some female talk about loving herself for who she is and all that. Hell, just go to a spa, take a vacation. I knew you'd get me, Eva. Why don't you have a sister?"

Eva shook her head. "No, it's not that. The wedding to herself sounds like a cool idea. Why wait around on a man to validate you? I totally get it," Eva yelled over the rapping.

Vin rolled his eyes skyward. "Oh, damn. I should have known that crazy traveled in packs."

Eva just rolled her eyes. "No, what I don't get is what happened between her and Thomas. I thought for sure he was getting close to asking her to marry him."

Vin pulled up short. He knew there was a guy who'd stood her up at her sister's wedding, but he didn't know they were that far gone so as other people thought marriage was an option. "Oh, well, maybe he wised up. You guys see how hot-tempered she can be."

Eva shrugged. "I don't know about wising up. From where I'm standing it sure looks like he's trying his best to win her back."

Vin felt his brows pull together as all the muscles in his body tensed up. He turned and looked in the

direction Eva was indicating, and he saw Lily and
The Suit, who he now knew to be her ex, Thomas. He
had her up against the railing over the dance floor, his
arms trapping her on either side while he whispered
something in her ear.

Vin knew it was wrong—he had already made an
ass of himself once, but why not go for two and then
see if he could round it out to a triple? He strode
away from his friends and toward Lily and The Suit.

By the time Vin made it over to Lily, The Suit had
her almost completely boxed in, and though she
didn't look like she was being threatened in any way,
she also didn't look completely at ease.

She said something to The Suit, and Vin saw him
lean back, giving her space to slip past one of his
arms. *Good*, Vin thought. *Maybe I can just go*. She
hadn't seen Vin yet, so maybe he could fade into
the background or play it off like he was going to the
bathroom. Vin tipped backward while he watched
Lily head for the stairs, but then The Suit reached out
a hand and grabbed at her elbow, causing her to turn
sharply and almost fall. The near fall gave The Suit
the leeway he needed to pull her into him.

"What the hell?" Vin mumbled to himself as he involuntarily stepped forward, now close enough to
hear them.

"I told you to leave me alone. If you didn't want
me when you had me, there is no need to be concerned about me now. Now let me go and stop
causing a scene." Lily's words were low, but Vin still
made them out. Vin could hear the faint edge of
panic, and he could tell she was the one trying not to
cause a scene; The Suit was banking on that. Of
course, a woman like Lily, so perfect on the outside

and one to go thumbing her nose at convention with her declarations, would still in the end not want to do anything to jeopardize her reputation or cause talk.

Good thing he could give a shit about that. Vin stepped in. "Lily! Damn, woman, you gonna do me like that? I leave to go hit the head and already somebody trying to get with you." He looked down at The Suit's hand and then back at his face. Because The Suit was a hair shorter, Vin had to look down slightly to stare straight into his eyes. The Suit removed his hand, and Lily stepped back.

"You know him?" Thomas said to Lily as if the "him" was shit he'd just stepped in.

Vin tapped him on his shoulder. Not speaking until Thomas was facing him fully. "The question you should be asking is if I'm going to know you."

Lil C finished his song, and the air seemed extra charged in the brief pause between the end of that tune and the start of the next. Thomas shook his head and then looked back up at Vin through eyes that Vin could tell were slightly unfocused. The haze of alcohol clear. "Man, do you know who I am? You don't want to mess with me. I could have you thrown out of this party." Thomas said then nodded in Lily's direction. Seemingly oblivious to the outburst a short brunette with enough hips and ass to throw a buffet on came over. "It don't matter," Thomas continued, his attention now on the behind of the brunette. "I'm good anyway, as you can see."

Vin stepped up, close to his face. "You just make sure you stay that way and keep your hands to yourself, if you want to keep them attached, that is."

He saw Aidan and Carter walk up behind The Suit and gave them an "I'm good" nod just as the buffet girl put an arm through The Suit's. "What is going on? You said we were leaving here to go back to Lil C's hotel for the after-party. I want to get in there early before the other girls get all the good spots."

Vin stayed stoic but gave him a look that said going and partying with Lil C was probably a lot smarter than what he was doing.

The Suit turned to the girl and gave her a pat on the ass. "Sure, let's go. There is nothing here for me anyway."

"Just so you remember it," Vin said as The Suit and the girl walked past to head down the stairs.

He looked over at Aidan and Carter. "What a dick. I don't get why Lily would even mess with him." He turned to ask her that exact question, but the space she had just occupied behind him was now empty.

He looked back to his friends just as Eva walked over, and he raised his hands. "She's gone. She gave her good-byes to each of you," she said to Aidan and Carter before turning to Vin. "And to you, she was kind enough to not have me pass on any message except check your phone."

Vin reached into his pocket and pulled out his phone, looking for a text. As mad as he was, he hadn't felt it vibrate. He clicked the app to read Lily's text.

The next time you're looking for someone to save, start with yourself. I got this and don't need you or any other man to save me.

Well, that was that. A night wasted and he didn't come out with anything for it but an unsatisfying argument and the possibility that he may have lost any chance with Lily. Again. Shit! At least if he'd gotten a punch off The Suit, all wouldn't have been for nothing.

As soon as Vin got on his bike, he knew he wasn't heading home.

He also knew he had no business heading to Lily's house, but after texting Simon and getting threatened with brother-in-law bodily harm, he finally finagled her home address from him and was now parked in front of her building, holding his phone as if it were some sort of life line. He tried calling her cell but she wouldn't pick up, so he was texting in hopes she would at least hear out his apology.

I know you don't want to hear from me but I'm sorry. I was an ass.

Lily responded:

Well you got it right on both fronts. Good to know you're not as dumb as me.

Vin chuckled.

OK, you got me. Now will you let me apologize in person? I want to make it up to you. Make sure we're still cool.

There was a long pause as Vin stared at the phone waiting for her reply. Just then a black car pulled up in front of the building, and a few seconds later there she was, getting out and looking more beautiful than she had earlier. She turned and looked his way.

"What are you doing here? How did you know where I lived?"

Vin held up a hand and went jogging across the street to her. She folded her arms across her chest and stepped back as if weary of him, and the movement caused his heart to plummet to his feet. "Trust me, I'd never hurt you. I just wanted to say I was sorry in person. To let you truly see that I am."

Lily still looked at him wearily.

"Trust me. If I do anything to hurt you, or to make you any madder, Simon and your growing army of brothers-in-law will have my ass. Simon let me know where you lived only because I promised I'd be cool."

As if on cue, Lily's phone buzzed with a text. She looked down, quickly typing something before looking back at him seriously. "That was Sophie checking to see if I'm okay and probably to determine if Simon has to put a hit out on you."

Vin raised a brow. "I hoped you told him to stand down."

She tilted her head to the side, the motion sending a curl into her face. Vin wanted so badly to reach out and move it from in front of her pretty brown eyes. "I told her I was fine. Let's hope it stays that way."

Vin swallowed and stepped forward. "You never have to be afraid when you're with me."

Lily let out a frustrated sigh. "But that's just it. I'm not with you. And you don't have a right to stake any sort of macho claim on me."

He closed his eyes and then opened them back up, looking at her deeply. "You're right, and I fucked up. It's just, I can't deal when I see any woman—well, anyone I care about—hurting or possibly being hurt. I was the only one around to protect my mom when she was here, and I did my best to do my job." Shit, he was screwing this up. Vin ran a hand over his head frustratedly and paced back and forth on the sidewalk before turning back to Lily. "You know, I'm just making things worse. I really just wanted you to know I'm sorry. I saw that dude being all possessive over you and you didn't look particularly comfortable, and I went too far. You are right. It was your place to ask for help if you wanted it and not my job to go stepping in. For all I know, you have a deep history." He let out a strangled breath, fighting the intense need he had to stop talking and start kissing her. Show her the depth of his feelings for her.

"I'll just go. I hope we can still find a way to work together."

Vin turned to head back to his bike when her hand shot out and touched his. It was so light if he wanted he could have mistaken it for a breeze, but still he turned.

"It's okay," she said softly, her eyes bright under the light of the street lamps. "Maybe you're not the only one who should be apologizing. I shouldn't have gotten on you like I did in front of your friends. It was uncalled for, and I'm embarrassed by my behavior. I should have stayed instead of jumping into a cab, a slow one at that, and he gouged me for an extra ten after taking the wrong route." She waved her hand after looking frustratingly down the street. Lily looked back up at Vin. "That's neither here nor there. The fact is, we both played our part and not well. How about we just call a truce?"

It was less than what he wanted, but he'd take what he could get. Vin put out his hand to shake hers. "So, back in business?"

Lily nodded and put her hand in his. Slow and easy she caressed his palm and came toward him, stretching up and moving close to his mouth with her full, pouty lips. "We're back in business."

Chapter 15

One moment she was arguing with him and the next she was all over him in her elevator. Or maybe he was all over her. No matter, Lily thought. They were all over each other, exiting the elevator and then making their way to her apartment door. Lily suddenly stilled, and Vin looked down at her lips and eyes and, oh Lord, his broad shoulders. "I can still go, you know. You don't have to invite me in." His gravelly tone revealed his hurt.

Lily let out a breath and looked down to find the right key. Surprised at how calm and steady her hands were, she opened the door and then looked up at him. "I'm inviting you in."

Vin smiled. The sweetness of it mixed with a definite hint of heated danger had her practically melting. Lily led the way in, thankful that the tiny apartment wasn't too much of a mess. She closed the door behind them and hit the deadbolt. "Should I be afraid?"

It was her turn to smile. "I don't know, maybe you should." Pushing him slowly backward, Lily directed him into the living space. She eased his jacket off his shoulders, taking her time to feel that insanely broad chest of his and his corded muscles as the jacket slid to the floor.

Once again his lips were on hers. Full and heavy. His breath becoming hers and hers becoming his. For a man so large, he took things slow. Lily was hungry and eager, ready to devour him in one gulp, but he forced her to slow down and keep time with the languid strokes of his tongue. Lily felt her body heating past what was certainly considered normal and her legs turning to jelly underneath her. She pulled back and gulped some air, and Vin held her gently by both of her forearms.

"Are you all right? Are things all right? I can still leave, you know. It's okay."

"If you leave now, I don't think I'd be able to take it."

He let out what seemed like a relieved breath and smiled at her. "Good. Because if you asked me to, I'm sure I would, but you might find me collapsed outside your door come morning."

Lily laughed at this. He was always such a surprise. On the outside he looked so stoic, so tough, and then he would go and say something like that. Lily turned away from him to display the back of her dress. "Can you unzip me?"

Like everything else, he did it slow, bringing the zipper down and slowly kissing her spine as he did so. She leaned into him as he came back up, spreading the back of her dress open and kissing the spot between her neck and shoulders. Lily felt her body shudder, and she blinked, then opened her eyes and focused on the scene she was in the middle of creating. It all seemed too perfect. The apartment was lit by the perfect level of moonlight and city streetlight. She stood half naked with easily the hottest man she ever had, or ever would, in her living room. And he made her shudder. When was the last time anyone had made her shudder?

She wanted more. Turning, she nibbled at her bottom lip and took Vin by the hand. "Come with me."

And there went that quirky brow. His reaction caused her to replay what she'd just said over again in her mind and she caught herself and the double entendre. Giggling, Lily was surprised by the sudden playfulness of the moment. She didn't laugh during sex or before. Was a person even supposed to do that?

He leaned down and kissed her quickly. "Sorry, you set it up. Let's go."

She shook her head and, as sexily as she could on not-well-thought-out heels and wobbly legs, started to walk toward her bedroom. She flipped on the light, and the brightness came on fast, almost breaking the spell. Lily quickly flipped it back off. "No need for all that."

Vin chuckled behind her and walked over to turn on her bedside lamp. "I'd really like to see you, if you don't mind."

She let out a sigh. "Okay, but it's at your own risk."

And with that Vin tugged off his shirt. The sight of that much of him made her mouth immediately water. The light was a good idea. Shit, she should have had her camera phone handy. The man was disgustingly bragworthy. She fell back down, sitting on the edge of her bed, taking him in as he kicked off his boots. Then he went to his knees before her. God, he was a lot to take. His mouth was once again on hers, and then suddenly she was leaning back and he was over her, going from her lips to her collarbone with his tongue leading the way as he traveled lower. Head between her breasts, he lingered, flipping open the back of her bra like some one-handed master, and then, there they were. Her breasts loose and heavy, and there for his taking.

And he did. Teasing one breast with his tongue while his hands traveled along her body in some crazed, hypnotic way that had her legs spreading and inviting him to go even further. When he touched her center and she gasped, she felt his smile spread across her breasts, those deliciously wiry hairs on his cheeks teasing her even more.

Completely impatient, Lily pushed up and pushed off her heels. With a tug she let her half-on/half-off dress slide to the floor, and the useless bra was next. She stood before him in her panties, waiting for some hint of judgment or dissatisfaction to show on his face. Perhaps her hips were too big or her stomach too heavy. But all Vin did was stare, taking her in from head to toe and then back up again. When he came to meet her eyes, his voice was a low hum. "God, I've waited a long time to see you like this. What an idiot I was." He swallowed and then leaned forward, kissing her stomach and then easing his large hands into the sides of her panties. With another slow motion he kissed her as he uncovered her and, when Lily finally was naked before him, picking her up and laying her gently on the bed.

She looked up at him. So much hard muscle and just barely reigned-in emotion. The weight of it all was almost too much to take. But take him she would. Happily. "I'm feeling way underdressed for this party."

He grinned. "Well, let me take care of that. Fair is fair."

Lily watched, barely breathing as Vin's jeans came off and she took in the full extent of him. She leaned forward and looked up. "Maybe I was the idiot," she said.

Vin crawled over her, a slow and sexy panther, and gently spread her legs. "Let's just call this one a draw and say we both screwed up."

Lily nodded as Vin once again captured her with his mouth while using his hands to drive her completely insane. When her breaths were coming in shorter and shorter gasps, he came up and gave her a bit of air, only to continue the torture by rubbing his stubble down the length of her body until she was open and wide before him. His tongue snaked out, at first slow and easy, tasting each spot except the one she knew would break her apart. He reached up and massaged her breast, teasing at her nipple so that her whole body was nothing more than one big, heightened nerve ending. All it would take was the slightest pressure and she knew she would blow. Vin let out a torturous breath of air on that spot, and she whimpered. He did it again, and she just may have whined. Then his tongue snaked out once more, swirling and flicking right at her center, and Lily heard a low, deep moan that she knew she'd later deny was her own. She felt the quake come on, but it was faster than she could prepare for. She reached out for the sheets, grabbing at them, twisting hard at Vin's strong muscles, searching for some type of escape from his exquisite torture. When he finally let up, and she sucked in a much needed breath of air, he was over her again, ripping a condom packet open with his teeth and then rolling it over his hardness.

Lily swallowed as she inched back on the bed as a

way of preparing herself, looking him in the eyes. Vin returned a steady gaze. All playfulness was gone. His voice went impossibly low, making her insides go soft. "Tell me this is what you want. I need to know you're sure."

Lily sucked in a breath, then bit her lip. The answer was clear. Her body said it all. But her mind was still at war. Lily shook her head to shut out the little nagging voice that dared to deny her this need. She looked at him. "This is exactly what I want."

She licked her lips again and smiled. "Is there anything about me that gives off a hint of 'I'm not sure'? I'd like to see you try to make it out of this bedroom without finishing what you started."

It was his turn to smile. "It's always a challenge with you, isn't it?"

Lily looked down at his delicious hardness, then back up into his eyes. "I'm afraid so. But somehow I think you're up for it."

But when he entered her for the first time, all the challenge completely went away. The fight was drained from both of them and in its place was nothing but the beautiful need that each of them had to satisfy themselves and each other. It didn't take long until Lily was moaning once again as she was clamped around Vin, all her muscles tight as he wrapped his strong arms around her. He flipped her so that she was over him, riding him face-to-face. He kissed her hard as quakes rocked through her body, and she heard her name deep in the back of his throat as he started to shake along with her. Together they collapsed as one, wrung out like two marathoners crossing the finish line together. Lily wanted to say something fun and quippy to keep the mood light because, as she lay sprawled across his chest, his heart beating in sync with hers, her usual thread of fear started to weave its way into her belly. She pushed up and looked at him, then smiled, about to ask if he wanted something from the kitchen, but the way he gazed at her with those midnight eyes stopped the words in her throat. He looked deep, and for a moment Lily thought she saw more than a quick one-off or possibly two-off in his eyes. The thread of fear started from her stomach and wrapped around her heart.

Vin leaned forward and kissed the top of her head. "Shh," he said before she could even speak. "Just rest. I think we've both talked enough for one night."

Chapter 16

Vin was up before the sun. He didn't want to be a total jerk and slip out on Lily without a word, but he also knew he needed to get home and it was too early to wake her. He had deliveries to take, not to mention the kids who were coming by from the Boys Club for their surf lessons. He didn't know how he'd come to enjoy volunteering and teaching the kids as much as he did, but somehow it happened.

After being wrangled into giving tips to a couple of boys who hung around on his side of the beach, that small thing had grown into a full, semi-organized class hosted by the local Boys Club. Although the kids were a handful, Vin had really come to look forward to teaching them. The group of six came out with two volunteers who also subbed as lifeguards, but thankfully there hadn't been any emergencies larger than the occasional scrape from a wayward shell.

Vin let out a breath as he pulled Lily's warm curves closer to his body. The sea was fine, but damn there was nothing better than this. Better than her. He stilled his breathing and let himself relax for a few minutes more, recalling the amazing night they'd just shared. God, she had rocked him and hard. From the inside out. And now it was confirmed just like he was afraid it would be, he was totally sprung. He felt himself harden against her and knew if he didn't move soon he definitely would be waking her, and then he wouldn't leave at all. At least not before having her once again.

Vin inhaled deeply, taking in her sweet spring rain smell before he slowly loosened his grasp around Lily's waist and attempted to ease away. He quickly slipped out of the bed and reaching for his haphazardly discarded underwear.

"I didn't peg you for the type to dine and dash."

Lily's voice caused him to turn around. She looked beautiful with sleepy eyes and tousled bed hair. Vin let out a low breath. "Shit, I'm sorry. I didn't want to wake you."

Lily gave him a lazy smile. "No worries. I'm a light sleeper anyway." She leaned up on one elbow, and the sway of her breasts barely covered by the sheets almost did him in. Vin leaned back down to give her a good morning kiss, her breasts swaying freely, just a thin sheet separating him from heaven. He moaned and pulled back reluctantly. "I'm sorry, but I need to get to the restaurant. It's a busy morning. I have deliveries, and then my kids are coming over to my place for their surfing lesson. . . ."

Lily's brows drew together, and Vin was quick to explain. "Not my kids, but kids from the local Boys Club who come to surf. I help them out with tips when it's in season."

He saw her visibly relax, then smile. "That's so

nice of you. I bet you're great with them, and they must really look up to you."

Vin shook his head as he eased into his underwear and went to pick up his jeans. "I don't know about all that. Though I do know that it surprised me how much I actually enjoy the time I spend with them."

She pulled herself up, letting the sheet drop to her waist, causing Vin to let out a groan as Lily moved forward and wrapped her arms around him. She leaned on his chest, the warmth of her body heating him in the best of ways. "You're going to make me late for sure," Vin said, dropping his jeans and reaching around to hold her.

But Lily pulled back. "No, you've got to go. You can't be late for the kids."

When he frowned at her, she shooed him away. "Just go. I couldn't live with myself if I was responsible for their teacher being a no-show. Especially when the class sounds like such fun."

"Fun?" Vin asked. "Would you like to come with me? Give it a try yourself. I have a board you can use."

Lily's eyes went wide. "Me? No way. It looks too treacherous for something I'd enjoy trying. Two left feet. I'm way too uncoordinated for that."

Vin leaned down and kissed her, pulling back as he looked in her eyes and smiled. "I've seen your moves, and I'd definitely not describe you as uncoordinated."

She leveled him with a look. "Cute, but no. I'll take it as a compliment and keep my feet as firmly planted on solid ground as I can."

Vin dressed quickly before he changed his mind. Lily had laid back down, and her eyes still had that heavy, in between two worlds look to them. He turned back to give her one more kiss. "Will you come and see me later?" *Damn, that came out needy.*

But instead of laughing in his face, Lily looked up at him, and he thought he felt a signal for something more emotionally as she did so.

"So, will you? That is, if you're not too busy. I could make you brunch, or maybe come out later and have a late dinner. Whatever you like."

He could tell she was thinking hard and looking for a way to measure her words. "I don't know. I wouldn't want to get in your way. Besides, this was nice, but I think it's best if we don't get it cloudy."

Nice? Cloudy? What the hell? Did they have two totally different experiences last night? Vin shook his head and stood after silently putting on his boots. He turned and looked at her once more. "Look, it's no big deal, or hell, maybe it is. I thought it was more than nice, and as for things getting cloudy, I guess that's just one more thing about you I don't under- stand. But cool. I'm here if you change your mind, and you can text me your schedule for working the events."

They stared at each other in silence for a moment, and he watched as she let out a long breath. "It's not like that. Last night was great; it's just, I think we should keep things light. Like I said from the start— a working relationship and, as we like, a playing association. I just don't want either of us to fool our- selves into thinking this is a romantic relationship."

Vin looked away from her and toward the window. The sun was getting brighter, and he really had to leave. Going thirteen rounds with Lily just didn't fit into his schedule. He headed out of the bedroom and she got up, wrapping the sheet haphazardly around her sexy body. He wouldn't be pulled in, though. Getting things right in Lily Perry's eyes was a lot more than he had the energy for. And why do it anyway? Maybe she was right. Just like Carter said at the club, with the scenario she was presenting, and after last night, she was turning out to be the perfect women. Beautiful, a hot body, and sex that blew his mind. All he had to do was get past the way she pushed all his warning buttons. If she could separate emotion so easily, then he could too.

As he made it to the door, Vin turned back to Lily and pulled her in toward him. He let his hand run down the length of her back and caress her ass as he bent to kiss her. Slow and easy he let his tongue say his good-bye. When he pulled back, she swayed in his arms. He smiled. "No worries, Lil. Like I said, I'm around when you want me. This is your show. I'm just here to enjoy the performance."

Chapter 17

It was closing time, and Vin had just hit the send button on his phone.

It's getting late. Thinking of you. V.

But as he looked down at his phone he cursed himself for sending the text and wished more than anything he could pull it back. He was so stupid. The woman clearly didn't want any attachments and was doing more than sending signals for him to back off; she was flat-out telling him to do so. If her words weren't enough of an indication of her true feelings, then her actions definitely were. He watched the phone as if it were some new invention, but she didn't answer the text, and as a matter of fact, she had gone completely silent for the past week.

He let out a low growl, which was unfortunately picked up by the all-hearing Manny, who apparently couldn't let a damn thing slide.

"Why don't you just give her a call?" Manny said while bagging the last of the food he'd be dropping off at a shelter on his way home. They had a food policy that any leftovers would be given away to a charity. Vin knew of many restaurants that didn't do this and considered it a terrible waste. He'd had his share of slim days when he was young. It wasn't uncommon for his mother and him to live from one meal to the next. With a past like that, he couldn't see throwing food away.

His attention was focused on Manny after hearing what he'd said. "How do you know it's even her I'm thinking about?" he said over his shoulder, toward Manny. "I have other things on my mind, you know, like keeping this restaurant going and paying overly nosy jerks like you. Besides, she's not the only woman in the world. You know me. I keep plenty busy."

"Yeah, yeah," Manny said. "If you say so. That may have been the old you, but we had plenty of gorgeous women who came in tonight. Though I hate to admit it, half of them were more into peeping you out through the kitchen view window than they were into the food or the drinks, and that was with me spending two hours behind the bar."

Vin raised a brow. "Maybe that has nothing to do with me but is due to your dwindling charm. Maybe your game is off."

Manny snorted. "Trust me, there is nothing wrong with my game. All my shots are three-pointers. I'm the MVP of this house." Just then a horn honked and Manny grinned. "Speaking of, I've got to go. That would be my ride for the night."

Vin shook his head. "Go. I can deliver those."

Manny shook his head. "No, I've got it. There is nothing sexier to a woman than a guy giving time to charity. This here is a little box of ready-made foreplay without the heavy lifting."

Vin gave Manny a side-eyed look. "I wouldn't repeat that, like anywhere."

Manny laughed and gave his hand a shake. "But you didn't tell me I was wrong." He walked out laughing at his own wit and left Vin in silence. The rest of the staff was gone, so Vin had nothing left to do but put the lights out, lock up, and take Dex out for a walk.

Nothing against the dog, but as Vin and Dex headed back down the stairs from his apartment, neither the walk nor his plans of watching the game appealed to him. They did a quick lap up and down the boardwalk. The warm breeze of the night showed signs of the warm season to come. Even though Vin wanted to let Dex run free, he knew he couldn't. Despite the late hour and the fact that the beach was officially closed, the sand was still sprinkled with a few couples taking advantage of the beautiful evening. He saw them dotted along the sand in intimate embraces or walking hand in hand along the shore. He looked down at Dex, who was tugging at his leash to be free. "Sorry, bud, this really blows. But it looks like neither of us is getting what we want tonight."

As he neared Canela, he heard the unmistakable loud sputter of her engine. It gave a roar, then seemed to cough, then nothing. Vin didn't know whether to laugh or be annoyed by her late-night intrusion. He snorted to himself. Who was he fooling? He was practically getting hard over just the rumble of her car's in need of a tune up engine. Clearly someone was in the mood for a booty call. Carter's words about the perfect women echoed through his mind at the same time the stupid need for something more pricked at the back of his mind.

Vin started to walk over to her car, taking in the

view of her from behind as she sat and looked at the restaurant. He hung back and just watched her. She sat there staring. Not moving and not getting out. As if feeling the war she was having with herself, he took a step to offer her a lifeline. But then she started up the car. Damn, she was ditching him again. But the poor old car could barely get up enough steam to cough before it died again.

Dex started to bark, and she jumped as Vin stepped forward.

"You lost?" he asked.

Lily looked at him, and for a moment she seemed like a child caught at playing hide-and-go-seek. As if she thought if she stood still and was silent he wouldn't see her. Finally she spoke. "It would seem so. Lost and stuck. It won't start. Again."

He'd never seen her look so vulnerable, and it pulled at him when he was really trying his best to stay strong and be steady. Dex pulled at him, trying his best to get to her. "Dex no." He looked back her way. "I think you'd better come out and say hello so he doesn't hurt himself trying to get to you or scratch the side of your car."

Lily leaned over the open window and looked down at Dex, then back up at Vin. "He's sweet. And it doesn't matter if this heap gets scratched. It's on its last leg anyway." Lily got out and slammed the car door behind her. She looked great, as usual, dressed casually in simple jeans that were rolled at the cuff and hugged her curves perfectly. She wore a boatneck tee that left just a hint of her toned belly showing. Vin looked down at her, then quickly back up again, telling himself to keep some sort of perspective on things despite his feelings and the late hour.

"So," Vin started. "Are you lost, or did you come up my side of the hill for a specific reason? Because from where I'm standing it looked like you were about to pull back out."

Lily looked at him sheepishly, then shrugged. "Honestly, I was. I don't know if what I was thinking was a good idea."

Vin let out a breath and ran a hand over his scalp while frustration nipped at his heels. "You know what? That's cool," he said. "You do you. You need to call anyone? The number of a cab?" He just needed to get up to his place and away from here. It was official. She was more than he could handle.

She took a step and reached out. Put her hand on his chest. Softly and gently. The simple touch stilling him. "Don't you want to know what I was thinking?"

He looked at her and let out a breath. "Not if it's just going to frustrate me. Not if it has anything to do with you denying that you're here because you want me right now as much as I want you."

Lily opened her mouth to speak, then closed it quickly.

Vin was about to walk away and go around into his apartment, but Dex wanted to be wrapped around her legs. "Come on, man. You stay or you go. I'm not begging you."

"I was going to ask you to make me breakfast."

"What?" Vin's gaze went from Dex to Lily and back to her vulnerable expression.

"I said I was going to ask you to make me breakfast."

He shook his head. "Woman, you know it's almost midnight, don't you?"

She nodded. "What? You think I can't tell time?"

* * *

Lily woke to the sound of crashing waves and the smell of the sea. She smiled. It had been a long time since she'd woken to that smell. It made her miss home more than she knew she did. But it was early and she was still tired after her eventful evening.

The thought had her reaching out for Vin and sadly coming up empty. She pushed herself up and looked around Vin's bedroom. It looked different in the haze of the morning light compared to the night before. Not that she paid that much attention the night before. No, all she'd had eyes for was Vin as he'd picked her up and carried her up the stairs to his place. The poor dog had barely made it in before Vin had kicked the door closed behind them.

He was so different than he'd been at her place. Last night, at least the first time they'd made love, he hasn't taken his time. He'd had her in his apartment, on his bed, and was inside of her before they could both get fully undressed. It was wild and passionate and not like anything she knew she wanted. But she did. She wanted him bad. Too bad he wasn't still there.

Stretching, Lily got up and looked around for something to put on. She spied Vin's black tee from the night before and slipped it on over her head. Inhaling, she let the spicy scent of him surround her and take her back with a sweet shudder of satisfaction. Lily went to the bathroom to relieve herself. Looking in the mirror she splashed her face with cool water, trying hard to see if she could bring a little bit of herself to the reflection of the reckless woman that was staring back at her. It didn't work.

Coming out, Lily did a quick scan of the place. It was an open plan—just a large living room/bedroom combo and the kitchen. She shook her head when she saw that Vin lived like mostly every other guy she'd woken up with, right down to the dark leather couch and ridiculously oversized TV. She let out a sigh. And down to the fact that she was waking up alone.

Maybe she should take the hint and gather her things and leave. It had been a fun night. Why stay around? *Because you want to, silly.* Crap, she could practically hear Bobbi's voice now. "Want and need are two different things," Bobbi would probably say. "And sometimes it's not about what you need but getting exactly what you want." And last night she'd surely gotten what she wanted and then some.

Maybe she wasn't even awake yet. Maybe she was still asleep and having a postorgasm hallucinogenic dream. But of course she wasn't. This was real. It was another morning after, and she was stuck with wondering about the right thing to do.

Coffee. Coffee was always right.

Looking around, she saw that at least Vin's kitchen was well lived in, though not at all fancy. He had knives in a well-used block. A well-seasoned cast-iron pan was on the stove, a couple of dishes were in the sink, and his fridge was better stocked than her own, with cheese, eggs, and nonexpired milk. Sadly, though, he had not an automatic, single-serve coffeemaker like she did but an intricate-looking press thing that she was sure needed a graduate of Le Cordon Bleu to operate it. After examining it, Lily decided it was way above her pay grade and put it back with a sigh, reaching for his teakettle and taking it to the sink to fill.

Over the sink was a shelf with a photo of what must have been of him and his mother. Lily recognized her as the women in the photo downstairs in the restaurant. Lily frowned and felt her brows pull together. In all the time in her own head and planning her ceremony Lily hadn't noticed that Vin didn't talk about his mom or any of his family. Hell, maybe she did notice but she'd spent so much time trying to actively distance herself emotionally from him that she'd made sure not to see him as any more than the components of his parts. Chef, surfer, good in bed. To attach a loving soul to that would be attaching emotions she was afraid of getting attached to. But seeing this photo in such a place of honor, she knew the woman must mean a lot to him. She also couldn't help but notice the lack of a father in any of the photos. It gave her pause. A red flag that popped up in the back of her brain.

Just then the front door opened and in bounded the overly friendly retriever from the night before, and he was going straight for her thighs. He was bigger than she remembered, and Lily jumped back with a loud squeak.

"Dex! Down," Vin said, all deep toned and stern. The poor dog immediately stilled and looked up at Lily with eyes that said "Save me." Lily smiled as she put the teakettle on the stove and reached out to give the dog's blond fur a pat.

"I know he can be rough, but he only looks mean," she said softly to Dex.

"Oh no, love. Don't go filling his head with lies. I'm just as mean as I look," Vin replied.

Lily looked at him. Tall, muscular, dark eyed, sexy, and scruffy, but mean? No, at the moment she couldn't cosign on that. He was smiling at her, and the fact that he did relieved Lily in a way that she didn't know she needed. But she was playing it cool. She turned toward the stove and picked up the coffee press. "What's this monstrosity you have masquerading as a coffeepot? How is anyone supposed to figure it out?"

She watched as Vin placed Dex's leash on a table by the door, then come over to her and took the coffee press from her hands. "I'll have you know this is top of the line and state of the art," he said.

Lily crossed her arms in front of her chest. "State of the art and top of the line for when? The forties? Don't you have a Keurig or at least a Mr. Coffee?"

Vin's eyes went skyward before he looked back at her. "I don't know what sort of terrible life you've been leading, love, but I'm about to change all that." He leaned in close to her, bringing the fresh sea smell with him and surrounding her with it as he brought his cool lips down on her and kissed her, then brought his hands to her bare thighs and up to cup her naked behind. Lily was quick to lean in and take what he was giving. The more he gave, the hungrier she seemed to be for him. His large hands squeezed her in close, and Lily let out a sigh as she felt him harden through his jeans as he rubbed against her belly. By the time Vin finally pulled away from the good morning kiss, Lily was breathless and all thoughts of coffee were gone. But he remembered, his comments bringing her back to earth. "You want me to make your coffee for you now? It will only take a few minutes. And I can brew you up a quick breakfast."

Lily shook her head and leaned back in to nuzzle

at his neck, then looked up into his dark eyes. "No, I'm not quite as hungry for food as I was a few minutes ago."

He looked at her through his dark eyes, seeing all. "Really? Lost your appetite, have you?"

"Not exactly. Just lost it for food. Though I am feeling like a hot shower might be just the thing I need to bring my appetite back."

Vin grinned, leaned down, and lifted her with both hands as she wrapped her legs around his waist. "Love, I like the way you think."

The water was hot but nothing compared to the two of them. As the steam rose, so did Lily's temperature. She didn't know how he did it, if it was a special skill of his from working in the kitchen and being adept at multitasking, but the man was a master at seeming to be everywhere at once. Just when she thought he was concentrating on one part of her body and working her into a frenzy that way, there would go a clever hand to seek out some body part that she didn't even know she liked having touched just so. But he was touching it and she was liking it all the way from one explosion to another.

Lily tried her best to keep time with him. Give as good as she got. Let her hands roam over all that exquisite muscle of his. He had these little bruises, some old scars that let her know he hadn't lived a gentle life. No, he'd been active and still was. As she came across each, she had the distinct urge to kiss the long-ago hurts and make them all better. When finally her kisses got lower on his belly and she kissed right below his belly button and above his glorious hardness, he shuddered in anticipation of what he hoped would come next but didn't open his mouth to

ask for. He didn't have to. Lily was happily enjoying
the smooth feel of him on her tongue, the tightness of
his backside as he tried to hold himself together
under her ministrations.

Finally, it was too much and he growled, a sound
she had anticipated with pleasure. Pulling her up
quickly, he flashed barely checked desire in his midnight eyes, and everything within her went liquid.
"Now, love. I must have you now. I mean right now."

Lily nodded her acceptance, and he shook his
head.

"I want to hear you say it. Tell me it's okay."

She bit her lip and looked at him hard, trying to
take in what he wanted from her. She blinked when
the only word she could come up with was something
she didn't know if she was quite ready to give. Trust.
But still, Lily let out a ragged breath, then nodded
again. "It's okay. Now," she said.

Then with surprising tenderness Vin turned her
around and placed her hands against the cool tiles,
pushing her slightly forward as he entered her from
behind. He filled her slowly and completely. Then he
wrapped his arms around her to steady her, one at her
breast as it lifted and caressed her and the other between her legs, finding her perfect spot. Instantly her
breathing hitched as tiny sparks of fire blazed through
her, burning her from the inside out. Suddenly she
was pushing back against him with all she had while
the water attempted to run between them from overhead but didn't succeed. They were too close. Fused
together. One. So much so that nothing could get in
between them.

Vin bent and kissed her on the back of her neck,
the side of her cheek. She felt his teeth gently scratch

at her shoulder, and she exploded as he squeezed her tighter and went surprisingly deeper, joining her on the ride to oblivion.

After what seemed like a long while, but was only moments, he led her out of the shower and toweled her off. Lily didn't say a word. She didn't want to screw up and risk breaking the spell they were under. The only sound between them was their gentle breathing and the crashing of the waves on the beach below. Pulling back the covers, Vin laid Lily out on the bed, then lay his large frame next to her. Spooning his body to hers before pulling the sheet over them both. Gently, he kissed her once more between her neck and shoulder. She was starting to think of that space as his spot. He let out a long breath. "Rest now, babe. Later I'll cook breakfast for you."

Lily smiled as she looked out the large sliding doors that led to his deck and beyond and took in the sky, which was promising a beautiful cloudless day. Vin rubbed lazily at her thigh. The easy movements were almost hypnotic. He'd just made love to her, gently tucked her into bed, and he said he'd cook for her. Lily felt her eyes flutter closed as she finally found her words again. "Breakfast sounds real nice."

Chapter 18

By all fault of her own, they fell quickly into a routine. Vin's had a friend of his come and tow her car, and it turned out to be both an oil and a starter problem. Lily thought about just leaving the car with him and selling it for parts, but still something wouldn't let her. Stubbornly she shelled out the money to get it repaired. She knew a new car was in her future, but she wasn't quite ready to give up on the old one just yet.

That first morning's breakfast was perfection. Eggs fried perfectly with some type of spicy and sweet sausage that she'd never tried before but was instantly addicted to. But that seemed to be the way with Vin. He had her trying new things, with her falling for them, hard.

She washed the dishes while Vin sat at the counter answering e-mails. "You know you don't have to wash the dishes just because I cooked the food. It's not like you're working downstairs. This isn't a *quid pro quo* situation," Vin said.

"It's no problem. I want to be useful and you really

have been doing a lot of cooking for me. If I don't watch out or get more active I'm going to regret it and not fit into any of my clothes anymore."

Vin gave a snort, causing her to do a quick turn, and he laughed.

"What was that for?"

Vin shook his head and looked down at her body before looking back up at her face. "Sweetheart, from where I'm sitting it looks like everything is landing in just the right places."

Lily didn't have a comeback and she felt her face heat with a blush, so she turned back to the dishes. Starting to wash again she looked at the photo over the sink. "I love this picture of you." Lily made her comment light.

Vin barely grunted.

"Hello. I said I love this picture of you. That's you and your mother, right? You look like her, you know. It's all in the eyes. So expressive."

Vin looked up from his laptop and over at her. "Thanks. I'll take that as a compliment. I think she was beautiful."

Lily nodded her agreement but could tell by Vin's sudden lengthening of his spine that she was treading into murky waters. "How long ago did she pass away?"

She saw him visibly tense. The telltale muscle in his jaw flexed. Lily turned away to the dishes. "I'm sorry. You don't have to talk about it. I can see it's hard; I didn't mean to pry."

He shook his head then. "No, no, it's okay," he said, though his smile was clearly forced. "It's going on two years."

Lily lowered her gaze a moment, the pain of his loss still almost palpable. Finally she looked back up at him and gave him a small smile. "I'm so sorry. Do you have any other family? Brothers?" She rolled her eyes dramatically. "Sisters?" And got a slight laugh out of him.

He shook his head.

"So it's just you and your father."

She watched his gaze harden as his jaw tightened again. "I don't have a father. It was just my mother and me. Now it's just me, and me alone."

"Once again," she said, "I'm so sorry."

He looked at her sharply, which almost made her want to take a wide step back. "Don't be. There is nothing to be sorry for. That's how life goes. Now, I think we've had enough with talking about subjects that have nothing to do with this moment and the here and now." Catching himself, Vin softened his tone and stood beside Lily. As he wrapped his arms around her, she washed the dishes, her lips clamped tightly shut, almost afraid to say something else that would upset him. The only sound the clanging dishes and the running water until she heard his sigh. His breath was soft against her ear. "I'm sorry. I just don't like to talk about her. She was all I had and I was all she had, and I failed her. And my father, well, he failed both of us so he's not worth any of my conversation."

Lily felt his muscles tense against her back, and she couldn't help but go slightly rigid herself. At her body's tightening, Vin gave her a nudge and a kiss on the side of her neck. "Come on, Lily. The last thing my ma would want me doing would be standing here in my kitchen like some sad sack when I have the opportunity to be making love to a beautiful woman."

Lily turned around then and gave him an arched brow. "Really? Somehow I highly doubt that."

Vin laughed once again, though she noticed his smile didn't quite reach his eyes, and it let her know that this conversation, at least the uncomfortable part, was closed. He kissed her, once again doing those sexy moves that worked like magic, taking all coherent thought from her mind and turning her body to one big mass of Vin pliable goo.

He had her, and she found herself doing just about anything to be with him, near him, but most of all be a part of him.

Once again waking with a groggy head and a limp though thoroughly sexually satisfied body, Lily reached for Vin with greedy hands in the early morning hours but came up empty as Vin was already slipping out of bed to hit the surf. "Really? You're going this early?" she asked.

Vin leaned back over in the bed and kissed her, his lips softly glancing off her own. "I'm going to take Dex out and get a little time on the water. I'll be back to make your coffee before you know it, though. Don't worry." He rubbed lightly on her behind before turning back away to dress in his trunks as she closed her eyes. "Though you know," he added nonchalantly, "you could just take a chance for once and come with me."

Lily cracked one closed eye back open. "Come with you where, and what do you mean 'for once'?"

He gave her that grin. She was starting to know the

inflections of his grins and, judging by how high or low it was, what boundary level he was going to push. This was the higher quirky grin plus a slight eyebrow raise. Lily knew it meant trouble. "I'm just saying, you should come out and give it a try. You'll never know if it's something you might like by watching from up here."

Lily gave him a frown. "I think at this point in my life I pretty much know if I should attempt something that really only Jesus should be doing. And mere mortals trying the wrath of God at their own risk."

Vin burst out laughing at that one. "I swear, your drama is legendary. Wrath of God type stuff. Only you would say that." His expression sobered as he looked at her deeper. "Seriously, come on out with me. I promise you it's safe. I teach kids and got certified for it."

Lily was unmoved as she looked at him. The idea did sound, if not like a good one, slightly intriguing. Like one of those bucket list things you wrote down but knew you'd never get to and were really perfectly fine with that. "I tell you what," she started. "You go and splash in the water for a while and I'll handle breakfast. I'll even do the coffee. I've seen you work that press thingy enough that I think I can handle it. I'm sure YouTube can teach me the rest."

Vin shook his head. "The fact that you call it a thingy tells me you can't handle it. Better you just wait till I get back." He got up silently. Lily was learning that it was his way to go only so far and not to push any one situation. She knew that a big part of it was his respecting the boundaries she had put up from the beginning and continued to, but at that point she wondered if she wasn't ready for some of the velvet ropes to come down. He turned her way and smiled from the bedroom's door frame. "It's no problem. Why don't you just relax and go back to sleep. I won't be long, and I'll do breakfast for you when I get back."

He was gone only a few minutes when Lily got up and looked out the back patio doors to see down to the beach before her. Something about the way he'd given up so easily and not pushed her started to bug her. It was as if he knew they wouldn't last, that she was on her way out, so why even take the time to put in the effort of the lesson? Lily bit at her bottom lip. Was she reading too much into this, or was that the signal she was giving off?

She watched him in his full-on body-hugging surf suit as he headed toward the water. Just then a younger boy walked up and greeted Vin. He was carrying a smaller board, and they chatted a few moments before going toward the water together. They attached their latches to their ankles and headed in to paddle out.

For a few moments Lily watched breathless while they paddled out, then disappeared from view. It was the longest twenty seconds of her life, but to see Vin as he came back up and stood firm and solid on his board with the younger boy just a few feet beside him was exhilarating. Both Vin and the boy looked happy and carefree as they balanced against the turbulent waves, and when they finally broke, each twisting off and into the water, they came up with bright, wet smiles that had Lily cheering on the inside. He'd wanted her to be a part of that, and she'd dismissed it out of hand. He wanted her to experience that type of joy, but she couldn't see further than the potential danger.

Lily changed quickly into the suit she'd brought with her from home that she'd been using for lounging on his deck. It was an intricate, black one-piece with lots of crisscross banding, so definitely better for lounging than surfing, but it was all she had. When Lily got to the beach and walked up to Vin, who was now saying good-bye to his little surfmate, he gave her a smile that was laced with questions. "What are you doing out here? I thought you went back to bed."

Lily shook her head. "Nah, I decided this seemed like a good morning for a lesson."

Vin leaned down and kissed her before she could get another word out, taking her breath away. "What was that for?"

He smiled wide, and it caused Lily's heart to dangerously trip over itself to see him so open and happy. "Just for you taking a chance and trusting me." But then he looked down at her and frowned. He looked her over critically, twisting her around and then back again.

Lily pulled a face. "Do you mind?"

"Yeah. This suit is not making it. It will do for today, but tomorrow we'll get you something proper to wear. For now, we'll just work on your balance in the water. If I have you slide up and down on the sand in that suit, it will be like the worst rug burn you could ever imagine." He frowned, realizing what he'd said. "Not that you'd know anything about that."

Lily reached out and stroked at his beard, which she was coming to love so well. "Of course not, darling."

It was a little over a month later, and though Lily wouldn't go so far as to call herself a beach bum, she had been bumming around the beach and Vincent's place enough to come scarily close. Her brown skin now held a deeper, more sunkissed glow and though she couldn't call herself a surfer either, she'd been out on the water with him enough to learn how to find her center, paddle out, judge a decent wave by the amount of white foam it had, and even hold her balance for all of 1.5 seconds. Sure she knew she'd never make a circuit with those numbers, but it was better than when she'd started. Still, it wasn't all sand, surf, and sex. Reality had to come, and it was coming in the forms of Christie Carlyle's graduation party and her own wedding to herself. For the past month she and Vin talked exclusively about everything but anything that really mattered.

Christie's party was fine because it didn't quite threaten to pop the fragile little bubble they'd built, but Lily kept any mention of each of their families, the past, or her upcoming ceremony off the table out of fear of coming back to earth. But her planner nature couldn't let it rest. It wasn't only her job, it was who she was. She lived by dates and efficacy, so she just couldn't let it lie. After Christie's party, decisions had to be made.

Lily was up and dressed early on the day before the graduation party to do one final walk through with Tori to be sure they had all they needed in terms of decorations, favors, and food. Lily and Tori were sitting at a table on Canela's patio, where most of the party's action would be happening. Their table was littered with charts and boards, as well as tablets and a laptop. Around them were boxes of new string lights in colors that would go with Lily's multicolor scheme, as well as a few extra palm trees she had brought in to green up the space.

Vin walked out with a tray of tapas for them and frowned when he couldn't find a place to set them. "It looks like you two are planning to go to war," he said.

Lily nodded and cleared some space. "Getting a party to run smoothly, especially when teens are involved, hey, you're not far off."

"Well, eat and keep up your strength." Vin put the tray down and Lily looked up, giving him a warm smile. He leaned down and kissed her easily on the top of her head. Tori raised a brow and gave her a smile. Lily gave her a tight look in return and pushed down a blush. They hadn't been particularly hiding their relationship. Not that they even tagged it as a relationship, but they also hadn't been flaunting it in front of anyone either. She came to his place most nights and left in the morning after a passionate night and maybe a lesson or two on the water. Vin was a masterful teacher of all things.

"You don't have to worry about the food," Vin said, pulling her back from her thoughts. "Remember, that's my department and I've got it covered."

"Just be sure you do," Lily replied. "Oh, and remind the staff that most of these guests will be eighteen and nineteen, so that means no alcohol. It's our signature alcohol-free drink for everyone unless there is a special order. Tori will be checking IDs and doing wristbands at the door. Rich teens are notorious for getting one over."

Vin nodded. "Oh yeah, I know that. I may be from the projects, but you don't run a place on the beach without seeing your fair share of tricks. Hell, you met

Carter and Aidan. Those two were always hell on wheels."

Lily raised a brow. She was shocked that Vin would mention his upbringing so casually in this setting when he'd not raised his past or his mother with her since she mentioned the picture. She pushed it aside, knowing that the right place to discuss this was not in front of Tori. "Yeah," she said with a half laugh, "and I'm sure you were a choir boy."

He gave her a wink. "Actually I was. But that's a story for another day." Vin grinned at her and stepped back, in the process tripping backward over one of the boxes and coming down hard on a planter, hitting his head.

Both Lily and Tori jumped up as Lily screamed his name. "Vin! Oh my God, are you all right?"

They both ran to his side as Manny and two wait-staff guys came out to see what the crash and commotion was all about. "Oh shit, boss, what the hell happened?" Manny said, rushing to pick Vin up.

Vin opened his eyes and shook his head, reaching to touch back behind his ear. When his hand came back with blood, Lily gasped. "Don't move him! Get a towel."

Vin looked at her and gave her a weak smile. "It's fine, love, don't worry yourself about it." He lifted his other hand and gave his wrist a twist, wincing.

"That too?" Lily said. "Oh God, you're going to the hospital."

He looked her straight in the eyes and then started to push himself up. "No. I'm not." His voice was steady and firm as Manny and Felix lifted him from under his shoulders.

They let him go and he was slightly unsteady. "I

don't know, boss," Felix said with worried eyes. "Maybe she's right and you should go and get checked out right quick."

Vin shot Felix a look that had him swallowing hard. "How about you just help clear up this mess and let me worry about me. I said, I'm fine."

It was Lily's turn to give Vin a sharp look. Why was he being such a jerk? They were all looking out for him. She grabbed a towel from Manny's apron, flipped it to the clean side, and put it to Vin's head. The gash didn't look too bad, but who knew with something like a concussion. She turned and looked at him. "Everyone is concerned about you. What if your wrist is sprained? What if you have a concussion and don't even know it? You need to be looked at and make sure all is well."

He looked her hard in the eyes, ignoring everyone around her. "What I need is for you to stop hovering and to listen for once. I'm not going to the hospital. I don't do them. End of story. Now, why don't you take care of your business and let me take care of mine. That's the arrangement, right?"

Lily blinked and counted backward in her head. There was no freaking way she'd tear up in front of him. If he wanted to be a jerk, then he'd do it without the payoff of her emotional toil. She nodded before moving out of his space. "Yep, that was the arrangement." Letting out a deep breath she turned to Felix as if Vin weren't still standing there and gave him a professional smile, as best she could. "Do you mind please moving these boxes to the corner until you and Punchy have time to string up the lights?"

Felix nodded and started to move the boxes. Manny gave her a look of pity and Vin one of contempt before heading back to the kitchen. Vin opened his mouth to speak, but Lily held up a hand. "Don't. Like you reminded me, I have work to do and it's about time I concentrated on getting it done."

Vin stared at her for a beat or two longer, then looked over at Tori with soft eyes before walking back into the restaurant. Lily sat back down and looked at Tori. "Where were we?"

Tori frowned. "Are you all right? That was a little intense."

Lily nodded. "I'm fine, and that was nothing. Besides, he was right. We need to work. This party isn't going to put on itself, and if it did we'd both be out of a job. So let's just focus."

But as she tried to focus, Lily could feel herself already pulling away. She had to. This was just the beginning. She knew how these things went. She and Vin had a good run where they were happy and easy with each other, but they could fall to the other side way too easily, and this proved it. She couldn't be with someone like that. Someone who could light her fuse like that, and she knew neither could he. Inevitably he'd be out the door. It was better to start the move toward letting go sooner rather than later.

Chapter 19

Vin knew he was wrong, but he also knew he couldn't help himself. Slamming the stainless steel saucepan down in the sink just felt right. It also felt petty as hell, but he wasn't about to admit that. He didn't have to. The hard, silent side eye he got from Manny was more than enough. He also knew the look wasn't about the saucepan. No, it was about the way he had talked to Lily. It was totally uncalled for, and he knew it. If he'd heard it from anyone else he'd be all about kicking that ass, so the fact that the nastiness came from him made the guilt that much worse.

He leaned his hands against the sink and winced in pain, only to hear a snort from Manny's side of the kitchen.

"I heard that," Vin growled.

"I meant for you to."

"Fuck," Vin said, turning around. "Leave it to me to be the guy with the mouthiest employees."

But Manny just looked at him. "You know that was wrong, boss, so you don't need me telling you so." Manny tilted his chin toward him. "I won't ask about the head because, unlike Lily, I know just how hard it is, but how's the wrist? You need me to wrap it, get you some ice?"

Vin frowned and tilted his wrist back and forth. The pain was definitely there but not unbearable. It was his left hand, so it may slow him down a little but wouldn't prevent him from working. He looked over at Manny. "I'll get the ice and put it on and off for a few minutes. If you don't mind helping with a wrap, I would take it."

Manny nodded but kept any comments he may have had to himself as he turned to retrieve the first aid kit from the back of the pantry. After coming back, he quickly pulled out the ace bandage and got to wrapping.

Vin frowned. "Not too tight."

Manny laughed. "Oh, don't get all wimpish on me now when you had all that lip before."

"What's this all about? Don't tell me my star player is getting sidelined?"

"Oh, hell. This day just gets better and better." Vin turned and looked at Carter. "What brings you out here today? Don't you have a studio to run? Some life to ruin with one of your not-so-real reality TV shows?"

Carter stepped back and feigned that he was affronted. "Great. So I see the emperor is in rare form." He tilted his chin at Manny. "Hey, Man. How goes it?"

"Oh, it goes," Manny said. "You?"

"I'm cool. Thought I'd come and check on my investment, and it's a good thing I did." He laughed.

"Hell, I may have to show my skills in the kitchen tonight."

Manny finished wrapping his wrist, and Vin stood, giving Carter a hard look. "Don't even think about stepping behind my stove."

Carter shook his head. "Still the same old territorial Vin."

"Yeah. About everything."

Carter chuckled as Manny shook his head. "So am I to assume this little tantrum had everything to do with that pretty planner sitting out on the patio?"

Manny snorted from the pantry, where he was pulling ingredients for the night's prep.

"All right. Enough out of you. I'm done with this," Vin said.

It was on that note and with impeccable timing that Lily appeared. Of course she'd heard him say he was done. Why would she not have with the loudness of his voice?

"Tori and I are out. Felix and Paunchy can handle the lights. We'll be back tomorrow about two hours before the party. Maybe less." Her tone was clipped and left no room for any opening for conversation. She stepped forward, and for a moment Vin stupidly hoped she'd actually reach up and kiss him good-bye, or better yet change her mind and go upstairs to meet him and let him make up for his assholery properly. But no, she just handed him a typed-up preparty checklist complete with a food outline and the timing on when each item should be brought out.

"I think everything you may need is here."

Vin looked from the list back to her. "I doubt that."

Lily stayed deadpan. "Well, I don't."

Once again Manny snorted, and this time Carter added his own snort to the mix. Good. Now Vin had legitimate places to land his anger. When she was gone, heads would roll. He gave Lily a half smile. "Till tomorrow."

"Till tomorrow."

Shit, tomorrow had come and Lily was dreading it. Freaking Vincent Caro. She shouldn't be thinking this way. It was an event day. Her game day. And normally on her game day she was pumped up, not waking up feeling drained and dejected. This was exactly why she was so careful to not let go of her tight reigns of control.

To say waking in her apartment alone after waking up with Vin most days in the last few weeks was a bummer was an understatement. The only part of it that kept her fueled up was the fact that she was still extremely mad at him. True, thanks to Tori and then after talking with Bobbi, her anger had reduced to a simmer, but she knew that it would take only the tiniest raise of her flame for it to boil right back over.

Tori had expressed that Vin's reaction seemed pretty out of character, but then there goes Bobbi. Her friend pointed out that though she and Vin were getting closer, he was the one doing most of the heavy lifting. That she still kept pushing the fact that there was no commitment between them and the sobering reality that they were at most friends with really good benefits.

Not that she really could see anything wrong with that, and if she didn't then why should he? Still, though they shouldn't, Bobbi's sobering words stung.

Lily's phone pinged with a message, and she reached over to her nightstand to check it.

I'm sorry. V.

Lily stared at the short message for a long time. Longer than she probably should have. Why did he do this? Couldn't he maybe be a little more verbal with it? Give her something more to go on? Rail against? This short, no-nonsense apology was so annoying and so like him that all it did was send her around the bend. Lily sucked in a breath and imagined him next to her. Those dark eyes as they raked along her skin, burning each part of her body they gazed upon. His big hands, so large but so gentle and expressive, taking her to heights that only he dared take her. Yeah, he'd show her just how sorry he was. But then what? How long would it last before she'd ask for too much? Before she'd demand more of him than just sexual satisfaction, a true sharing of not just his body but his mind and soul. His vulnerabilities.

No, he wouldn't be able to do that, and he wouldn't be able to take it from her either. It would be like his irrational hospital meltdown and close off all over again. Lily knew she couldn't handle a relationship in which she was constantly walking on eggshells to keep the peace and the guy was going into it wearing a mask hiding his true self behind a façade of perfection, keeping his real feelings, needs, fears, and desires hidden. She'd watched that drama play out with her parents. There was no need to live it all over again.

Lily thought then of their many intimate nights together and how fulfilling they had been. So packed with sexual acrobatics that there was no room for anything else. And whenever the space became empty and there was any attempt to fill it with actual meaningful talk, they both closed off.

Maybe Bobbi was right. Maybe it wasn't just him blocking things but her too. Frustrated, Lily put the phone aside and went to take a shower. She didn't answer him, because she had no words. At least not ones she was prepared to say out loud.

Chapter 20

It was getting on dusk, and Lily had successfully made it to party time without getting stuck alone with Vin once. Sure, there was some awkwardness between them and the staff after the incident the day before and from her not answering his text that morning, but to his credit and maturity he sailed right past it after she'd told him it was not the day to discuss it.

Vin just nodded and got back to work preparing the tapas for the celebration. The back patio had been transformed into a tropical oasis with the palm trees, rented teak tables, and new multicolored lights. Lily had also rented a free-standing bar where Manny, with his sparkling personality, would serve "The Christie," the special nonalcoholic fruit drink that looked like white sangria but, sadly for Lily, since she could have used it, packed none of the punch. She thought about indulging in one of the alcoholic red ones, but her policy was never to drink while on the job, so she didn't.

Chelsea Carlyle and her husband, Brandon, were the first to arrive and make sure everything was in shape for the party, Christie having opted to come in on the rented party bus with her friends.

Lily put on her best face when coaxing Vin out from the kitchen to come smile at the Carlyles.

"It's nice to meet you," he said, shaking both their hands quickly.

But Chelsea—all done up in shades of white from her designer jeans, to her silk blouse, right to the tips of her freshly bleached hair—made sure to let hers linger in his a beat longer as she licked her top lip and flipped her hair over her shoulder. She didn't give one whit about her husband, Mr. Bonded in Holy Matrimony, not to mention the bill footer, standing right next to her. But to his credit, or not, Brandon seemed not to notice, as his eyes were already wandering to some of the temp waitresses who had been hired for the event.

"I've been looking forward to meeting you, Mr. Caro. I have to say that when Lily approached me proposing your establishment as a venue I was not really into the idea, but upon researching you, I couldn't help being impressed. You've come from such humble beginnings and made such a name for yourself," she said, looking at him as if he were a sad charity case from an orphanage and at the same time were hot cornbread coming out of the oven when she was trying to do Atkins. "You're truly astounding."

Vin frowned as he slid his hand from hers. "Am I, now?" he asked innocently.

Chelsea nodded, all the while looking down at the crotch of his pants.

"I really don't think so, since I screwed my way to get all that I have."

Lily gasped and Chelsea blinked quickly, looking

up from Vin's crotch to his eyes. It was then that
Brandon turned around from checking out a waitresses
rack, and not of lamb, to get back in the conversation.
Vin laughed, turning his comment into one big joke.
The Carlyles laughed awkwardly with him, then took
an alcoholic sangria that Manny offered from the tray
he was carrying around for adult guests. Lily took the
opportunity to give Vin a hard pinch in his side.

He turned to her and quirked a brow. They stood
for a few seconds and stared at each other before Lily
spoke up. "If you all don't mind, I'm just going to
check on some final details with Vin for a moment."

Toni walked up and led the Carlyles out to the
patio. As soon as they were out of earshot, Lily let
loose through clenched teeth. "What the hell was that
about?"

Vin threw up his hands and went to the kitchen.
Lily followed. "That was me getting her eyes off my
dick and back where they belonged. Would have been
nice if you noticed."

Lily frowned. "Of course I noticed, but how is
your dick my responsibility?" she whispered.

Vin's eyes went wide. "How is it not? Seems
you've been taking care of it pretty well these past
few weeks. I kind of thought you cared about it."

"Of course I care about your dick, but it's yours,
not mine to rule over."

"What?" Vin said. "Just like your"—he looked
down to the V of her white jeans, then back up to her
eyes—"is not mine to rule over. Now, to cherish is
another story." Lily opened her mouth in shock, and
suddenly she wanted to cross her legs. She was hot
and tingling all over. She wanted to tell him that, but

wouldn't give him the satisfaction of knowing he'd gotten to her.

Was she seriously having this conversation in hushed tones in the middle of his kitchen when she had clients outside? Lily let out a long, frustrated growl. "Number one, you are not policing my private parts, and two, this is not the time or the place. I'm not having this conversation right now."

Thankfully, Tori peeked her head in to break up the heated tension. "Bus arrives in two minutes," she said, her eyes shifting uncomfortably between the two of them.

Lily looked up at Vin, her fire on four alarm. "I'm out."

She started to walk away, and then his hand shot out to cover the bare section of her upper arm. Lily looked down at his hand, and he released quickly but still stepped in close, leaning near her ear. "This is not over, Lil. You and I will have this conversation. You can't ignore my texts forever or run away from whatever it is we have going on here."

Lily snorted and stepped away. "Oh really? Just watch me."

Over a hundred teens later, not to mention fifty adults, a staff of twenty, and one brooding chef, and Lily was exhausted.

The party was finally winding down, and it seemed to have been a huge success. Lily was everywhere at once, but mostly she watched out for Christie, making sure that the honoree was having a great time. Thankfully, Christie spent most of the evening laughing and dancing. And for the four hours that the party lasted, she never looked bored and picked up her phone only for selfies that she Instagrammed. She even grabbed hold of Lily and Toni to snap a quick picture of the three of them for her gram, which Lily knew to be the highest form of praise for her set. Lily couldn't ask for more than that.

After the night ended with Lily getting everyone back on the party bus and out of her care, Lily thanked the Canela staff for their help with making the night a success. Lily gave Tori a hug and let her leave before the rental company came to break down the tables and chairs, with a ride to the train from Manny and a quick warning to stay safe. Tori gave her a laugh. "Yes, Mom."

Lily shook her head. "I'm sorry. I know that was over the line. I can't help it. I always play the big sister even if I'm your boss."

Tori patted her hand. "It's okay, and don't worry, I've got both eyes on him." She looked over Lily's shoulder to a still brooding Vin, who was hanging back and pretending not to be watching from the kitchen opening. "You watch yourself too."

Lily smiled. "Don't worry. I've got my eyes wide open."

"Yeah, but what about your heart?"

"Heart? What's that got to do with any of this?"

Tori shook her head as Manny appeared by her side. "You ready? I've just got to drop this food at the shelter on my way." He gave her a sly grin after making his statement, and Tori rolled her eyes.

"Do you, now?"

* * *

The rental company had taken the tables and the DJ was done packing up all the equipment as Lily was packing her tote. Vin came over to her. "So, are we going to do this now?" he asked.

Lily looked at him with tired eyes and shook her head. "No. No we are not going to do this now. This day . . . these past two days have been ridiculous."

He let out a long, exasperated breath. "Yes, they have, but the days before were great."

Lily nodded her agreement. "You're right, the days before were great. They've also been hot and sexy and exhilarating. But that's about it."

Vin pulled back as if he'd been punched, hard. "For some, even most, that would be enough."

Lily stepped forward into his space and put her hand lightly on his chest. He looked at her with hard-end eyes that she wasn't used to seeing from him. But Lily held still, unwavering under his gaze. "You're right. It is enough, or it should be. Honestly, it's what I expected from the beginning."

"Expected or set up?"

Lily's gaze went flat at his accusation. So they were doing this. "What are you trying to get at? I didn't set anything up from the beginning."

Vin's own gaze was laser sharp. "Like hell, you didn't. You have us, well, me, exactly where you want me, and you have from the start. A sexual scratching post waiting for you whenever you have an itch."

His words hit her hard, with their underlying thread of truth, but still Lily felt the need to protest. "That is completely unfair. You insist on being so closed off."

"And whose fault is that?" he challenged.

Lily shook her head, then looked back at him. "Mine, I guess. But can you honestly tell me that if I did anything different—say, opened myself up to you and poured my heart out and told you I wanted it all, said I wanted a real relationship maybe even a commitment from you—you would have been okay with that? Or even ready for it? Or would my words just be something else to placate your ego, make you feel validated while you strung me along until I got just close enough to be an annoyance under your skin? Something you'd have to cut loose."

Vin was quiet, the heavy silence saying more than any words could.

But still Lily couldn't help but go on. "And could you really share yourself with me? Go deeper? Tell me about your mother or dare I say, your father? Do you, or did you, even have a father?" She moved close to him and looked deeper into his eyes. She saw nothing there. The only hint at his emotion was the tightening of his jaw, the barest flaring of his nostrils.

But then his eyes softened and his voice fell. "You care to talk to me about yours?"

Lily sucked in a breath. "You are cold. You can't even make yourself vulnerable for one moment without deflecting. Hell, you couldn't even loosen up enough to tell me why you were afraid to go to the hospital without snapping my head off!"

Vin opened his mouth to speak and then closed it again, looking at her silently.

"That's what I thought," Lily said, now talking softer and pulling her hand away from his chest. She continued to pack her tote, then went to put it on her shoulder when he reached out to stop her. She looked up at him.

"You're still not anywhere near close to understanding why I'm having my wedding, are you? Nowhere near understanding who I am."

Vin shook his head and his eyes flashed. "Tell me, do you even understand yourself?"

His words were few, but they were mighty. Lily swallowed and turned away but not before Vin came up behind her and pulled her in toward him.

"I still want to be with you, you know," he growled out, then laughed. "Even if you are already promised to another."

Lily chuckled, then turned and looked up at him. "Believe me, I know. But the only wrinkle is, for how long?"

He gave a wry laugh, then bent to kiss her. His lips were soft, his need immediately hard. Lily felt her body begin to fold, compress into his and threaten to become not her own. "As long as it takes," he replied.

She pulled back and looked at him. He was beautiful and was looking at her like the answer to every need she could ever have. But something stopped her, and for the life of her she just couldn't let go and believe with her mind in the momentary happiness she was feeling in her heart. Her mind was telling her that what she was experiencing was all heat and hormones, and beyond that what? She was always happy when she was in his arms. So what? He was addictive like that. But Lily was smart enough to recognize that addictive quality and knew it was the reason she couldn't easily walk away. He was her drug, and more than anything right now she needed a fix.

Lily reached down and let her hand go under his T-shirt. She wanted to feel his warm skin under the pads of her fingers. "How about for as long as I let you," Lily said, going back to Vin's earlier point.

She kissed him, then with all she had and let her hand roam over his chest, tease at his nipples, move down into his pants. When she heard him groan she knew she had won, but the victory felt hollow. "Tell me this is what you want," she said on a low growl into his mouth.

He was silent once again, and Lily pulled back and looked into those midnight eyes. He tried to challenge her with all he had, and she challenged him right back. She took a small step, preparing to leave. "Tell me or not."

"You are the most infuriating woman I know."

Lily nodded. "That I am. Now tell me."

"You first."

Chapter 21

Lily woke before sunrise and reluctantly slipped her shoulders out from under Vin's arms. It wasn't as easy getting the lower half of her body from where it was wedged under his muscular thighs.

"Trying to sneak out again without waking me?" His voice was a low rumble, vibrating behind her back.

Lily turned and looked over her shoulder, catching the golden-hued image of him in faintly shadowed moonlight. "I was, but I see now that's not going to happen."

Vin reached up and pulled her body back down and in toward him. He snuggled her in close, her body fitting perfectly with his. He let out an exhale that let her know he was comforted, and she felt his lips kiss tenderly at the tip of her spine. "Stay, baby. I'll get up early with you. Take you into the city and have you home or wherever you need to be whenever you need to be."

Lily let out a sigh. She wasn't going anywhere, and she knew it. He'd had her at stay.

* * *

After the Carlyle party they'd come to a cool though, Lily told herself, modern and necessary, non-verbal don't-ask-don't-tell agreement where the status quo was kept and waters stayed calm. By day they each went about their business, never saying they were exclusive, never saying much of anything, but by night they'd find their way back into each other's arms and be lovers again. Lily told herself it was the perfect arrangement.

And in reality it was.

It was pretty much just like all her past relationships minus the fakery of the potential of something more. She was careful not to talk about a future past their next hookup, and he never spoke of anything that hinted at promises he couldn't keep. They were living fully and completely in the present, and Lily had reconciled in her mind that she was okay with that. She knew the day would come when some incident would happen—maybe big, maybe little—where he or most likely she would become intolerable and it would just be over. This way, when the time came, she told herself she'd be prepared.

It had happened to her plenty of times before, and there was no reason for her to think the same wouldn't happen with this relationship. If not some incident, then someone. There was always another someone. That was just the way of things, and the thought of "the someone" pulled her to the day's tasks. Coaxing her out of Vin's arms, where for the moment she was snuggled and warm. But she had meetings to set up with potential new clients. Work. Real work. And then there was meeting her father for lunch. That thought made her want to burrow deeper into the sanctuary of Vin's chest.

No longer able to dodge her father's calls, she'd finally talked to him and he'd pinned her down for lunch. Honestly, her time spent with Vin had infringed on all her time with her family. She'd missed two of the weekly dinners and even one shopping day with Mama Dee. But this thing with her father could no longer be avoided. She wasn't a child, and it was time to stop acting like one. She could hold on to the anger of his leaving them only for so long—no, that was a little too mature. Lily knew she could hold on to that anger forever. But holding it in while smiling on the outside just wasn't healthy.

Still, Lily had been hoping to at least meet him with the buffer of one or two of her sisters, but each of them claimed to be busy with one thing or another, so she was stuck. She didn't know why he was being so persistent. Just the thought of their sit down, and the possibility that he might bring his new fiancée, filled her with dread.

She let out a long sigh as the unwelcome thought fluttered through her mind while she was laying across Vin's chest. She really needed to get up and get her head on straight.

"What's bothering you?" he asked, the bass of his voice sending vibrations from him to her.

She shook her head and then was surprised to find a tear running from her eye and down her cheek. It escaped before she could catch it, and it hit Vin's bare skin. "Are you crying?"

She shook her head again and choked out as strong a "No" as she could.

Vin sat up, leaning over her. Then he flipped on

the bedside lamp and looked into her eyes. "Lily, what is going on with you?"

Lily turned away from him. "I said nothing. Okay? Now either be quiet or just let me go home."

Vin shook his head and rubbed at her hair. "God, you really are my little drama queen. You make it sound like I'm holding you here against your will."

"And you make it sound like you make this easy."

He held her tighter and kissed her shoulder. "Fine. You got me there, I don't. But I never promised I would."

"And neither did I."

Lily closed her eyes and went back to sleep. He was right. It was too early to be heading out, and she was tired.

Her father looked his usual handsome self, standing to greet her when she walked into the Gallery Diner. It had always been a favorite of his, along with most other folks in town, as it had been awarded "Best Coffee on the Island" ten years running.

Her dad was wearing his usual uniform of Levi's, a T-shirt, and baseball cap, which in her opinion was a little too young and casual for a man of his age. But it seemed to work for him; since leaving her mother, he has never been in want for a date. And always a much younger one than him at that. Maybe it was the jeans, or maybe it was the nice retirement plan that made him so appealing. Lily didn't know. She did know she was being cynical as all hell and felt a little bad for it.

Her dad leaned forward and hugged Lily immediately. "Hey, baby girl. I got started on my coffee already. I hope you don't mind."

Lily sat. "Of course not, Dad. Would you like to go
ahead and order? I have a lot on my plate this afternoon."

Her dad motioned for the waitress, Joan, to come
over. He and Lily had been coming to the Gallery for
many years, and Joan was a fixture with her tightly
wound curls and overly rouged cheeks. "Hey, Lily.
How are you?"

Lily fought to loosen her smile. "I'm fine, Joan,
how are you?"

Joan shrugged. "Can complain, but I won't. I'll be
a might happier when that son of mine gets out of my
basement and on with his life, but that is neither here
nor there. Can I get you a cup of coffee? You need a
menu, or do you know what you're having?" All of
this was said on one long exhale of breath, and Lily
marveled at how Joan did it.

"I'm glad to hear it. I'm ready to order. I'll just
have a coffee and a grilled cheese, thanks."

Joan nodded. "So, the usual?"

She turned to Lily's dad. "And you, Phil?"

Her dad smiled up at Joan. "Club sandwich, hold
the pickle. Oh, and a refill on my coffee, please."

Joan rolled her eyes playfully. "As if I don't know
you want a refill. I should hook you up intravenously,
the way you take it."

Lily raised her brow at her father as Joan walked
away. "Are you drinking too much coffee, Dad? You
know what too much does for your reflux."

Lily's father shook his head at her and then smiled
as he took a sip of his coffee. "And here I thought you
didn't care."

Now it was Lily who rolled her eyes and leaned
back as Joan brought her coffee. She sweetened it in

silence and added half-and-half. "What's this all about, Dad? Like I said, I have work to do."

"Like what?" her father countered. "Planning this wedding to yourself? The one I've yet to get an invitation to?"

"Damn Sophie."

Joan came over and dropped off their lunch.

"Don't blame Sophie. How do you think you can plan an event like that and not have it get back to me?" he asked. "Not to mention, why would you not want it to get back to me?"

Lily didn't know why. At first all she wanted was his approval. She felt sure she'd get it over her mother's, but after his own news and engagement she just wasn't sure anymore. She took a bite of her sandwich. It was delicious, as always. She took another bite before looking back at her father. He was smiling at her like he always did while he watched her eat, and in the moment it was infuriating.

"Tell me why it is you choose now to get married," Lily responded instead of answering her father's question.

Her father gave her a long look. "Why are you?"

Lily took a sip of her coffee and carefully measured her words. "Because I want people to know that I'm good. I'm okay and happy just how I am. That I don't need to be in a relationship to feel complete within myself."

Her father nodded as he took a bite of his club sandwich before looking up at her earnestly. "And by people I guess that excludes me."

Lily frowned. "It was not like that. Things," she paused. "Things have been moving fast and everything is not about you. Like I said, this is about me being fine with me."

He nodded. "Well, all right, baby girl. You're better than me. I have found that I'm the type that needs companionship, people around, family. I don't do well on my own."

Lily frowned. The cheese turned pasty in her mouth. "Funny, you had all that and threw it all away. It didn't seem so important to you back then."

Then it was her father's turn to frown. "What are you talking about, threw it away?"

Lily shook her head. "Can we just eat so I can go? I don't feel like doing this right now."

Her father nodded. "Yeah, I can see that."

They ate in silence for a while until Lily decided to speak up. "Why did you do it?"

"Do what, Lil?"

"Leave Mom. Leave us. All of us." Lily felt herself starting to lose control and fought to pull it back in. "We were doing fine. You told me that. You said we were fine. Then you left. How could you walk away from Mom like you did?"

Her father gave her a pained look, and Lily could tell he was struggling. Maybe she'd gone too far. She was the glue. The oldest. Everyone had a role to play in the family and she was the one that held it all together. Making waves was not Lily's roll. She shouldn't have gone there. "You know what, it's fine. It's none of my business, and of course you can come to my wedding. I'll send you an evite."

Her father looked at her then and for the first time his eyes hit her with what she could see was anger. It was anger mixed with a certain amount of pain. That part Lily knew well. "You know what, did you ever stop to think that she may have asked me to leave?"

The words stopped Lily cold and she couldn't help her shocked expression. She wanted to know more, but her father held his mouth firmly shut.

"Of course she didn't ask you to leave," Lily said, now dismissing his premise. "As soon as you were gone, in like a minute and a half you had another girlfriend, then another and another."

Her father shook his head. "Okay, you got me there. But that doesn't change the fact that she didn't want me anymore. That she was the one that said go. We fought a lot. She said I brought out the worst in her, and maybe I did. So she told me she didn't want me there, making her unhappy anymore. I loved your mother. Still do. More than anyone or anything. And the last thing I ever wanted to do was make her unhappy or have her not be her best self because of me."

Lily was stunned. She didn't know what to say or do about her father and his backward logic about love. Or maybe it wasn't so backward after all. Shit, how far was it from the craziness she had going on with Vin?

With a long sigh, she and her father finished eating their sandwiches in silence. Lily's phone pinged, and she looked down to see a message from Vin.

Dinner tonight? Breakfast tomorrow? V.

Lily smiled. She looked over at her father and didn't respond to Vin. Maybe after lunch she'd answer him. Right now she needed to just sit and be for a moment.

Chapter 22

By the time Lily got to Canela it was well past dinner, but she knew Vin would still whip her up something to eat. What she didn't expect was to find Manny serving a group of women still at the bar and Vin in deep conversation with skanky Lacy Colten, who, judging by her leanings, was more into his thighs than the drink in front of her. Lily hadn't seen Lacy since Sophie and Simon's wedding, but judging by how cozy she was, it was clear that she was no stranger to Canela.

Lily let out a sigh of capitulation as she took in the scene. Lacy leaning in, showing off her breasts and twisting her long weave. Vin being stoic but still engaged, giving off that tough, hard-to-get thing he does so well. Lily shook her head. And so it begins, Lily thought, as her eyes connected with Vin's and she gave him a nod before making her way up the back stairs to his apartment to undress and crawl into bed.

* * *

Lily woke to see Vin as he stood naked by the window, his body shadowed in the moonlight. For a moment she thought this time she must surely be dreaming, he was such an awe-inspiring vision. But then he turned to her and his eyes connected with hers, and it was as if her whole world opened up for a moment and she saw infinity.

He reached out his hand to her, and as if floating she rose from the bed and went to him under what felt like a spell. "What time is it?" she asked.

Vin pulled her to him and gently tugged the T-shirt she was wearing over her head. "It's late, but not too late."

The sliding doors to the deck were open and the night air was warm. The breeze hitting her now-exposed breasts caused her nipples to pebble immediately, or maybe it was the intense electric heat of his gaze. He reached out a hand, then brought his blunt fingertips from her collarbone down between her breasts to her navel, and then down to the V between her legs. Lily felt a shiver run through her body and liquid pool between her legs.

God, it was just one touch and already she was ready for him. Was that all it took? A touch, a look, and nothing more than that for him to take control? For a moment a shiver of fear went through her, and Vin leaned forward. "Don't do that, baby. Don't hold back. Let yourself go. You're safe with me."

She looked at him then. In that moment wanting more than anything to believe his words of safety. But was the heart ever really protected? Lily smiled what she knew was a weak smile. "I will if you will."

He gave her that grin then. The one that was both sweetness and sin. "Love, all you have to do is ask."

Then he took a nipple into his mouth as he lifted her around his waist to mount him. He leaned her against the sliding door glass. As the surf crashed in her ears he crashed against her soul.

Lily's cell rang early the next morning, and she picked it up groggily.

"Are we going shopping, or are you going to make this ditching your grandmother for a hot chef hunk a habit? Let me know now, because I only got so many good years left, and if there's a will to be amended I need to get on that."

Lily let out a deep breath. "Of course we're going shopping, and of course I didn't ditch you. I'll be there, my usual time."

"Great, just make sure you do."

All Lily got after that was the silence of the disconnected call leaving her shaking her head.

"Who was that?" Vin said from by her side.

"That was Mama Dee. Today is our shopping day. I'm taking her to look for her dress for the wedding this afternoon."

She thought she may have heard Vin give a grunt, but then he said, "Cool."

Lily snorted. "You think?"

Vin looked at her. "Yeah, I do."

Lily suddenly felt awful. He was right, and she loved her outings with Mama Dee. "You're right. It's just early and someone tired me out last night."

Vin brought his hands up from her waist to her breasts. "Well, it is pretty early, so we could technically close our eyes and pretend it's still night."

Lily smiled and turned fully into his embrace. "Yes, we could."

He leaned down and drew her nipple into his mouth, sending a thrilling shockwave throughout her body while she reached down for his hardness. He grinned. "You know, you sure don't seem like a woman about to get married."

Lily pushed herself up then and straddled him. "Well, sir, times are changing and everything ain't what it looks like."

Vin looked up at her with eyes full of admiration as he stroked her from her collarbone to her waist. "And thank God some things still are."

In a postsex haze Lily picked up Mama Dee promptly at eleven. She came out as if she was waiting right behind the door for her to show. Lily kissed the woman's cool cheek and smiled. Mama Dee looked cute in her purple shorts set with rosettes at the shirt neck. Like everyone's favorite grandmother. No one would suspect what a spitfire she was under all that sweetness.

"So where to today?" Lily asked. "Galleria or fancy mall?"

Mama Dee snorted. "You know in my day the Galleria was the fancy mall. You kids these days with your high standards." She let out a sigh, then she straightened herself in the seat. "Well, I've had my eye on a dress at Sears, so Galleria is fine by me. Though I don't know, I may just order one I saw at Penney's."

"No worries, we can hit both if you're up to it."

Mama Dee grinned. "Up to it? I've been looking forward to it."

Lily reached back for her purse in order to check her phone before they started off, but when she did it wasn't there. "Crap, I left my phone."

"At home? I guess you're lost for the day."

Lily felt the heat come to her cheeks. She really didn't want to have the conversation. But then again she really didn't want to go without her phone. "No, at Vin's. I was there earlier."

She didn't want to face her, but she could feel Mama Dee's eyes. "Were you, now? Well, his place is not far, I hear. I guess we should go and pick it up. I've been wanting to see that restaurant of his."

Lily snorted. "And how do you know where his place is?"

But Mama Dee was quick to snort back. "Oh please Lil' Miss. It will be a frozen day in hell when I don't know what's going on in this town, especially when it has something to do with one of my girls."

Sure, Lily knew she could put on airs about privacy and small towns but really it would just be her flapping her gums in the breeze for nothing. Mama Dee was old school and those women in the cartel knew things the NSA probably had trouble finding out.

Lily heard Mama Dee chuckle and shook her head. "What's so funny?"

"Oh, I was just thinking, isn't it perfect how things can work out sometimes?"

Lily raised a brow. "Yeah, I don't know if I'd call it that in this instance." But the annoyed tone in her voice only served to tickle Mama Dee that much more, and Lily knew she was in for it. The last thing she wanted was Vin and Mama Dee in the same room, but it seemed like that was going to be just what she got. She needed her phone, and that was all there was to it.

As they pulled up in front of Canela, Vin came outside, the loudness of the car announcing her arrival before she even came to a stop. He looked good in his usual tee and jeans. He seemed surprised but not too caught off guard by her pulling up with Mama Dee. He leaned over to the passenger seat to greet her. "It's good to see you again, Mrs. Perry."

"It's Henton, but please, child, call me Mama Dee."

He smiled. "Mama Dee, then." He looked over at Lily with a question in his eyes.

"I forgot my phone," she said. "I'll just run and get it. I'll just be a moment. Mama Dee, you wait here."

Mama Dee made a face then. "Where the hell do you think I'm going, I'd like to know?"

Lily watched as Mama Dee and Vin shared a conspiratorial look.

By the time Lily came back downstairs Mama Dee was in Canela's dining room looking around and surveying the place just as fine as can be. Lily looked at her with wide eyes. "I thought I told you to stay in the car, and don't we have some shopping to do?"

Mama Dee cut Lily with a sharp eye, then waved her hand. "I'm going to give you a pass on that one, since you're in front of your little friend here."

Lily felt her cheeks heat because, one, she'd been put in her place in front of Vin and, two, there was not a thing on him that could be described as little. She looked over at Vin, who was smiling at the "little" comment.

Mama Dee continued. "The stores ain't going nowhere, and I wanted to see where your ceremony is going to be." She turned to Vin. "Your place is lovely. You've done a fine job keeping it up from the previous owners, made some fine improvements, but have not strayed too far from the original. I like that. And I bet your food is a lot better than that jar sauce they used to try to pass off as homemade."

Lily opened her mouth in shock. "Mama Dee!"

"Oh, hush. I'm not saying nothing the whole town don't know." She took Vin's arm then and let him lead her to the patio. She looked out onto the beach, and Lily followed.

"Now, this is glorious." She turned to Lily. "Did I tell you how your grandfather and I used to love the beach?"

Lily shook her head.

"Well, he did. He loved the water and me. I daresay I won out over the water. He was in the navy, you know, and looked so fine in his suit. Navy, as well as swim. Not that I was a slacker back then, mind you." Lily thought about Vin and how fine he looked as he surfed.

Mama Dee gave the shoreline a long look and smiled. "Yes we used to have a fine time." She seemed to laugh to herself. Lily and Vin just looked at her. "We ran two temperatures, he and I—hot and hotter. There was no tepid for us. But I don't know if you young ones know about that." She waved her hand and turned to go back inside. "With you all it's PC this and don't offend that. No, that wasn't us. We leaped and looked afterward. You have only one life. Might as well live it while you can."

"Can I offer you something to eat or drink, Mama Dee?" Vin asked as they made their way back inside.

Mama Dee shook her head. "Not now, sweetheart,

but soon. I gather I'll get to try your skills at Lily's shindig if not before."

Vin looked to Lily and then nodded.

Over by the bar Mama Dee paused and looked at the photo of Vin's mother. "Is that your mother?"

Vin coughed and then nodded. "Was."

"Mama Dee, I think we'd better go if we're going to have time to shop."

But Mama Dee just stared at Vin. She reached up and touched his face. She smiled before getting solemn. "I knew that I knew those eyes of yours. They are so like hers. I'm so sorry for your loss, darling. She was a beautiful spirit. And so proud of you." Mama Dee smiled to herself, then looked back at Vin. "I loved your little stand on the beach. Your mama could cook. It's no wonder you got a gift," she said. "I'm sure she continues to surround you with her love and that beautiful spirit I remember so well."

Lily saw Vin's jaw tighten, and he swallowed hard.

Uh oh, Mama Dee was in off-limits territory, but he didn't try to brush her off and he wasn't abrasive or stiff. "Thank you for that," was all he said.

Lily came over and took Mama Dee's arm. "Come on, I really think we need to go."

Mama Dee laughed. "All right, but I don't want you complaining when I try on every dress in the store."

They got in the car, and Lily couldn't get away from Canela and to the mall quick enough.

"So what's the rush?" Mama Dee asked from the passenger seat.

"The rush was getting you out of there. Don't think I don't know what you were trying to do with all that talk about you and Granddaddy as if you were the most glorious love story ever."

"And who says we weren't, little Miss Know-It-All?"

Lily shook her head and let out a low breath.

Mama Dee did the same before she spoke. "Girl, you know you're my favorite, but that doesn't mean you don't have faults to spare. You need to get up and get out of your own head every once in a while. If not, one day that wall you got built up is going to topple right down on you and bury you."

"Geez, Mama Dee. And they say *I'm* dramatic."

"It's not dramatics if it's the truth. You need to look beyond yourself sometimes to see. Love and pain is all around. You don't have the monopoly on either. Besides, you've got a good one there. Not to mention he can cook. I'd think carefully if I were you before casually tossing that man aside."

Lily just shook her head and kept driving. This was going to be quite the long day.

Chapter 23

Lily didn't know why she'd agreed that this bachelorette party was a good idea. Not that a night out with gorgeous men is ever a bad idea. But when you added her sisters, Bobbi, her mom, and Mama Dee, who was the mad architect of all of this, well, things got a little dicey.

The wedding was two weeks away. Lily was annoyed that she was more nervous than she really should have been. Was this type of anxiety what all brides went through? If so, then she really should work on her Bride-Side Manner, so to speak, because she had constant twinges and pains in her stomach that alternated between simple butterflies over things going right to out-and-out banging boulders over her making a complete fool of herself.

She and Vin's truce over the wedding was holding steady, though try as hard as he did to keep thing cool and easy, she could tell it still wasn't sitting right with him, and though she refused to regret these months with him, she was coming to regret her part in pulling him in on something he clearly didn't want to be a part of. It was Canela's day to be closed, and she and Vin had plans to get out on the water early and then lounge in bed for most of the afternoon until it was time for her to head to her mom's to meet her friends and family for the start of the party. The early surfing didn't happen, but they were well into the bed portion when Lily's phone rang. She ignored it, but when a text ping came, she looked away from Vin, who was cleverly doing some magic with his tongue, and over to the nightstand.

"I think I should check that."

He looked up at her and raised a brow. "Have at it. I'll be down here. Don't mind me."

Lily laughed at his silliness as he made a show of burying his head back under the covers. She was enjoying the moment and never wanting it to end.

She reached for the phone while he tickled at her side. Wiggling she checked the message and jumped up. "Shit!"

Vin's head popped from under the covers. "It's my dress. They screwed up at the shop and messed up the order. They need me to come in right away and get measured again if I'm going to get my dress in time. With two weeks to go, how in the hell am I going to get my dress in time?" Lily's heart began to pound in triple-time. Dammit. That dress was the one wedding day detail she'd felt absolutely certain about. She blinked quickly as tears threatened.

Vin gave her a pat on the side of her naked thigh. "Come on."

She looked at him wide eyed. "What are you talking about? Didn't you just hear me? I can't go anywhere with you. I have to go check on this dress thing."

He nodded. "I know, love, so let's go. I'm taking you. You are getting yourself all worked up, and frankly you're exhausted. You don't look like you can walk down the stairs let alone drive yourself to the shop. Come on, let me help you get dressed and I'll take you over."

Lily swallowed and blinked faster.

Vin shook his head and gave her a stern look. "Don't you dare, Lil. I'm not having any crying out of you. This is supposed to be a happy time. And besides"—he leaned over, kissed her softly, and ran his hand up between her thighs before pulling back. "I was just about to be well on my way to heaven. If anyone should be crying, it ought to be me."

Lily dressed quickly and ran downstairs to find Vin already waiting. She fully expected him to get in the delivery van, but he went straight to his bike. "Are you nuts?"

He tilted his head at her. "Come on. You want to get there and find parking? You know how tight it can get on that shopping strip during the summer season. With my bike, I can ease right in. The van would just have to circle."

Lily knew his logic was semi-solid at best, and she also knew he'd been dying to get her on the back of his bike. This totally played into his hand. She let out a long sigh as he handed her a helmet. "You got me this time, V."

He grinned. "Just get on and hold on, babe. That's right, I got you."

The ride was more thrilling than Lily imagined,

and she couldn't wait to do it again. The bike, big and dangerous vibrating between her legs, and Vin in front of her gave her double the pleasure. Large and solid, totally and completely relaxed and in command. She liked that about him. No, loved that about him. Though they had their quick, volatile dustups, when he was in control, he was totally in control. He didn't waver, and she didn't feel any fear with him at the helm. She trusted him. The thought sobered her as she leaned on him more and rested her chest against his back.

They made it to the shop in good time and, as Vin had anticipated, there weren't any spots. Even with the bike he had to circle and wait for one to open. Lily hopped off and went in to get started with her refitting.

"I'm so sorry about this, Lily," Miss Benning, the shop owner, said as Lily stood on the dais in the middle of the salon. Her head seamstress, a much older woman than Miss Benning, named Valencia, was stooped down at Lily's feet pinning from her hip down to the dress's delicate train. Lily was worried she'd have trouble getting back up and didn't for the life of her know how her knotted fingers could do such detailed work but they did.

Lily loved the dress just as much as when she first tried it on, even if it was two sizes too big. The low back, the beautiful bow at her neck, the shapely draping—if she had dreamed up a dress, this would be it. "Are you sure you can get it done in time?" she said, her voice quivering with worry.

Valencia looked up at her and gave a reassuring smile. Her aged eyes full of promise. "Don't worry, don't worry. It will be done, I guarantee it."

Lily smiled back believing in the woman and her experience.

"You'll be a beautiful bride. Your fiancé will be the happiest of husbands."

Lily let out a low, weary breath. She didn't have it in her to do any correcting. Instead, she looked straight ahead, and when she did her eyes met Vin's in the mirror. She didn't even hear him come into the shop, as focused as she was on the fitting. His expression was completely and utterly blank as he took her in. She watched him swallow and saw his jaw twitch. "Yes, you're right. She will be a beautiful bride. Whomever she's marrying is very lucky."

They didn't talk about the shop beyond Vin telling her when she met him outside that her dress was beautiful. They tried to pick up where they left off and he took her for a ride down the coastline, and they shared a basket of seafood on the pier before going back to his place and making love. He was distant, though, and in reality so was she. She felt as if she were floating above, then watching two people going through the motions of what a real relationship should look like.

Lily knew there was something left in that shop. Left in their expressions in the mirror. Lily didn't know if they had already said good-bye, but she was starting to feel like they had.

Vin stood barefoot in the sand with Dex at his side and looked out into the dark of the ocean, hoping to find peace in the turbulent waters.

It took all Vin had in him, saying good-bye to Lily and watching her leave to go to her bachelorette party.

The afternoon weighed heavy on his chest, and as they went through the motions of smiling and laughing he felt like someone completely outside himself looking back in. Who was this man riding around with, a beautiful woman at his back and suddenly the ridiculous hope of possibilities in his heart? Just thinking about it made him want to back away. Put up a shield and protect himself. That or kick the poor idiot off the bike and knock some sense into his head.

Vin told himself to think rationally. Tried to channel what his mother would want for him and just open up and let go, enjoy his time with Lily. But for all his trying he couldn't do it. Something in him didn't feel worthy enough of a treasure such as her. Not that she was all in with offering. It was as if she knew there was something hidden within him that would inevitably screw it up. Maybe that was why she held herself at arm's length.

He wasn't made like his friends. Not like Aidan, who for all his talk of not settling down had seamlessly fallen in with Eva. Or Simon, who fit with Sophie as if they were born for each other. But what did he know? All he'd known was that he'd had a father who ran out on his mother at the first opportunity, and according to his history he was pretty much like him.

Vin thought once again of the first day he'd seen Lily. Out with Simon and Sophie. How it was so soon after his mother had died, and how for the very first time in he didn't know how many months he smiled, seeing her smile, and it was real. Not something his mind told him to do because it was the right thing and society expected it or they'd back away from him permanently. And how when she kissed him that time under the dock, and made him feel, made him forget the pain he'd shrouded himself in that was so strong it was now a part of his persona. Well, he didn't know how to react. Those moments of forgetfulness left him open and vulnerable. Two things he'd never wanted to be ever again. So he just ran. Not in the literal sense, but in the metaphorical sense for sure. He couldn't call her. Couldn't open up to her and feel. Back then he didn't want to be happy, and honestly even now he wasn't really sure he knew how to be.

Frustrated, Vin kicked at the sand and Dex looked up at him with a look that said, "What's your problem?" Vin shrugged at the dog and pulled off his shirt, peeled off his pants, and got down to his boxers. He was happy to feel the warm night breeze against his body. Walking forward he stepped into the foamy water while Dex hung back and just looked. The coolness of the water was a welcome pinprick against his skin.

Vin closed his eyes for a moment and remembered Lily's tense expression as she first tried to balance herself on the board, and then her smile when she realized he had her and that he would not let her fall. Vin frowned and ducked his head under the water. He came up again and opened his eyes to the moonlight and the vision of her in that white wedding dress. So beautiful. So full of promise. The vision a mockery of what they'd both told themselves they didn't want. But here they were playing at the motions of it.

He wondered if they were both fools running from pasts that they never had any control over or smart

pragmatists avoiding a future that would only lead to
the pain of history repeating itself. He never wanted
to be the man his father was. The man that Lily already pegged him and all men to be. He couldn't
bring himself to make promises he knew in his heart
he may not keep. Vin laughed to himself. The echo of
it in his chest was almost painful. Hell, maybe she
was right all along. Better to get out now, before
either of them went so deep they couldn't get back
to shore.

By the time Lily got to her mother's, she wasn't
exactly in a bachelorette, male stripper mood, but
since faking it was the call for the day, Lily put on the
bridal sash given to her by Bobbi and the tiara given
to her by her sisters and proceeded to get her party on
as they headed out to Talia's Temptation, The island's
premier ladies lounge. And by premier we're talking
nowhere near close to Magic Mike, but it was good
enough to maybe be called Fake It 'Till You Make It
Harry.

Lily could only laugh at the picture they must
make, a group of women ranging in age from twenty-
one to well over seventy piling into the slightly seedy
club. But it wasn't as bad as Lily anticipated. The
guys were all friendly and in no way overly intrusive.
There were no unwanted penises in the face, though
there was an abundance of oil and glitter, and Lily
saw some pole acrobatics that were truly impressive
and had her rethinking her ab game.

The highlight of the night, though, was Mama Dee.
No one was having more fun than she was. Though
there was a strict no-touching policy at Talia's, Mama

Dee came prepared to make it rain, and she was fully getting her money's worth out of all the guys. Lily feared she'd be covered in gold glitter for weeks.

When Lily was pulled up on stage in a traditional überembarrassing bridal lap dance, she wasn't surprised to hear Mama Dee whooping it up the loudest. She *was* surprised, though, to hear her mother's cheers above the crowd. It got her thinking of her father and their talk and what he'd said about her being her best self. She wondered more and more at the truth of that. Maybe it was her mother's choice. Maybe she was living the life she wanted to live.

Lily made it back to her table and downed her drink before giving her mother a tight hug. "Thank you," she said.

Her mother pulled back and looked her in the eyes. "For what?"

Lily smiled. "For everything."

Lily's mom shook her head and laughed. "Oh, honey, I think you're drunk."

Lily sniffled and blinked back tears. "I may be." There was a loud whoop, and they looked over to see Mama Dee doing the bump with a guy in a gold thong. "I think we all are."

Leaving the party, they tumbled out of the club like weary warriors who came, saw, and conquered the strippers of Long Island. Lily threw her hands in the air before getting into their rented van for the night. "Victorious!" she yelled as she looked across the street at the other strip bars that littered that part of town. But the words died in her mouth as she saw Vin stumble out of the club arm in arm with Lacy Colten.

The pain in her chest was real as her heart sank and Sophie walked up beside her. "What the hell is he doing with freaking Lacy Colten?"

Lily swallowed. The sheen and sparkle of their night at the strip club faded to ash. She turned to her sister. "Living his life just like I'm living mine."

Chapter 24

Lily was awakened along with the rest of the house to the sound of her mother screaming into the phone in panic. They had been home from the club only a few hours. What was her mother going on about? And why did she sound so desperate? It had to be a dream. But no, it wasn't a dream. No, this was Lily's worst nightmare.

It was Mama Dee. She was sitting in the kitchen in the same spot where she'd sat after coming home from the club, when she said she'd just needed a cool drink after all those hot boys. But now there she was slumped over and barely responsive. The paramedics arrived quickly, and Lily's mother accompanied Mama Dee to the hospital in the ambulance. Lily and Violet couldn't fit, and Lily was so on edge that she didn't think she could drive, so Lily was more than happy when Violet offered to get behind the wheel. What was wrong with her? She was the oldest. She was supposed to be the strong one.

True to form for her family, by the time Mama Dee was admitted everyone was there. Sisters with new husbands, and even her father sans the fiancée. They all paced, cried, and huddled together until the sun rose and the doctor came out to give Mama Dee's condition. There were thanks and praises to God when the doc told them that Mama Dee had, thankfully, a mild arrhythmia, which Lily knew more than likely was due to the wild time that night. Her blood pressure had fallen alarmingly low as well, so due to her prior conditions, they wanted to keep her for a few days for observation.

Despite rules of only two visitors at a time, the doctor kindly let all the sisters file in along with Lily's mom and dad for a few minutes just to see her. The word was she was asking for them all and being "quite persuasive." Lily had never been happier to hear such a report on Mama Dee's stubbornness. The brothers-in-laws opted to stand outside the little viewing window and send their love that way.

But as soon as Lily saw her grandmother in a hospital bed, her larger-than-life spirit looking so frail and fragile, with an IV in her arm and tubes in her nose, Lily choked back sobs just like the rest of her sisters and her mother. She looked over to her father and saw him wiping a tear too. But true to form, Mama Dee looked at them all and shook her head. "Lord, if I haven't died I'd better have, otherwise there are some asses to be kicked. Now, we had too good a time tonight, girls, don't go and let this little thing ruin it. And I'll not have no tears out of you all. I don't care even if you were at my funeral."

Her saying that only caused Lily's mother to sniffle harder. "Renée, you just cut that blubbering right out. Your sister and that husband of hers are going to be here any moment. I'm sure they're not here 'cause she's still squeezing into a girdle. I'm going to need you to be strong to deal with her."

"Yes, Mama." Lily's mom sniffled, more dutifully than Lily had ever heard her.

Mama Dee turned to Lily. "I'm going to need you to buck up and act like the woman I know you are. Using me as an example for these silly sisters of yours."

"Hey!" Sophie protested loudly, not caring that Mama Dee was in the hospital and maybe she should be a little quiet.

Mama Dee winked, knowing she had broken the mood. "Oh, hush, girl. Go on out there and get some coffee for your husband. You all do that. Tell my boys I love them and I'm fine. I need to talk with Lily a minute."

As everyone reluctantly filed out, Mama Dee reached for Lily's hand. Her touch was cool and had Lily pulling her blanket farther up her chest. She shooed it off. "It's all right, honey," she said to Lily. "I want you to know everything is all right. I want you to stop doing what you're doing right now with all that blame and let it go."

Lily wiped at the tears that were falling freely from her eyes. "But if we didn't have that silly party, if I didn't start with this wedding nonsense, then none of this would have happened.".

Mama Dee laughed. The labor of it caused her to cough. Lily frowned. "What are you laughing about, lady? This is serious. I'm serious."

Mama Dee shook her head. "That right there is what I'm laughing about. You are the most dramatic person I know."

Lily stilled. The words that Vin had said so often

echoed out of Mama Dee's mouth were sobering. "You think you can control the world. As if the sun waits for you to wake before it rises. Honey, you've got to lighten up. The quicker you realize that this all is not your show and there are other forces in control everywhere, the easier your path will be. You can only control you, and hell, sometimes you can't even control that. Humph. I've been in and out of love enough to know that's the truth."

Lily swallowed, not wanting to meet her grandmother's all-seeing eyes. "Do you love him?"

The four words were so heavy that Lily felt the need to sit on the edge of the bed. Finally she answered, "I don't want to love him."

Mama Dee nodded, looking to the window that separated her room from the hospital hallway. "Funny, by the pained look on that boy's face right now, I get the feeling he don't want to love you either."

Lily turned to look, and there was Vin, standing outside the room. He was with the rest of her family but slightly apart, and he was watching her and Mama Dee with an expression of so much longing and pain that Lily thought it would break her heart.

She turned back to Mama Dee. "I—I don't know what he's doing here."

Mama Dee nodded. "I think you do." Then she let out a breath. "You know, I remember him from a few years ago. His mama too. I knew them vaguely from their food stand, but more importantly back when I was still volunteering here, he brought his mother in for some test that, according to her, would be routine. Well, one thing led to another and there was a quick surgery and next thing you know, that poor woman was gone just like that. It couldn't have been more than a day and it was all over." Mama Dee sighed. "I'll never forget the sight of that big man as he collapsed to the floor in a heap. A man turned back into a child. He was just about inconsolable at the loss of his mother. One of the saddest things I've ever seen and I've seen a lot of love and a lot of loss in my life. I tried to comfort him, me along with the chaplain and some other volunteers. I don't think he saw or remembers any of us." Mama Dee looked back at Vin and gave him a smile and a wave. "But I sure remember him. That one there. He loves hard. And it's taking all he has to be standing in the spot he's standing in right now."

Vin gave Mama Dee a small wave back. The gesture was so sweet that Lily thought her heart might explode from her chest. It was then that the enormity and the reasoning behind his earlier outburst and refusal to go to a hospital came to her.

"Yep, it must have taken everything for him to come here today," Mama Dee said. "And I know he didn't do it for me. He did it for you. Now go now, chile'. I got some resting up to do so that I can dance at your wedding." She let out a sigh. "I also got to get my strength up for that dang Ruby and Gene. If they don't work a nerve."

Chapter 25

Poor Tori was running around like a chicken with two heads after they'd been cut off. "Hey, it's okay," Lily told her, stilling her with a hand on her forearm. "You've done all you can and the day will be wonderful. Now go, and I'll meet you at Canela."

Lily looked at herself in the full-length mirror one last time and prayed she wasn't lying. She had no idea how the day would go. Thankfully Mama Dee, true to her fighting spirit, was well on the mend and could attend the ceremony. Lily had offered to cancel the whole thing, and part of her was maybe looking for the out, but Mama Dee said absolutely no way. She was looking forward to seeing her do this amazing thing and nothing would stop it from happening. She was currently going around town telling the story that St. Peter had called her but she said, Sorry you gonna have to call back. I've got a granddaughter to see married.

Lily had to laugh over how Mama Dee had taken her wedding-for-one commitment and used it to turn herself into a local legend. It was perfectly Mama Dee.

She was catching a breather from her family. Her sisters had just filed out. They all looked beautiful and went with her suggestion of different dresses, but instead of ivory they decided at the last minute to go for different shades of purple, Mama Dee's favorite color, and Lily couldn't be happier. The control freak in her would usually lose it over a last-minute change like that, but that was not what this day was about. This day was about love and acceptance, and for the first time she was starting to truly accept that. Her mother came in and gave her a warm smile. "You are so beautiful. This is a day I didn't think I'd ever see."

Lily raised a brow. "What, Mom, this ceremony or me looking beautiful?"

Her mother shook her head. "Don't start. You know exactly what I'm talking about. Now, here." She handed Lily a box.

"What is this?"

"Just open it and see."

Inside was a thin gold band twisted into countless infinity symbols. Lily picked up the band. It was lovely in its delicateness and symbolism. "Thank you, Mom. It's beautiful and probably more than I deserve."

"Well, I didn't know if you'd gone and gotten a ring, so I thought that maybe this could be your something old and take two places. And as for more than you deserve"—she shook her head and Lily saw tears threaten the tips of her lashes—"this is nothing. You deserve every good thing in the world. It's all I've ever wanted and ever want for you."

Lily blinked quickly. She could take a lot, but she

couldn't take her tough mother getting mushy and crying over her. And worse yet, being accepting of her wishes and dreams. It was almost too much.

Lily looked down at the pretty band. She hadn't gotten a ring. She'd talked to her friend, Fran, who was officiating the ceremony, and had decided to skip over the ring part mainly because she just didn't have it in her to shop for it alone, as wimpy as that sounded. Lily looked to her mother. "How old is it?"

Her mom smiled. "Older than you. I got it for myself as a birthday present back when I was eighteen. Bought with money from my summer job, and I was excited to wear it as I headed off to college." Lily looked at her mother confused. She didn't go to college. Lily hadn't known that she'd made it in or wanted to. Her mother never shared that. Her mother had her when she was nineteen.

"Oh, Ma." Lily gave her a hug. "I'm so proud of you. Of all of you girls. Live and live in your dream. I don't know if you can have it all, but promise me you won't give up on trying."

"I won't," Lily said as the image of Vin jumped into her mind.

He was the first person she saw when she slipped into the back loading area of Canela. They paused at the same time and stared at each other. It was as if the world stopped for a moment just so they could have this time to take each other in.

Vin looked fantastic in his dark suit, white shirt, and black tie. Breathtaking really. He was freshly shaven and his beard was trimmed, but she could see by the slight shadows under his eyes that he'd not gotten a lot of sleep. They'd talked for a few minutes the night he'd come to the hospital. She'd thanked him and he'd explained that he'd heard about Mama Dee, that he knew how much she meant to Lily, and that he was worried.

But it went no further than that. Lily hadn't been ready to face all Mama Dee said, she was also still curious over the whole Lacy thing. Seeing him in his suit, though, with tired eyes, caused all her feelings to bubble up. She let out a deep breath before she greeted him.

"Hi," she whispered.

"Hi," he answered, his voice like rough bark.

He looked at her then, long and hard. Taking in her dress and the white flowers in her pinned-up hair. He cleared his throat. "You look even more beautiful than I thought you would."

Lilly frowned. "Thought?"

"Not thought, well, imagined. Come on, Lil, you know what I mean."

She smiled. Putting him on the defensive wasn't fair, but it strangely calmed her nerves. "Yeah, I do. And thanks."

A car drove past where they were standing, and Vin frowned. "Come on, you should go to my office until the ceremony. People shouldn't see the bride before the wedding."

Lily watched as Vin peeked around the corner and slipped her off to his office behind the kitchen. On the way she saw Manny, who gave her a smile and a wave. When she got to the small office she turned to Vin. "Thank you for everything. I know today will go well and it's all because of you and your place."

He shook his head. "You don't have to thank me."

She stared at him, seeing the weariness in his eyes as he struggled to meet hers. Lily could hear laughter and lots of talking as folks started to fill the outside patio set for the ceremony. She swallowed. This was not the time to say what she wanted to say. To ask what she wanted to ask. There were guests. She had to get through her ceremony.

Vin started to turn to walk away. "Well, I'd better go. I'm sure everything will be starting soon."

She nodded as he started to leave, but then her mouth just came open. "Did you sleep with Lacy Colten?"

Vin turned slowly, and the look he gave her almost burned her from her toes on up. "Are you freaking serious with this?"

Lily instantly got mad. "Why would I not be? I saw the way she hung on you, and I saw you leaving a club with her the night of my party."

Vin raked his hand over his head in frustration. "I swear, you drive me insane. First, that you'd think I'd be one to sleep with someone like Lacy. No. And second, that you'd think I'd go from your bed straight to another's. Don't you get how I feel about you at all? Can't you tell when someone is in love with you?"

Lily stepped back as if punched, and in that instant he might as well have knocked her out cold. *Love?* What the hell. "You're telling me now that you love me right when I'm about to walk down the aisle?"

He looked at her dumbfounded. "What the hell difference does it make? It's not *The Graduate*. It's not like I'm stopping you from marrying the wrong guy. I can't keep you from yourself, though God I wish at times I could."

Vin threw up his hands and shook his head just as Tori and Bobbi came around the corner. "It's time," Tori said, but her words died out when she saw Vin.

"Thank goodness," he said, riled up. "Get this woman hitched, why don't you." He started to walk away leaving the three women looking dumbstruck, but then he turned back and came straight for Lily. "But first I'd like to kiss the bride."

She looked at him hard. "Vin. Don't. My makeup."

He strode right up to her and pulled her to him, capturing her mouth and kissing her with all he had before pulling back and straightening his tie. "Fuck your makeup." He nodded to Bobbi and Tori. "Ladies. I'll see you out there."

Chapter 26

Vin couldn't deny that Lily was a vision as he looked at her from where he stood off to the side of the patio. He knew that he had screwed up royally with his declaration of love, but there it was. He loved her, and if this would be the day he lost her because he'd taken a chance and said so, then so be it. At least he went all in. His mother would be proud. Now only if he could slow his heartrate down and get back to some form of normalcy, a hint of his old cool, then just maybe he could find a way to get through this day.

But trying was futile since in that moment Vin felt like he was standing outside of himself. A spectator looking in on his own life.

He let out a breath. One then another. He loved her. He said it to himself once again and astonishingly, this time, his heartrate did seem to slow down as the declaration brought with it a sense of warmth and calm. Like whatever the outcome he'd somehow make it through and it would be all right. He watched

the scene of all the guests seated on the patio on top
of a rented wooden extension that led out to the sand
on the beach. Lily had thought of everything, and that
included the guests not getting beach sand in their
shoes but still having the effect of a beach wedding.
There were ghost chairs flanking each side of a white
runner that led to a beautiful rose-covered archway
that had the Atlantic as its backdrop.

Somehow in that moment Vin knew that she was
his future as she appeared with her father at the
back of the patio to the sound of lyrical harp music.
Her dad kissed her hand, spun her like an angel, and
then passed her off to her sister Sylvie as the music
changed to a more up-tempo beat and the guests
cheered as the sisters danced to a song about the
power of women and the bond of sisterly love. Next
came Sophie and Audrey, who showered her with
rose petals as she joined in on the dance. Peggy joined
them next and then Violet as they made their way
down the aisle with the crowd cheering and dancing
along all the way with the beautiful Perry sisters.

Vin was shocked to find himself swaying along,
for the life of him not able to put a cynical spin on
the beautiful display of love before him with Lily
at the center. The music died down as the officiant
asked, "Who gives this woman away?" and up
popped Mama Dee from her seat with a loud "I do."
Everyone clapped. All were happy to see her grandmother fully recovered from her hospital scare.
Mama Dee then turned to the crowd. "We all do.
Freely and with love."

Lily came forward and kissed her grandmother
lovingly. Tears slid down all their cheeks as she

climbed the few steps to the raised dais flanked by her mother, grandmother, and her sisters before the assembled crowd and the officiant began.

"Dear friends, we are gathered here today in celebration of the commitment of the life and love of Lilian Annalise Perry."

Everyone cheered with whoops and hollers, and Vin found himself raising his fist. This was Lil's day. There was no hate from the people here. Only love for what she was doing.

The officiant spoke again. "Lily has now prepared vows she'd like to share with all of you."

Lily turned then, and Vin could see that despite the outpouring of love, she was slightly nervous. She nibbled lightly at her bottom lip, and for a moment he thought he saw her hand quiver. But in true Lily fashion she steeled her back and let out a breath, and she smiled. Big and wide. Brave and strong.

Vin pushed back against his base instinct. More than anything he wanted to sweep her up in his arms and cover her with protection she didn't need and didn't ask for. She turned and looked at the gathered crowd. Her gaze locked with his for a moment, and she gave him a reassuring smile that warmed his heart. Her gaze then moved from his to the rest of the crowd of friends and family, and she smiled wider. "Thank you all so much for being here today. You have truly made this day extraspecial." She looked at each of her sisters and then, with a nod, began.

"Today I'm here to declare that I vow to love and cherish myself always. To be a friend to myself, to be patient, to be kind, and to most of all be forgiving, because even when I am weak, I am still more than enough. I vow not to be judgmental"—with that Sophie smirked and Lily laughed before continuing—"or"—and she looked at Mama Dee—"too cautious." Lily smiled at her mother, who to her surprise pulled out a thin gold band with one perfect pearl as its ornament and slid it on Lily's right hand finger and kissed her cheek. "To live my life to the fullest," she said while choking back tears of joy. Lily turned back to the crowd, and her eyes hit Vin's once again. "To love fearlessly until I can't love anymore. Because above all I am worth it."

Once again up went a cheer.

Lily beamed then and turned back to the officiate. "And, in this wonderfully nontraditional commitment ceremony, I now pronounce you Lily Perry, as you always were and always will be, perfect just as you are. And all you ever need or needed to be. Amen."

Lily turned and whispered something to the officiant, who frowned but then smiled as the crowd looked on expectantly.

Vin frowned too and his heartbeat sped up as he wondered what else Lily had up her sleeve now. This ceremony was being held on his property, but he half expected surprise doves to come out of nowhere. Fireworks, maybe?

"Okay," the officiant said to Lily, "this is your show." She then addressed the assembled guests. "Lily would like to know if anybody would like to kiss the bride."

Suddenly no less than four men in the group raised their hands all at once in a jumbled chorus of "I do," "Pick me," and "I've got next."

Lily laughed, looking past them all and straight

at Vin, and gave him a wink. Then she turned to the officiant. "I think I know someone who's got that covered."

Lifting the hem of her dress, she walked back down the aisle and over to Vin. When she got close to him she dropped her hem and tripped, once again her shoe getting caught just like it had at Sophie's wedding, and she practically fell right into his waiting arms.

Vin laughed. "Why do I feel like we've been here before?"

Lily shook her head and looked up at him with a wide grin. "Because we have." She pushed a wayward hair back behind her ear and licked at her top lip. That damned tantalizing tongue of hers was about to send this perfect family function up a rating. "So you going to congratulate the bride or what?" she asked.

Vin leaned in close as he put his arms around her and pulled her in tight.

"Tell me this is what you want," he said.

Lily looked him in the eyes. "You are exactly what I want," she said. "Now and always."

Vin grinned, his heart damn near bursting with joy. "Then, my love, I'm going to congratulate you so good that you're not going to remember your name."

Lily looked at him with a spark in her eye. "Oh, I'll remember it all right. Let's see how well you remember yours."

As they kissed, this time it was to the cheer of friends and family and, for the first time that Lily or Vin could think of, it was without fear of the future or thoughts of the past, only hope for all the joy that was to come.

Vin's laugh came free and unbidden when he finally came up for air and looked once again into her eyes. "Miss Perry, you can call me whatever you want. Vin, Vincent, Caro, hey you, or even Mr. Perry, if I'm lucky. Just as long as you never stop calling me, I'll forever be a happy man."

COLLECT THEM ALL
The Unconventional Bride Series

Insert Groom Here

Eva Ward has won a lavish wedding on the nation's
hottest morning show and can't wait to kick off
her happily-ever-after in style. Too bad her fiancé
backs out on the air. The only way Eva can save
face and keep her perfect nuptial plans on track is
to star in a new "find-a-groom" reality segment.
But finding Mr. Right in eight weeks means
ignoring Aidan Walker—her handsome new
producer—and getting their instant,
exasperating attraction out of her system . . .

ON SALE NOW

The Betting Vow

Leila Darling's got the talent to be a serious actress,
but the industry sees her as a high-maintenance,
impulsive party girl with a reputation for leaving
men in the dust. TV producer Carter Bain's had
his eye on Leila for years, so when a bet gives
him a chance to get close to her, he accepts.
With the goal of getting Leila the image
makeover she needs and Carter the star he desires,
the game in on. But as their "I do" turns up all
kinds of heat, Leila and Carter find they have
more in common than they ever imagined . . .

COMING SOON

Enjoy the following excerpt from *Insert Groom Here* ...

Chapter 1

"I can't marry you."

Eva Ward knew words were being murmured over her shoulder, but for the life of her she couldn't quite make them out. The red light above the camera transfixed her, and Kevin's voice sounded like it came from somewhere far away, as if from down a long corridor. To top things off, she was fighting a chill. The temperature in the blasted television studio had to be set at fifty degrees at the highest. Eva thought about the frigid air a moment and hoped the cold didn't show on her face—or, lord help her—anywhere else on her anatomy. That would be all she needed, for her nipples to make a surprise appearance on national morning television. Eva pushed back a frown as she brought her thoughts back to that blasted red light and Kevin. *Okay, focus time. What is he going on about?*

"I can't marry you," Kevin repeated, and Eva blinked.

Wait. What?

"Wait. What?!" Jim Bauer, *The Morning Show*'s

co-host, took Eva's confused thoughts and echoed them out loud, punctuated with his usual everyman laugh. But this was a bad time to laugh. In fact, it was the absolute worst time to laugh. "I don't think we heard you correctly, Kevin. It sounded for a moment like you were calling off the wedding."

Eva fought to keep her smile in place as Kevin turned from her to Jim. "That's right, Jim. I am."

She blinked again as the words really begin to sink in. *He is calling off what?* Anger bubbled up, heating Eva more quickly than could possibly be safe. She caught another glimpse of the red light and forced herself to push it back down. *Hold on there. This is not the time to go off the rails,* Eva told herself. She could do this. She'd practiced being on live TV, and she'd been put on the spot plenty of times. She was trained for these moments. Media relations was her job, for chrissake.

Eva pulled her attention away from the maddening red light that reminded her millions of people were watching this debacle over their morning coffee and toast. Instead, she plastered on a well-trained smile and focused on what her fiancé, Kevin, and the talk show's co-hosts were now saying. But try as she might, she couldn't wrap her head around the words as they trickled toward her in dribs and drabs.

Something about being "confused," Kevin said. "Just not the right time," he went on. And wait, did she really hear the words "moving too fast"?

Hold up, this was madness! It was as if she was having some sort of odd bout of both inner and out-of-body experience, and she couldn't get the two to gel. But she had to, because Kevin was talking about her as if she wasn't there, sitting by his side on TV. National freaking TV! It was time to take control of the situation.

Eva blinked again, her lashes feeling thick and gloppy from the extra coats of mascara plus the individual false lashes the makeup woman had put on her that morning. She had thought they were a bit much at the time. Now she was afraid that with all the ridiculous blinking she was doing, she probably looked like Bambi gone drag. Eva forced her eyes wide, as if that would somehow make her appear saner, and stared at Kevin. Oh hell, Mr. Smooth was starting to sweat, despite the fact that if it was two degrees colder, you'd be able to see your breath as you welcomed Satan into the studio. His sleek, ultra-groomed, dark cocoa skin was starting to glisten, and Eva now noticed a hint of fear in his eyes.

Eva's heart raced, but despite this, she caught Kevin's eye and gave him a smile that she hoped said, "Come on, honey, don't lose your cool now," as she reached over and gave his hand a pat. She could do this. Just a little damage control, and she'd reel this right in.

Eva turned to her other side and looked at Diane Parker, one of *The Morning Show*'s other co-hosts, but Diane's blue eyes only seemed to mirror Eva's own internal confusion.

Just perfect. No help from blondie.

So Eva turned her gaze to Jim. Good ol' Jim. Surely Mr. All America would help save the day. But in that moment, a clear sound finally reached Eva's ears, punctuated by good ol' Jim's good ol' laugh. The loud, false pang rang against her eardrums. "Har,

har! Good one, Kevin," Jim said, as Eva took in the obvious tension playing around the corners of his mouth, causing some of his pancake makeup to crease. "Of course you're joking."

"No, Jim, I'm not," Kevin said, his voice clear, strong, and surprisingly absolute as he turned Eva's way. "I'm sorry, Eva. I can't go through with this."

Despite her best efforts at bracing, Eva winced as the words penetrated. The full impact hit her like a crosstown bus trying to make up for lost time.

This was not happening. It couldn't be happening. Not here. Not now. Not to her.

But Kevin continued, his voice getting higher with each word. The more his lips moved and the words washed over her, the more of a blur he became. His handsome features, smooth skin, close-cropped hair, fine button-down oxford shirt, new three-button jacket, pocket square—all becoming a washed-out mass of swirly rejection under the bright studio lights. For a moment, Eva felt like she might be sick, so she bent her head, her gaze hitting Kevin's highly polished leather shoes. The ones that she had picked up for him last week so he would be perfect for their big television appearance this morning. Eva felt her chest tighten as her throat squeezed shut.

"I really am sorry, babe. But I can't do it. It's all too much, and I've realized I'm not ready to get married."

It was like a physical blow. Like he had kicked her in the gut while wearing the shoes she paid for.

Eva's head snapped up then, away from the shoes and away from Kevin too. She saw the camera and the red light as it flashed before her like a beacon.

She shut her eyes for a moment and thought once again about how many people watched this while they sipped their morning coffee and ate their sugar-toasted oats. What were they thinking as they stared at the seemingly normal-looking woman in her pink twinset and sharply pleated skirt? Damn it, she was wearing her grandmother's pearls. How does one go about getting dumped in heirloom pearls?

The nausea twisted at her again, and Eva had the distinct feeling that her normally caramel-hued skin was probably taking on a green cast to match the bile now churning in her belly. She wondered if the color would be picked up and broadcast in HD. Now there was ideal breakfast entertainment for you.

And then it hit her, and her worry doubled. Practically tripled. Shit. Her mother was watching this. Watching and most likely fuming. She could imagine the look on Valerie Ward's face right now. She was sure to be yelling into a phone right that moment to have her assistant and the rest of the staff come in early to get started on damage control. The thought sent Eva over the edge. Probably even more than experiencing disappointment herself, she hated the idea of letting her mother down. She'd had enough of that in her life, and though she came off as a human fire-breather, Eva knew it was mostly a mask to cover past hurts.

Not ready to get married.

Kevin's words echoed through Eva's head, along with visions of her mother's impending tirade, and she felt the heat rise. First, it was a burning in the soles of her feet, then it licked up her legs, moving on to radiate through her stomach before finally making its way to her face.

She paused, her breathing virtually stopping a moment as the stomach churning turned to a full-on boil. Was this bastard really breaking up with her on national television merely months, hell, practically weeks, before her perfectly planned wedding?

Eva finally turned and looked at Kevin, fighting hard to keep her emotions in line. She laughed. A belly laugh that would make even ol' Jim proud. *It's a joke. It has to be.* Diane and Jim cautiously joined her in the chuckle and bolstered her spirits. *Whew.* She couldn't believe she'd almost fallen for it. Of course, Kevin would never do that to her. He also had too much riding on this marriage. Too much riding on them. It must have been some silly producer thing. They were always doing something to try and jack up the ratings. And she played along and fell for it, for a moment. She should have known it was a stunt. What better fodder for the gossip mill and ratings than an on-air breakup and makeup from America's, at least for the moment, sweetheart couple? But Kevin knew how important this was. How much this wedding meant to her. To them and their future. Both personally and professionally. But he had been a fool to go for it in the first place and not let her in on the joke.

Eva strained out a smile. "Funny. But come on, sweetie. Joke's over," she said. "Now tell me you were just playing." She turned to the camera and raised a perfectly arched brow. "Tell America you were playing. We will be married and have our dream wedding right here on *The Morning Show* courtesy of Tied Knot Style and Bliss." Eva smiled wide. Her mother would appreciate the advertiser tie-in. One never missed out on the opportunity to thank a sponsor. It was a cardinal rule of marketing. Always keep the sponsors happy and coming back to write another check.

But instead of laughing with her and getting in on the joke, good ol' Jim clammed up and flipped through his blue cards, looking confused, and Diane, well, she was still a grinning zero as she nodded in a bobbleheaded way that couldn't quite be declared for or against the joke theory. And wait, was that sweat on her brow now too? *Holy hell.*

Eva looked back at Kevin for reassurance, and he shrugged. *The bastard shrugged!*

"I really am sorry, Eva. You know I always cared for you."

Cared? Did he say *cared?* A rock thudded where her heart was supposed to be. Cared. As in, what you do for your late grandmother, as in how you felt about your childhood dog. Cared, "ed," as in past tense?

Kevin turned to the camera and laid on that old Kevin charm, looking ever so innocent and sincere. "I'm, um, sorry, America. I'd like to apologize to you too. And this is not Eva's fault. It's all me."

Jim piped in, "Well, I'm not really sure what to say here. We'll, well, take a commercial break and be right back?" He then held his ear and with an awkward look turned to Eva. "Oh, uh, I really am sorry; it seems we can't go to commercial. Not for ninety more seconds." Jim gave Eva a look that said, "Tough break, kid."

Eva bit her lip and tried to steady her breathing,

since her heart was beating so hard and fast she was sure the mics must be picking up every erratic thump. Crap! In ninety seconds, she was sure to be dead from humiliation.

Diane shifted her eyes away before speaking to the camera. Her voice took on a funereal tone. "We are truly sad to hear of this development. We were all looking forward to your wedding. But I guess now, given the circumstances, and as per the rules of the competition, we'll have to choose another couple." Diane smiled and changed her voice on a dime. "Luckily, we still have Sherri and Brad from Des Moines, who are our runner-up couple. Hey, as they say, it's for the best to find out before the marriage that the two of you don't suit. Don't you think?"

Just perfect. It's now that she turns into a freaking all-star chatterbox, spouting rules and crap.

"No."

The word came out before Eva could stop to think about what she was saying.

"Excuse me?" Diane asked, her wispy brows drawing together. "Maybe you didn't hear what Kevin said. He does not want to marry you."

Eva shot Diane a look that said *Thanks, but no thanks for the clarification,* then turned back to Kevin as he piped up again.

"Yes, Eva." Kevin put his hand across her forearm. "What are you talking about? I said I won't marry you. There won't be a wedding." He rubbed his hand gently across her forearm. Eva looked down at it, not knowing if it was supposed to be comforting or controlling. It didn't matter.

It wasn't either.

She looked up at him, eyes blazing, and jerked her

arm away. Then, catching the red light out of the corner of her eye, Eva thought briefly of her mother, before giving Kevin a huge smile that would probably make the most venomous snake proud. "I don't give a damn what you said. I will have my wedding with or without you." It was like a fire had ignited and was rushing through her veins, threatening to burn out of control.

Kevin pulled back, shaking his head. "Eva, come on. Stop, you're not making sense." Then he lowered his voice to a stage whisper, as if the mics still couldn't pick him up. "Plus you're embarrassing yourself."

For the second time that morning, Eva laughed inappropriately on national TV. *Goody, maybe hysterics are setting in.* She supposed it was natural, given the circumstances.

"Oh, really? Tell me, how can I embarrass myself any more than you already have? Freaking all of America is watching my national dumpation!" She waved her hands wildly in a gesture to the studio. Beyond them there were multiple cameras and overhead lights, and you could see the silhouettes of the burly cameramen nodding their heads in the distance. Behind Eva, Jim, Diane, and Kevin was a large window with people jockeying for their moment of fame, holding up signs saying hi to mom. Eva blew a guy in a cheese hat a kiss when he made an obscene gesture toward his crotch.

She turned back to Kevin and nodded. "See there! I'm already fielding promising offers."

A mumble of laughter traveled throughout the studio. Kevin looked down at the floor. Coward. She should have known he wasn't up to the challenge when she had to push him to retake the bar exam. No, he was ready, after one little setback, to squander it all and spend his life living between her couch and his rich stepfather's bungalow, making it party-hopping off his good looks and charm. Well, no more.

Eva jabbed a finger into his chest, and Kevin looked back up. This time satisfaction nipped at her as she saw a glimmer of anger in his eyes. "Six years! I have wasted six years dealing with your wishy-washy indecisiveness, and here we are about at the finish line, and you go and back out now. Stopping in the fourth quarter? Eighth inning? On the last lap? What kind of man are you? Well, I'll tell you. You're the type to use up all the best years a woman has, and then when it's time to commit, you bail." As she said the words, she felt a lump form in her throat and tears well in her eyes.

Oh hell no. There was no way she would let that happen. No way would she let Kevin know he'd gotten to her.

She swallowed and then continued, "Well, I've got news for you. There are plenty of men who I'm sure would be happy to take your place. Just ask Cheese Head." Eva looked back to the window, but Cheese Head was gone. She guessed the cheese was fine, but apparently pointing out your sausage was a bit much for morning TV. She turned back to Kevin and continued, "No matter, I will still have my wedding. You are replaceable. The question is, Who's got next? I will have my wedding! And I'll have it on the date as planned!" She pointed to the empty spot beside her. "All I have to do is just insert groom here!"

It was then that Eva detected a murmur going through the studio. Oh crap. Did she really say what she had just said out loud? She looked up and saw the red light flashing like a beacon out to New York, Chicago, Iowa, and beyond. And did she really just say it to not only Kevin, but to Jim, Diane, and the rest of America?

Eva closed her eyes. *Oh God. Please make this a bad dream. It has to be.* But when she opened them and focused on everyone around the studio, the same people who had smiled at her with admiration moments ago were all staring at her now like she was the Wicked Witch of the West or someone ready for a straitjacket. Shit. This dream is way too real.

Panicked, Eva jumped off the raised stool; pushing back sharply, she heard it crash to the ground behind her as she ran off the set.

"Well, um, that was spirited. We'll be right back, folks, and in our next half hour, bringing romance back into the kitchen!" The irony of Jim's words almost had Eva cringing as they echoed through the studio's speakers. His ridiculous "Har, har, har" laugh kept time with the clanking of Eva's retreating heels.

Connect with Us

Visit us online at
KensingtonBooks.com
to read more from your favorite authors, see books
by series, view reading group guides, and more.